for Judy

Sea Above
Sky Below

Best wishes

Richard Medrington

Sea Above
Sky Below

RICHARD MEDRINGTON

CURIOUS TREE

First published in Great Britain in 2017 by
CURIOUS TREE
www.curioustree.co.uk

Typeset in Garamond with additional chapter and character fonts:
Chapter Titles: A Song For Jennifer by Brittney Murphy
Alma: DJB Annalise by Darcy Baldwin
Stinkhorn: Tkachenko by Sergiy S. Tkachenko
Poet: Italiano by Rob Leuschke

Typesetting and cover design by Wendy Ball
www.wendyball.org

Cover generated using illustrations
designed by Freepik.com

Curious Tree illustration by Paul Ballingall

ISBN 978-1-9997748-0-6

For Paul

"It is above all by the imagination that we achieve perception and compassion and hope."

- Ursula K Le Guin

Contents

Preface

I started writing this story in the year 2000. It began with a poem about a strange creature called Stinkhorn who lives in a hedge, feeding on poisonous things and bits of himself, and it became a story about a girl called Alma. A momentum built up, the likes of which I had never experienced. I was writing solidly for four and five hours a day – normal perhaps for real authors but unheard of for me. Going to bed at night I had a sense of excitement, knowing that the characters were sleeping and wondering what adventures they would have the following day. At times it was more like listening to a story than making one up, but as I got nearer to the conclusion, for reasons I cannot quite explain I lost confidence and abandoned it.

It lay in its box for more than ten years, during which time I couldn't bring myself look at it, but thanks to the encouragement of friends and a little story by JRR Tolkien called *Leaf by Niggle*, I eventually lifted the lid and took out a chapter, fully expecting to hate it. It wasn't as bad as I had feared, so I read some more. It was like reading a book that you've read a long time ago and can only half-remember. Somewhere near the end I was in tears. I couldn't understand why I'd stopped so close to the finishing line.

It needed a lot of work. I think I have done all I can to it now and so it must leave the nest and find its way in the world. I apologise to it for letting it sit down there in the darkness for so long.

Seeing that we can be certain about so little beyond the material world, I feel that the imagination is the best tool for approaching so-called eternal questions. We have managed to turn the subject of metaphysics into something timid and doom-laden, instead of seeing it as a realm we can enter safely and playfully with hopeful ideas and strange imaginings.

CHAPTER ONE

Onto the Page

THE BOOK OF SLIGHTS
Faults

Hair: ginger and too curly.

Freckles: too many and running into one another. Julia calls me "The Freckle" and keeps pushing me away and saying she doesn't want to catch freckles from me.

Nose: too big and slightly turned up.

Accent: Granny keeps talking about elocution lessons and **that dreadful Primary School**, which I liked a lot better than The Grange.

Body: the wrong shape. Clothes don't fit well. I'm small for my age. People think I'm much younger than I am.

Teeth: having gaps and white stains.

Eyes: too small and a watery blue like my father's.

Ears: stick out.

Belly button: bulges.

Shoulders: hunched. "Will you SIT UP STRAIGHT!"

Face: chin dimpled, but not in an attractive way.

Nothing is attractive.

What is the opposite of attraction?

Repulsion.

Yesterday I went to school with my hair tied up at the back and Rosa said

"Repulsive! Repulsive! Let down your hair!"

Attitude: lazy, a dreamer. I'm not really lazy, but people think I am because I like to think about things and do them properly and they want me to do things fast.

Name: hate it. Nobody knows that I call myself Alma.

There was a box of special stationery that she had been given for her ninth birthday – the sort of present you don't appreciate immediately. The paper was thick and ridged and when Alma wrote her thank-you letter the felt tip bumped over the ridges. If she let the pen rest on the paper it soaked up the ink, but the ridges made it easier to write in straight lines. She used one sheet and one envelope for the letter, then put the box in a drawer and didn't touch it again until three years later, when she began to write *The Book of Slights*, where she wrote down things that had gone wrong. There seemed to be a lot more things that had gone wrong than things that had gone right, though it may have been that the things that had gone right didn't seem as important. Good things she forgot quickly, whereas the things that went wrong lingered. These were the things that Alma thought about while trying to go to sleep. Sometimes she thought she was never going to get to sleep at all, and often in the morning she would claim to have been awake all night.

Her father said, "You were asleep when I looked in on you before I went to bed."

"If you find you worry about things," he went on, "then write them down – that takes them out of your mind and onto the page." So she had started *The Book of Slights*. She kept the pages in a drawer in a brown folder, which she sealed each time with a new piece of tape.

There was a gap beneath the work surface in the kitchen where they kept the bin. There were pipes and taps which suggested that at one time it had been used to house a dishwasher, though due to the strange shape of the kitchen it was at least two feet deeper than normal dishwasher size. Alma's mother didn't believe in dishwashers, she liked to get her hands into some hot soapy water. When her mother wasn't in the kitchen Alma would sometimes crawl into this space behind the bin. It was a dark place, and often her mother would come into the room and not notice her at all. She once sat there undetected for half an hour while her mother was getting a meal ready. When she went upstairs to call her down, Alma went into the living room and pretended she'd been there all the time. In their old house she had had a similar hiding place – a corner of the larder, under a stone shelf, a hide from which she could listen to the world without being a part of it. When they had moved to this house she had still felt the need for a refuge. The space behind the bin wasn't ideal – it was smellier for one thing, but she didn't mind that, and once she had got in and pulled the bin across the opening she felt safe.

One hot Wednesday afternoon towards the end of the summer holidays she crawled in behind the bin and sat in the coolness. Her mother had gone upstairs for her rest, and Alma knew she had at least an hour to herself. The kitchen floor was covered with dark green carpet tiles, each one about sixteen inches square. They were showing signs of age and her mother had been lobbying for some smart new laminate flooring. Her father favoured the tiles for their practicality – they were hard wearing and if one got stained it could, theoretically, be replaced.

In the darkness of her hiding place, Alma noticed the corner of one of the tiles sticking out from the wall, its edge curling like a piece of stale toast. It was loose and when she pulled it there was a lot more of it than she had expected. She couldn't understand where it was coming from because this should have been an outside wall, which meant that she must be pulling the carpet through from the garden. She kept pulling and it turned out to be a complete sixteen inch square carpet tile. She pushed it back and it went quite easily.

Out in the garden Alma tried to work out where the tile could be going. The brickwork at the back of the house was uneven, showing signs of alterations that had been made to the house. There was a window above the sink, then a couple of paces on from there the place where the pipes came out of the wall. She looked for some sort of gap where the carpet tile could have come from, but there was nothing – just ordinary bricks and mortar.

Back in the hiding place she couldn't actually see the brickwork because a piece of hardboard had been cut to size and fitted into the gap. She tapped on the hardboard and it sounded hollow. She was still surprised that there could be such a wide gap between the hardboard and the wall, unless the carpet tile was somehow sliding up into the cavity when she pushed it. This could explain the curled corner, and yet even as she was thinking this with one part of her mind, another part was telling her that it didn't feel like that at all when she pushed it: the tile was going into a large space, not a narrow one. She tried to prise a corner of the hardboard out from the wall, and getting right down on the floor she peered round the edge of it: only darkness. Letting go, the hardboard snapped back into place. Immediately she decided not to tell anyone.

Alma had reasons for wanting to keep this a secret. At their old house there had been a patch of lawn near the compost heap where she had found a four-leafed clover, which she knew meant good luck. Then she had found another, and another: she had even found a five-leafed clover. The whole patch three feet square had been full of four- and five-leafed clovers. She'd gone running to her mother with a handful saying, "Look, we're going to be so lucky..." That weekend she had been pleased to see her father with his silver watering can, watering her special four-leafed clover patch. But a few days later the clover was all brown and dead. It turned out that the watering can had been full of weed killer. She suspected that he had been under instructions from her mother, who didn't really believe in luck.

So she kept the thing with the carpet tile to herself, and it seemed right to have something like that in the secret place where she hid, to have something which didn't make any sense. She would push the carpet tile in and out and imagine that it was moving in a place that didn't exist. It was like a tiny miracle, and she touched it when it came back through and sniffed it. It felt cold and smelled musty.

It reminded her of a story her father had told her, in the days when he used to tell her bedtime stories. These had usually had something to do with mathematics, which was what he taught. This time he was telling her about the square root of minus one. She had pictured something like a chopped turnip. He had explained that the square root of minus one was an imaginary number, a number like infinity, which didn't really exist in this world, but if you took that number and put it into certain calculations it helped you get the right answer. Long after he had turned out her light she had lain awake wondering about things that could be imaginary and real at the same time.

CHAPTER TWO

The Message

An idea came to her as she sat on the stairs watching the mail being pushed through the letterbox by the postman. She wrote some questions on a piece of her good paper and without quite knowing why put the paper on the tile and pushed it through the wall behind the bin. After a largely silent Sunday lunch, when the house was quiet, Alma crawled back into the hiding place. She listened for a moment, then pulled the carpet tile gently out from the wall. The paper tore as she pulled it out, which was odd, as it had gone in quite easily. She pulled back the hardboard but she could only retrieve a few pieces. What she had written was:

> Where does this go to?
> Is there anyone there?
> Please give me a sign.
> What is the meaning of life?

This had been written on a whole piece of paper, but now there were just a few small scraps left. She put them on the floor and smoothed them out. She moved them around for a moment, rearranging the order, then stopped. Trembling slightly, she went up to her room and took out another piece of paper. On this she wrote:

What is the meaning of life?

Underneath she stuck four of the fragments:

to... give... life... meaning

THE BOOK OF SLIGHTS

This is not a slight so much as a frustration. I went down into the kitchen but Mum was in there. "Okay?" she said.

"Yes."

"That's good." She was doing the washing up very slowly and carefully, and I sat at the table and watched her back. She was muttering, praying under her breath, "Oh, Sanderby, Sanderby Coriander."

When the House Group come round on a Wednesday night for Bible Study I can hear them all praying and singing and making strange noises. It's called 'Praying in Tongues'. Quite a few of them make similar noises to Mum. When she first became Pentecostal I found it worrying, but now it's sort of comforting. It never gets out of control – sometimes it builds to a crescendo and the women go really high and the men stay low, and then they start singing one of their choruses.

Mum pulled off her rubber gloves and let the water out.

"Right, all done here," she said, and she looked at me and gave that little sigh, which means she's worried about me, and a few minutes later I could hear her upstairs in the bedroom praying for me.

If I had any friends I wouldn't ask them home. At my last school, the ordinary primary school, I asked some friends home and my mother asked them if they went to Sunday School, and the next day Janice said, "Your mother is seriously weird."

I asked Sarah in the Sunday School if she had given her heart to Jesus and she said she did it last year. Then she looked at the ground and said, "Jesus is okay."

Alma's next question was the one she assumed everyone had asked themselves at some time or other. It was like the other questions only more specific. She took another sheet and wrote in large letters:

WHY WAS I BORN?

Then she crossed out the question mark and added:

AT ALL?

She waited until she heard the sound of her mother praying upstairs. Ducking in under the worktop she squatted down behind the bin, pulled out the carpet tile, carefully placed the note on top of it and pushed it back into the wall. It went in so easily that an idea occurred to her. She went over to her school bag which was hanging on the back of the kitchen door and took out a plastic ruler, then she got down on her knees again and tried to push the ruler into the wall, but it wouldn't go. She put it right on top of the carpet tile and tried to slide it through in the same way she had pushed through the folded pieces of paper. The end of it just scraped against hard brick.

She pulled the tile out and tried again, but still the ruler seemed to be too thick to go through. Then she pushed the tile with the note back in again – once again it went in easily, but when she pulled the carpet tile back out, the note didn't come with it.

It made her think of the time when her father had taken her to the beach with a message in a bottle. It wasn't really a message, just her name and address on a rolled up piece of paper. They had thrown it into the water and watched it float away; then after watching and waiting for a while they had turned and walked home without saying a word.

She pushed the tile in again, then pulled it out as slowly as she could, moving it from side to side, until finally a white corner appeared. She went up to the bathroom and got the tweezers from the cabinet, went back downstairs again and at last managed to pull it through. It came out in one piece, just a little crumpled. She had half-hoped it might tear again and reveal some new word order that would answer her question. But the question had come back unanswered: *Why were you born at all?* She folded up the piece of paper and was about to throw it into the bin when she felt a sudden thrill. She remembered quite clearly writing, *Why was I born...* and then crossing out the question mark and adding *...at all?* But the note now said, *Why were you born at all?* And even if she had put *were you* instead of *was I*, and forgotten about it, she was certain she could not be mistaken about the crossed out question mark. Now that she looked, not only was the paper different, but the handwriting was not her own – it was very similar, but jerkier somehow, as if someone had copied it out, altering those two words, reposing the question.

CHAPTER THREE

The Stations

THE BOOK OF SLIGHTS

I have a recurring nightmare. I've had it three or four times I think, and it is always the same. I tried to draw a picture of it once and it looked like a fried egg at the top of a ladder, but I don't remember what the picture had to do with the dream, all I remember is that I am in a place that is completely dark, and I am paralysed and I have lost my memory. When people say to you, imagine the size of the Universe, or imagine infinity, if you go as far as you can go what would you find? I always think of a brick wall, and then I ask myself, so what is on the other side of the brick wall? And I wonder if it is like that, a place that is completely dark, and no light can get there. Because when you think of the emptiness of space and the blackness of space, it isn't really black or dark because there is either light from the sun or from the moon or from the stars: space is actually full of light, only the background is dark, like a blackboard. If you went into a room with black walls and you switched on the light, the room would still be black, but it would be full of light. But the place in my dream is like the black room with the light turned out. So when I'm there I don't know if I've gone blind, but also I've lost my memory and I'm paralysed so I can't move my arms or kick my legs or do anything at all. There is nothing, and I'm just aware of nothing. And then from somewhere deep inside I start to call for help, only I make no sound, and no one comes. But when I'm awake, I think something else. I think that maybe the place over the wall at the edge of the Universe is really full of a strange new kind of light. And when you are in that light you know everything, you find the answer to all your questions, and all the things you've lost are waiting for you there, and it is full of love.

But probably you can only get there when you die.

Even as the holidays ebbed away and the first day of term approached, Alma had a warm feeling inside because of the secret. Living in a house on the school campus she had to cope not just with the idea of going back to school, but of having school come back to her. Her privacy would once again be invaded: the garden would cease to be a place where she could feel safe and even her bedroom was overlooked by school buildings. She tried to keep the curtains drawn but her mother would come and open them and open the window, which meant that she couldn't play her CDs for fear of someone hearing and mocking her taste in music.

But the presence beyond the wall in the kitchen – this was something entirely private, something invisible, and so secret that even she didn't know what it was, only that it was. But then she would have doubts: she would tell herself there must be some *perfectly logical explanation*. This was her father's attitude to any so-called mystery. When her mother would mention a miracle performed in a church somewhere, (usually it was in America, or for the really extreme stories a church in Africa) her father would listen and then say, "There will be some perfectly logical explanation."

Alma felt torn, because in a way she admired his rational mind, but in another way she desperately wanted to believe in the supernatural, especially if it was a supernatural that took some notice of her. Something beyond the wall, something perhaps in another dimension, had possibly answered one question and certainly rephrased another, and that meant that everything she had been taught about the way the world worked was wrong.

Unless of course there *was* some logical explanation. She didn't like to investigate too closely for fear of finding one.

As the holiday entered its final week Alma had the sense that time was speeding up. She was taken to shop for clothes and equipment, and meanwhile the campus was visited by delivery vans and workmen carrying out last minute repairs. This final week was almost like a week of term, and time itself went past so quickly. Alma tried everything she could think of to slow it down: she would find a difficult book and force herself to read it; she would set herself targets like twenty pages in a morning, and even if she had to re-read each page two or three times before she understood it, she wouldn't mind because at least it was time that belonged to her. But she was always under pressure to get things ready. *Ready for what?* she wanted to say. *We are getting things ready so that we can go to school and get things ready for life. But when does life actually start? Isn't life supposed to have started?*

Alma spent most of Wednesday morning in her room trying to formulate her next question. The paper was stretched out neatly on the table before her. She gripped the pen, but nothing would come. *What do I want to know?* she thought. *What have I always wanted to know?* Then she felt her hand writing something:

What is on the other side of the wall?

On Wednesday evenings there was a prayer meeting at the church, so her mother hurried out after an early supper. Her father went into the dining room to work. When the house was quiet Alma went up and took the piece of paper out of the lockable drawer at the bottom of her wardrobe where she kept her poems and stories and *The Book of Slights*.

She had decided to use one of the special envelopes that matched the paper. For a moment she couldn't think what to put on the front of the envelope, then she wrote in capital letters:

TO WHOM IT MAY CONCERN

She folded the paper and put it into the envelope. Then she took a box out of the drawer. Inside was a piece of green sealing wax, a brass stamp shaped like a tiny truncheon and a box of matches. She struck a match and held it against the sealing wax. A wisp of black smoke snaked up and she inhaled some of it. Though she didn't like the smell, nevertheless it was exciting – the essence of a secret. She pressed the stamp into the pool of wax that was beginning to congeal on the back of the envelope and pushed down hard. When she lifted it away it made a snapping, cracking sound and she was pleased to see the perfect imprint of a five-pointed star.

Downstairs the kitchen was dark except for the yellow light from the street lamp outside. Alma crawled in behind the bin and felt for the corner of the carpet tile. She pulled about half the tile through and placed the envelope on it. Then, because the occasion seemed so important, she decided that perhaps this time she should make a kind of ritual out of it. She had heard about how Catholics performed something called the *Stations of the Cross*. She had always associated this with the four stations on a Monopoly board, except that she had an idea there were meant to be seven of them, seven being such a significant number. She went back to the kitchen door and surveyed the floor plan. The green carpet tiles stretched out before her like a chessboard. Alma closed her eyes and tried to imagine where each station might be and what symbols would represent them. There was King's Cross, Fenchurch Street, Euston and Marylebone. Euston seemed to not quite fit: there was nothing holy or mysterious sounding about the word Euston; it made her think of uselessness, but then holy things were often of little practical use. She decided this was okay, but she needed three more to have the seven stations. There was a women's dance group at the church called the *Dancers of St Asaph* and her father had once referred to them as the

Shunters of St Pancras. It had made her mother smile for a moment before she had checked herself and told him not to be critical. But you were being critical too, Alma had thought, otherwise you wouldn't have smiled.

St Pancras made five. Two to go.

She went to the bookshelf and pulled out the A to Z of London. She had been to London twice, both times by train and then they had travelled on the underground. She tried to remember the names of some of the underground stations. Was there one called Mortlake? That seemed familiar. She knew that Mort meant dead in French: a lake of death? That was a possible *Station of the Cross*, surely. So that was six, one to go.

She flicked through the A to Z and found the map of the underground system. There was one called New Cross but it sounded too modern to be part of a ritual. She felt she was dealing with an ancient religion here, one that went back to a time when people sang dirges in Latin and wore cloaks made of itchy cloth. There was another called Charing Cross. Charing sounded like a mixture of caring and charity. She closed the book and put it back on the shelf.

Back up in the bedroom she ripped some pages out of an exercise book, wrote the name of each station on a piece of paper, then went back down to the kitchen. She could hear her father talking to himself in the dining room, the way he did when he was absorbed in marking or preparing lesson plans. She thought carefully about where to place the stations – there needed to be some sort of logical progression, but she couldn't think where to start. She spread out the sheets before her on the kitchen table: Euston-less. Was that a starting point or a final destination? Surely a starting point. The Holy Station of Uselessness from which we all set out on our journey to find meaning in life. From there we progress to... probably Fenchurch Street. That is just like a church: not a very exciting place, and quite close to useless. Then where? St Pancras, who must have been a good person; perhaps he was the patron saint of something or other – trains possibly. Where next? Not quite at the cross yet, so maybe to Marylebone? She couldn't make this fit very well, until she remembered that *bon* in French meant good, so perhaps it was Mary the Good rather than something to do with one of her bones. Okay, so we go through the Virgin Mary and then...? She sensed that Mortlake would be the last place she would come to, so that meant that the two crosses were next: Charing Cross first, then the King's Cross which is Jesus' cross and then – the Lake of Death!

A few minutes were spent placing the pages carefully on various carpet tiles so that the bin could be reached by stepping from one to the other in the right order. Alma moved the bin aside so that she would have easy access to her hiding place. She had put a number on each page, and now she spaced them not more than two squares apart. She toyed with the idea of making it work like a game of draughts, but soon gave this up as being too complicated. "This is no game," she thought, "this is religion."

Still, the game idea would be a useful excuse if her father came in and asked what she was doing. Having placed all the stations she went back and stood on the one marked Euston, just inside the door. She closed her eyes for a moment and composed herself. "Perhaps I should say a little prayer," but all that came into her mind was, "Sanderby Coriander, Oh Sanderby Coriander".

She stepped onto Fenchurch Street and said in a whisper, "I move from Uselessness – I am no longer useless, I am now at the Church in the Fen." Then on to the next station saying: "In the name of St Pancras..." And then again, because it sounded like a nice thing when she said it, "In the holy name of St Pancras!"

She was now standing by the cooker, and the next step took her to the corner of the room by the crockery cupboard.

"By the love of Mary the Good. Then I come to the Cross of Charity, and now to the Cross of the King."

She closed her eyes and pictured a blue and orange kingfisher diving into the still waters of a lake. She bent down and, hanging on to the edge of the worktop, swung herself onto the final square. It seemed important not to stand on any of the other squares: if she had done this she felt she would have had to go back to the beginning and start all over again. The final square was just next to her magic tile.

"Now I have passed through death and can finally ask my question."

She took the envelope out of her pocket and placed it face up on the carpet tile. As she did so she heard a faint whistling, like the sound the wind makes blowing under a door. There were bits of fluff and dust and she could see that they were being drawn towards the gap in the wall, the carpet fibres were moving in that direction too.

She pushed the tile, with the envelope, into the wall. But there was some resistance – usually its movement into and out of the wall was quite smooth, but now it was snagging on something. She pushed it in again, more forcefully this time. Then she screamed and let go of the tile.

Something on the other side had given it a tug.

CHAPTER FOUR

The Reply

"You all right Veronica?" called her father. The sound of her footsteps running up the stairs had brought him out of the dining room.

"I'm okay!" she called from the landing. Her breath was coming quickly, her heart pounding. She looked down at him and tried to appear calm.

"Are you sure you're all right?"

"Yes I'm fine. I think I'm going to go to bed early tonight."

"Okay... Now is there any work you have to be doing for the new term?"

"No, I think I've done everything."

"Well make sure you're properly prepared this time."

He was fingering the thin hair on top of his head. This was what he always did when he was nervous. People at school said he was counting his hairs to see how many he'd lost that day.

She shoved the pieces of paper, which she had hastily gathered from the kitchen floor, into her secret drawer. Then she sat on her bed and switched on the lamp. She was both terrified and excited. There really was something on the other side of the wall...

"Or..." said a voice inside her head, "Or, something *in* the wall. And we all know what lives in walls, don't we."

She nodded her head slowly, then sighed.

"What lives in walls?" said the voice.

"Rats," she said.

THE BOOK OF SLIGHTS

The Last Christmas we were in our old house, just before we moved here, I heard the grown-ups say something really bad. I was in my old hiding place, and my Auntie Rachel was staying as well and she and Granny were talking about my parents and they had all been drinking champagne and it was just before Christmas lunch so they should have been merry but they weren't, nobody was. My mother was in a bad mood, and my Auntie lowered her voice and said, "How do you think they're getting on?" And Granny said "Well!" like she was blowing it out with a big puff of air. "Well, what can you expect? Chalk and cheese, chalk and cheese." And my Auntie said, "I thought they were doing better since Irene got religion." And Granny said, "Well it's kept them in the same house, but of course they should have separated long ago..."

My Auntie said, "Yes, they so nearly did..."

And Granny said, "Yes but... can't be helped."

"Could have been helped," said my Auntie. "She should have been more careful."

"Well," said Granny, "at least you and John are

both happy."

"Happy<u>ish</u>," said my Auntie.

It was three days before the start of term and Alma could feel the tension in the house rising. There was a lull after lunch when her father went to a staff meeting and her mother disappeared upstairs for what she called her *quiet time*. Now that the ground floor belonged to her, Alma went into the kitchen and squeezed herself in behind the bin. Some marmalade had dribbled down the back of it and a bit got onto her shirt, so she licked her finger and tried to wipe it off. She didn't pull out the piece of carpet immediately, but got down close to the floor and checked to see if the wind was still whistling through the gap. All was still. She put her ear to the hardboard and listened for sounds of scratching or squeaking, but there was nothing, just the gentle pulse of her body.

She remembered, back in the old house, lying awake at night listening to what she took to be footsteps climbing the stairs yet never getting to the landing. She had thought that someone was playing a trick on her by walking on the spot, but it went on and on, this relentless tramp, tramp, tramp, and a picture had come into her mind of an old man walking up a staircase that went spiralling into the sky. It might have been an escalator, but because it was suspended in space you couldn't tell if it was moving up or down or standing still. She had become fascinated by this image and all its possibilities: if it was a down escalator, it would mean that the man was making no progress at all, just remaining in the same place.

And if it was an up escalator then he might as well stand still and try to enjoy the ride. The man looked very weary, as if he had been climbing for years, yet he seemed unable to stop. She had called out for her father, then called again and again, louder and louder until she was almost screaming, and finally she had heard a door open and her father's equally weary footsteps on the stairs. When she told him about the sound he had explained how the heart makes the blood flow around the body. Taking hold of her wrist with thumb and forefinger he had found her pulse, then he guided her own fingers to the place.

"There, can you feel that? That is like the beating of your heart, the pulse of the blood moving around your body, and there are several places where you can feel it. There's one in your thumb for example, which is why doctors never feel for a pulse with their thumbs, but with the tips of their fingers. You can feel a pulse in someone's neck. And if you go into a really well soundproofed room you will hear the sound of your own heart beating. That is what you are hearing when you put your head on the pillow, if the room is very quiet, and perhaps if you are a bit excited and your heart is beating unusually fast."

"I thought it was someone climbing the stairs forever."

"No. It was just the sound of your own heart beating, and that goes on forever."

"Or until I die."

"And that won't be for a long time."

"It might be a short time. Perhaps we're only allowed so many heartbeats, and when those run out we die."

Alma took her ear away from the hardboard and the

thrumming sound ceased. Even if there were rats, she didn't see how they would be able to get through such a tiny gap, so there was really no danger. She listened to make sure that her mother was still upstairs and heard the familiar sound: "*Oh, Sanderby Coriander, Sanderby, Sanderby Coriander...*"

Alma tugged at the carpet tile and it slid smoothly out from the wall. She caught a faint whiff of something unpleasant, but it might have been from the bin. When half the tile was through she saw the corner of her envelope, just as she had left it – untouched and un-nibbled. On the back the green wax seal was still intact. She considered putting it back and leaving it for a while longer, just in case. This was a setback, but there was still the message that had been changed and nothing could take that away.

"Oh come off it," said the voice in her head, "you just forgot what you wrote. There is nothing on the other side; it is just a wall with a wide cavity in it. This is an old house."

She was surprised by how empty she felt.

"You need to grow up," said the voice, "you're not a little girl any more."

She reached up and dropped the letter into the bin, then wriggled out of the hiding place and ran upstairs. Once in the bedroom she got into bed and pulled the duvet up over her head. Outside she heard the people calling to one another and the cars and vans driving around. The sounds, muffled by the duvet, seemed to come from far away.

"I still have two days," she thought. "There is the rest of today then two whole clear days – Tuesday and Wednesday before... before it all starts again... at 8.30 on Thursday. So I have nearly three days."

Alma dragged herself off the bed and stood to one side of the window. Without looking out she slowly closed the curtains. The darkness felt safer. She got back under the duvet and within a few minutes she was asleep. When she woke up she knew she had been dreaming about something, but all she could remember was a blue feather sticking out of an inkwell, and someone saying, "Two of the clock and all's well."

The clock by her bedside said it was just after two. Alma sat up, and whether because of the sleep or the dreams, she felt like she'd been spring-cleaned. She got out of bed and went downstairs. Back in the kitchen there was still no sign of her mother or father. She went over to the bin and fished out the message. Perhaps the problem had been with the envelope. She would take the message out of the envelope and put it on the carpet tile face up and see if anything happened. It might be that some of the words would be nibbled away revealing a different message.

Breaking the seal she opened the envelope, unfolded the message and felt her heart do a somersault. The message had been scribbled across in angry wavy lines of black crayon, and scrawled across the bottom of the page was the single word:

GARBAGE

"What have you got there dear?"

Alma jumped and put the message behind her back. Her mother was standing at the kitchen door.

"What have you got there?"

"Nothing... That is... It's just a game... I was playing a game."

"Let me see."

Reluctantly she handed her the message. Her mother's usual look of concern deepened as she examined the letter. She turned it over, then looked at Alma.

"What does this mean?"

Alma tried to sound casual. "It's just a game I was playing. I was pretending to send messages to myself."

Her mother kept looking at the message, turning it over, holding it up to the light.

"I think I'd better keep this and show it to your father when he gets home."

"Why, what have I done wrong?"

"Why are you writing things like this?"

"I told you, I was just pretending."

"What were you pretending?"

Alma thought for a moment. How could she possibly explain that she had received a message from something or someone living inside the wall cavity, and a rather rude message at that?

"I was trying to write a story," she said, "and I was going to call it something, and then I realised that wasn't what I wanted to call it at all, and for some reason... For some reason I got really angry with myself and I crossed it all out and wrote *garbage* at the bottom, and now I was just trying to think of what I should call it instead."

She could see her mother's face beginning to relax slightly, so she went on, "I think I must be a bit of a perfectionist or something."

Her mother was still looking at the sheet of paper.

"You're too old to be playing these games, Veronica.

You should be getting things ready for school instead of daydreaming all the time and writing silly stories. And this is your nice paper – what a waste."

"No it isn't, because I can use the other side."

And she held out her hand to receive it. Her mother still seemed to want to hang onto the evidence to show to her father, or worse still to her grandmother, as yet another example of Alma's strange behaviour. Reluctantly, the sheet was returned.

"Right, well, I'd better get on with it," said Alma, and hurried back upstairs.

Once in her room and with the door locked, she began to study the paper in detail. She got out her magnifying glass and looked at it under the light. She took out the envelope which she had stuffed into her pocket and studied that. The seal was now broken of course, but she was almost sure that it had not been tampered with before – there were the remains of the five pointed star, so it had not been opened and resealed by anyone else, unless they had an identical stamp. "The only possible explanation," she thought, "is that I went downstairs in my sleep and opened the envelope and took out the letter, scribbled on it and wrote GARBAGE, then resealed it and put it back, and that I did all that in my sleep, and forgot all about it."

She went over to the locked drawer and took out the box containing the envelopes; there were ten left and there had been eleven to start with, not counting the one she had used for her thank-you letter. So if she had opened the envelope and resealed it, she must have done it incredibly carefully, and scraped off all traces of the first batch of sealing wax, and then resealed it. And to do all that in her sleep...?

But then she thought of a more disturbing possibility. Perhaps she was altering the messages herself before pushing them through the wall, but doing so unconsciously.

A mad person could do things like that and have no memory of doing them.

*

When the alarm went off she felt like she had been dragged back to earth from another dimension. She pressed the snooze button, but just as she was going back to sleep she remembered why she had set the alarm especially early. She felt under her pillow for the letter.

Pulling on her dressing gown she tiptoed to the door and opened it as slowly as possible. There was the rhythmical sound of her father's snoring. She had made sure to finish the glass of water by her bed so that if questioned she could say she'd woken up and felt thirsty. Softly, softly, down the stairs, into the moon- and lamp-lit kitchen.

In behind the bin she pressed her ear to the hardboard, but there was no sound or movement, only the beat of her own life-support system. She made a fist and tapped gently on the hardboard. She waited for a reply, but there was no sound at all. She reached down and took hold of the carpet tile, pushed it in and pulled it out several times, then tapped again. Still there was nothing. Then she remembered the *Stations of the Cross*: when she had approached that way before there had been a special sort of feeling, and she had received the clearest reply to date. The pieces of paper with the names on them were upstairs in her locked drawer, but she thought she could remember the order and more or less where they had been placed on the floor. She went back and stood on the square just in front of the door.

"Right, this was Euselessness," she thought, "and from here we went to... The Church in the Fens." She stepped to the square by the table. That seemed about right. "From here we went over towards the cooker, it would have been that square – now which station was that?" She squatted down to think and in a moment it came to her: "Shunters! It was St Pancras!" She skipped lightly onto the square. She knew the next one was Mary the Good, but wasn't quite sure where it had been. It did seem important to get this right, and to do it just the same as last time. "It's doubly important to follow a ritual when it's one you've made up yourself," she whispered. Being pretty sure it was one of two tiles over in the direction of the bin, she chose the left hand one.

And from here it was a short step to Charing Cross. "I re-member that one because it had the rhubarb stain on it." But looking down she saw that the one with the stain was next to the one where she was standing. She could have simply shifted to the right square and continued from there, but the order would have been wrong.

"If a thing's worth doing, it's worth doing right!" she said, and realised with a shudder that she was quoting her grand-mother. She walked back to the door and started again from Euselessness: Euston, Fenchurch, Pancras, Marylebone to the right, then Charing Cross with the rhubarb stain, then Kings Cross straight ahead and finally...

She took a deep breath, leant forward, took hold of the

worktop and prepared to swing herself onto the last tile.

"And finally, The Lake of Death!"

It seemed to be the right thing to do this with her eyes closed. She felt with her foot, sliding it about to make sure she was on the right tile, then swung her other foot across, but as she did so she slipped and fell against the side of the unit. She hadn't hurt herself, but she was sure her parents would wake up and think it was a burglar. She held her breath and strained to listen. Outside a van pulled up and there was a jingle of bottles – the milkman delivering to the people next door. After a minute it pulled away again. There was no sound in the house, so Alma got ready to knock again.

"But how should I knock?" she thought. "Is there a special way I ought to knock? Some sort of code?" All she could think of was the one piece of Morse Code she knew: SOS – *Save Our Souls*. It seemed appropriate, so she gave three quick knocks followed by three slow ones, then three quick ones again. But even as she knocked she sensed that there would be no response. The tingling she had felt the first time was missing. What had she done wrong? Perhaps the mistake had come when she had slipped off the Mortlake tile onto the one next to it, a tile without any significance, thereby breaking the spell. She got up and went back to the door. But now she knew where she was going and could visualise the path stretching out in front of her. She moved from Euselessness to Fenchurch... There was the tingling down her back, then from Fenchurch to Pancras... Yes this was working: from Pancras to Mary the Good. She watched her foot land right in the middle of the square... Then on to Charing Cross – right on the rhubarb stain. And now The

Cross of the King... She stood with both feet on the square, lifted her heels and raised her arms like a diver. She leant forward and reaching out for the worktop allowed her weight to fall forward onto her arms. She jumped, swung and landed with both feet right on the square she was aiming for.

"Mortlake!" she whispered, and once again she saw the Kingfisher plop into the mist-covered water.

She leant back in her usual position and raised a fist.

"This time it will work!" she thought.

BEEP – BEEP – BEEP – BEEP.

From somewhere in the house an alarm was sounding. At first she thought it was her parents' alarm going off, but it was too early for that, it was only just after five. Then she realised it was her own alarm – she had only pressed the snooze button, and her ten minutes were up! She squeezed out of the hiding place and hurried up the stairs.

Once on the landing she saw the light go on under her parents door. She dived into her room and turned off the alarm. She got under the duvet just as the door opened.

"What's going on?" said her father, "It's the middle of the night."

"Sorry," she said, "I must have set my alarm wrong."

He grunted and closed the door.

She lay awake for a long time. It was too late to go back and try again, but at least she knew now exactly what she had to do. Next time she would get it right.

CHAPTER FIVE

The Trapdoor

"Veronica, what's this on your shirt?"

"Where?"

"Here on your good white shirt. There's something horrid all down the side of it and on the sleeve."

"I don't know what it is."

"Well, you must know."

"I don't."

"You've leant against something. You had it on yesterday, what did you lean against?"

Alma looked into her mother's eyes and felt that something which had been growing very thin was about to tear. Suspicions had been aroused by the letter yesterday, and by the alarm going off this morning. They were in the kitchen and her mother was standing by the washing machine holding the shirt with its orange stain. She sniffed it.

"Smells like marmalade."

She turned and looked at the bin. Then back to Alma, who could feel her cheeks beginning to burn.

"What have you been doing?"

There was that note of worry in her mother's voice. She went over and pulled the bin out from under the worktop;

turning it round she saw the patch on its side where the marmalade had spilled.

"Have you been getting in behind the bin?"

"I... I dropped something..."

"What have you been doing down there? Have you been spying again?"

"I don't spy!"

"You've hidden down there before, haven't you."

"No."

"Granny has told me that she's seen you hiding before now, hiding and listening to people's private conversations."

"I haven't..."

"You can go up to your room, and I don't want to catch you going anywhere near that bin other than to put something in it. And I'm going to tell your father about this when he gets home."

Up in her room Alma lay down on her bed. She didn't really mind being sent here, and she knew her father wouldn't do anything when he came home apart from giving her one of *his* worried looks. So what did it matter if they thought she was strange? Everyone thought she was strange. She had heard her grandmother use the word about her, when she thought she wasn't listening. And so what if she did spy on people? That was the only way you ever got to hear what people really thought about you, because adults never said what they thought straight to your face.

Around lunchtime she heard her father come home, and there were voices at the bottom of the stairs, then his slow steps and the knock on her door.

"Yes."

He looked in, gave her a reproving look and shook his head. Then he went away.

On Wednesday morning the alarm once again woke her at five o'clock. She had it with her under the bedclothes so that it shouldn't disturb her parents, and this time she made sure it was properly switched off.

When she reached the kitchen there was no moonlight, just the stark yellow of the street lamp. Outside the rain was falling. She pulled her dressing gown more tightly around her. The house was cold and she felt afraid, partly that her parents might catch her and make a fuss, and partly because she knew that if they didn't catch her, something strange was probably going to happen.

She went through the ritual again, and with each step felt the shivers up and down her spine. At Kings Cross she once again stood on tiptoe, raised her arms and pretended to be the beautiful bird. And there she was, under the worktop and the house was silent except for the pattering of rain on the window. She put her fingers near to the gap and thought she could just feel the air being drawn past them under the hardboard. She raised her hand and rapped on the board: tap tap tap – TAP TAP TAP – tap tap tap. Then she held her breath and waited.

At first she heard nothing, except perhaps a very distant noise, which could have been anything, but was probably the milkman's van approaching. She could hear the faintest tinkling; no, more of a scraping sound.

Something brushed gently against her ankle. She almost

cried out, and the shivering moved from her spine to wash cold across her whole body. Looking down she saw the carpet tile was being pushed steadily out from the wall, and there, at its very centre, was a small, round piece of card.

"What are you?" she hissed, bending down towards the gap in the wall.

"What are you and where are you?"

But there was no answer. The tile paused, then began to withdraw. Seeing what was happening she just managed to grab the piece of card before it disappeared into the wall.

Back up in her room, she switched on the bedside light, her hands shaking as she did so. She looked at the piece of cardboard. It lay in the palm of her hand, and she thought of Blind Pugh in *Treasure Island* and the Black Spot.

"If it is a black spot," she thought, "that probably means I'm going to die soon."

With a shrug she slapped her other palm down on top of the fragment, turned her hands over, removed the top hand and peered at some words written in the same jerky black crayon:

COME SEE

*

They had difficulty waking her that morning. Her mother had to come in three times and still she didn't get out of bed.

"Veronica!" she called from the door. "Are you feeling all right?"

There was still a coldness in her voice left over from the day before. After a telling-off it would sometimes be three or four days before the voice was back to normal, and even then Alma could feel that they were a little further apart after each disagreement. This didn't seem right seeing as her mother was always going on about the importance of forgiveness. Alma thought she could remember a time when they had been much closer. Certainly her parents had got on better once her mother started going to the church; there weren't so many arguments, but instead there was a different kind of gulf growing between them all – they were standing on pieces of ice that had cracked and begun to drift apart.

She came over and put her cold hand on Alma's forehead.

"You've got a fever," she said.

"Have I?"

"Wait, I'll get the thermometer."

Alma lay back on the pillow. A fever could mean flu, and a couple of days in bed, one of which would be her last day of freedom, and the next the first day of school. She would then have to go back on the second day of school, and all the teachers and the other children would wonder where she'd been and they'd think she hadn't come back because she was afraid and pretending to be ill. But she didn't feel very well, and to get up and dress would have required an enormous effort.

She had hoped to have the kitchen to herself today during her mother's *quiet time* so that she could get in behind the bin with a screwdriver and try to prise the hardboard away from the wall and shine in a light, but now she would have to stay in her room for the next couple of days, and then it would be back to school.

She slept through most of Thursday, and on the Friday

lay in bed and listened to the children passing the house. They were out there playing and arguing and strengthening alliances, and she could feel herself getting left even further behind. No one came to see her, though some books were sent by her form teacher, and she had to read her English book and do some maths exercises.

On the Sunday she was allowed downstairs to watch *Songs of Praise* and *Antiques Roadshow*.

When Alma went to bed on Sunday night her mother took her temperature and said she could go to school in the morning, provided her temperature was still down.

She didn't set an alarm, but when she woke up and looked at her clock it was just before 5 am. She felt better – no fever, so her return to school was just three and a half hours away. She thought, "I will have to start getting dressed at 7.30, and they will be getting up at 7, but if I don't go back to sleep now I could have at least two hours to myself."

She slid out of bed and put on her dressing gown and slippers. In one pocket she placed the box of matches and in the other the little round scrap of card. She tiptoed down to the kitchen – it was getting easier to move soundlessly around the house now that she knew where the noisy floorboards were.

In the kitchen she went over to the tool drawer and eased it open. Everything was laid out neatly: on the left hand side she found a box of candles, and in an old biscuit tin a tent peg with a looped end. Solemnly, she performed the ritual of the Stations, ending with the dive into the lake.

Under the worktop she got out the matches and lit the candle. She found an empty jam jar and let a few drops of wax fall into it to help the candle stand upright. Then she inspected the edges of the hardboard and tried to see how it was attached to the wall. There were no signs of nails or screws – it seemed to have been cut exactly to fit the space and then simply pushed into place, but it was tightly wedged all round except for a gap on the right hand side, close to the top corner, where it had been cut to fit around the pipes. She pushed the looped end of the skewer into this gap and turned it through 90 degrees. When she pulled the hardboard began to come away from the wall with surprising ease. She drew it out a few inches and stopped, not certain what to do. If this is someone's front door, she thought, it would be very rude to just burst in.

She gave her Morse Code SOS knock again and waited. There was absolute silence. She watched the carpet tile to see if it moved... Nothing. She had hoped there might be some response, but now there was none, and she was almost sure that if she managed to pull out the hardboard she would find only a brick wall behind it. Also her ritual approach had not had the same tingling specialness about it that she had experienced the last time. The candle was not guttering, as it would have done had there been a draught of any kind. She looked out of the hiding place to the clock on the wall – it was 5.20. She took hold of the skewer and pulled at the hardboard. She had to move the bin and the candle out into the room so that she could swing it away from the wall properly.

Even though her body was blocking the light, she could tell that the wall was not solid. As she held up the candle, the light fell on an open doorway framed by a stone lintel.

The carpet tile was lying half way through it, and beyond she could see other carpet tiles disappearing into the darkness.

She reached her hand through the doorway; the air on the other side felt cool and damp. The only explanation was that this was an underground room. Perhaps the ground outside was higher than it seemed and the doorway led downwards, creating some sort of optical illusion.

There had to be a *logical explanation*.

She listened – but no sound came from either the house or the place beyond the door.

Still holding the candle she began to crawl on her knees through the opening. There was just room for her to fit through without hurting herself. She crawled right in, the carpet tiles slightly damp through the knees of her pyjamas. She hoped it wouldn't be too dirty, or she'd have to do some more explaining to her mother. Once inside she turned and looked out into the kitchen: there was the silhouette of the bin and the table beyond it. Still kneeling, she sat back on her ankles and slowly lifted her eyes above the level of the top of the doorway. The wall continued up further than it could possibly have done if they were under the garden outside the kitchen. There were at least another four feet of brick wall, then a ceiling with what looked like concrete girders. She tilted her head back, then turned around, lifting the candle. She was in a small rectangular room with bare brick walls; the mortar hung from between the bricks like the filling in a cake. The floor was dusty and there were cobwebs all around the walls and ceiling.

Nothing made sense. She wondered if it could be an air raid shelter, but she knew perfectly well what the garden looked like from the kitchen window, and that there was no shed or room or anything of this size, indeed the kitchen window should look into this room! But the room had no windows and only this one tiny door.

Alma got to her feet but found it difficult to stand upright because part of her brain was telling her that this room couldn't actually be there, and she felt she was going to bump her head. When this didn't happen she decided to have a look round. What she knew for sure was that someone had been in this room – the person who had doctored her notes and sent a message, an invitation of their own, but there was no one here at the moment and no sign that anyone could ever have got in here at all. She inspected the floor for footprints – it was very dusty and seemed to have been disturbed quite recently, though she wasn't sure if she was the one who had disturbed it while walking round the room. Then she stepped on a part of the floor that felt different. Most of the carpet tiles were laid directly onto a hard stone or cement floor, but she had just stepped on one carpet tile, close to the centre of the room, which seemed springier than those around it. She knelt down to inspect it: the tile was stuck to the floor but when she tapped, it made a hollow sound.

"A trap door!" she whispered.

Feeling around the edges she found a place where she could get a handhold. She lifted it up just enough to see a chink of light. She put it down quickly, and sat back, her heart racing.

"Oh God," she said, "I want to wake up now, I really want to wake up."

Something about what she had seen had made her feel

quite ill. She felt the blood pumping in her temples like the *tramp, tramp* of the feet coming up the stairs. Or coming down the stairs... Coming down the stairs! She scuttled across the floor on her knees and squeezed through the doorway; then, not caring about the noise, she heaved the hardboard back into place, dragged the bin across the floor, blew out the candle and dropped it into the bin. Standing up she brushed off the worst of the dust, and with a calmness she did not feel, got a glass from the cupboard, went to the tap and filled it.

Alma stood panting in the darkness waiting to be asked for an explanation, but nothing happened. As the silence returned all she could hear in the darkened kitchen was the sound of her own breathing, and upstairs the gentle rhythm of her father's snoring.

Still holding her glass of water she went upstairs to her room. She took off her dressing gown and gave it a good shake, then got into bed and lay quite still.

She was trembling all over, but it was not from cold or fever, but because when she had opened the trapdoor, she had been looking *down* at a patch of grey sky.

CHAPTER SIX

The Wastelands

THE BOOK OF SLIGHTS

It felt much better walking from classroom to classroom, sitting in the dining room. I didn't mind no one talking to me because all the time I was thinking, I know something, I have seen something that would astound you. And while Mr Stephens was trying to teach us trigonometry I was thinking, I have seen something that he could not explain if he studied it for the rest of his life.

And mostly they left me alone – they didn't seem to notice that I hadn't been there last week, which is fine by me.

I have somewhere to go, and there is someone waiting for me. I know there is someone on the other side of the wall, through the trap door.

Much to her parents surprise, by eight o'clock that night Alma had done her homework and was ready for bed. Her mother felt her forehead.

"Well, you seem all right."

"I feel all right, I'm just a bit tired."

"How was school?" her father called as she passed the dining room, but he was doing some marking and didn't look at her.

"It was okay."

"Well I hope you're going to have a good term."

The unspoken part of this sentence was, "for once," but it didn't worry her. Alma felt she was above all these things now; she had had a tiny glimpse of a world beyond the school and her family. Even being handed the phone for a conversation with her grandmother didn't depress her as much as it would normally have done. Once that was over she went to bed.

She didn't set her alarm. Something told her that she would wake up at the right time if she trusted... What? Herself? God? Well, if she just *trusted*.

It seemed she had hardly turned over when she heard someone calling her name. Only they were not calling Alma or Veronica, they were calling some other name; it was her name, yet it was a name she hadn't heard for a very long time, if indeed she had ever heard it, but she knew for sure it was her name, much more than anything she had been called in her whole life. It was a name that not only belonged to her, it also described her, and it was filled with affection. It was like a nickname that someone who loves you invents and uses as a signal to let you know how much they think of you; a warm thing, like a private joke.

She opened her eyes. Now that she was wide awake she couldn't remember what the word was. It had melted away; it was nothing more than a hint of an idea from a distant place.

She looked at the clock: it was 4.15.

Alma got out of bed and began putting on her clothes. She had them all ready: her old jeans and a jersey. In her pocket was the torch she had bought at the corner shop after school. She put on socks and a pair of gym shoes. She considered wearing a hat but decided that it was going to be hard enough to explain why she was dressed if she should get caught – a hat would suggest she was intending to go outside, which could mean serious trouble. In the kitchen she went straight to the drawer and took out the skewer, then she turned on the torch, moved the bin out of the way and went to work on the hardboard. Her hands were shaking as she slipped the hoop into the hole and gave it a half turn. The metal caught and she pulled gently. The hardboard came away just as it had the night before, but there was no draught of cool air, and when she shone the torch on the place where the door had been there was a solid brick wall.

She knelt forward and put her face to the floor with her hands over her head. So, it had just been her imagination, or a dream. Or perhaps it was just that her mind had made it all up because she wanted it so badly; she was an ordinary, uninteresting person with an empty life, and she had had to fabricate something to make her seem special, if only to herself.

She got up and pushed the hardboard back into place, then the bin. She went to the drawer and put back the skewer. Then she noticed a dark patch on the floor by her foot: it was the rhubarb stain. In her excitement she had completely forgotten about the ritual! The surge of energy almost made her laugh out loud. Taking the skewer and torch she put them on the floor next to the Mortlake square and pulled out the bin so that her path was clear. Then standing in the door she mouthed the holy word "Euselessness" and stepped forward.

"Church in the Fens, St. Pancras, Mary the Good, Charing Cross, Cross of the King. I lift my arms and leap to Mortlake."

Even before she pulled back the hardboard she knew that this time it was going to work, but she was not expecting the doorway to be full of light. As she looked into the room she felt the dizziness come over her again. She tried to make sense of what she was seeing: in the middle of the room the trap door had been flung back and a pale light was filling the room. Instinctively she turned her head on one side, her brain trying to make a window of the trap door if it could not make a skylight, for through it she could see the pale grey sky. She crept into the room, then turned and looked back through the door to the window on the far side of the kitchen. There was the street lamp and the black night sky beyond. She took a deep breath and reached out for the bin. Before she pulled the hardboard back into place she managed to drag the bin more or less into its usual position. Now she was in the secret room, apparently outside her own world, but whether she was sitting on the floor or the ceiling she could not tell.

"This is going to be strange," she thought as she edged nearer to the trap door, and peered down... Or rather, peered up at the grey sky.

The torch was not needed now, so she switched it off and put it on the floor. She thought that if she tried to get through the trap door either she would have to climb out or else she would fall out. And if she fell out, when would she stop falling? She might just go on and on through the clouds and out into space. A gentle wind was blowing in the upside-down world, drawing through air from the room and occasionally blowing it back. When the air came back, it smelled pretty bad.

She held her arm over the opening and tried to gauge which way the gravity was working. She didn't feel as though her hand wanted to lift up towards what she still thought of as the ceiling. She reached an arm through the trap door and back up under the floor; her hand touched something that felt slimy and unpleasant. She brought her hand back, sniffed it and realised she had just squeezed a rotten banana.

She wondered if there might be someone close at hand who could help, so she tried calling softly, still worried about waking her parents.

"Hello! Hello!"

There was no reply. She stuck her arm through and waved it around and waited, but there was still no response. It seemed she was just going to have to risk it. Up until now she had been lying flat on her stomach, but now she sat up and gingerly brought her legs round, swinging them over the edge of the opening. She felt as if she were about to jump out of an aeroplane without a parachute.

"Okay on the count of three – and if I fall, I fall. One, two, three..."

But she could not bring herself to do it: the thought of falling forever and ever was just too scary. By way of a compromise she turned round, lay on her belly again and eased her legs further and further through the hole, supporting herself with her arms. Her legs went straight down, or up, she wasn't sure which, until at a certain point she felt her feet begin to topple over, and as she let them fall, so the rest of her body went through the hole and she just avoided bashing the back of her head on the far edge of the trapdoor.

Thus Alma made the transition between two worlds and found herself lying on her front looking down at the ceiling of the secret room, with her legs resting in a patch of rotten fruit and vegetables.

"Well that wasn't so bad," she thought, "and there can't be many people who've done that."

She sat up and looked around her. Her eyes and her nose told her that she had arrived in a rubbish heap. The smell was strong and slightly sweet – grass clippings, rotten fruit, a hint of fish. The landscape didn't look too promising either. There were trees and hills in the distance but in her immediate vicinity nothing but piles of earth and rubbish: paper and plastic and packaging mixed with fish heads and vegetables, with here and there bits of twisted metal, a rusted shopping trolley, a pram with huge wheels and broken chairs half buried in a mound of grass clippings. There were no birds in the sky and apart from the sighing of the breeze there were no sounds or signs of life.

She squelched through the rubbish that surrounded her and headed for the top of one of the mounds to get a better view. On three sides there were hills in the far distance, but in the fourth direction, which she decided must be the east, the sky was slightly brighter, and she could see light reflecting on a large body of water.

For no particular reason she thought, "That is where I should be heading!"

From where she stood the ground fell away to sea level over a distance of several miles. In between there were wooded areas, as well as fields and hedges, to be negotiated. The first clump of trees was only about a hundred yards away and as she looked she saw something moving about among them. The light was not quite good enough for her to make out what it was but it seemed to be an animal. It was walking on its hind legs and she hoped it wasn't a bear, though this didn't look like the kind of country that would have bears. She watched it for a few moments – its movements seemed almost human, yet it was covered in fur; she wondered if it could be a chimpanzee. Then it disappeared into the trees.

Alma looked back down from the mound to the trap door, which was in a little dip in the midst of all the rubbish. She realised that unless she set up some sort of marker it was going to be quite difficult to find her way home again. It took her a few minutes and she had to watch where she stepped, but in the end she managed to drag the shopping trolley up to the top of the mound as a signpost. She looked at her watch: it was still only 4.25, plenty of time for a look round. Moving quietly she set off in the direction of the trees.

"Wait a minute!" she suddenly said out loud. "Why am I still trying to be quiet? Who is there to hear me? I am here underground – and very possibly in quite another world."

She put back her head and shouted the first thing that came into her head: "This is MY WORLD!"

The words echoed around her; she couldn't remember the last time she had said anything in such a loud voice, and there was something liberating about it.

"I can say WHATEVER I LIKE!"

She waited for someone to tell her to be quiet, but nobody did. She looked over towards the trees to see if the creature might have heard her and come to have a look. Nothing stirred. The wind seemed to blow her words back to her, and she repeated softly to herself, "I can say whatever I like... What shall I say?" She thought for a minute and was disappointed to discover how few things there were that she actually wanted to say. She put her hands into the pockets of her jeans and found a piece of Blu Tack.

"I shall start with some pure nonsense," she said.

"Okay: I AM A BLU TACK MAGNATE. I OWN THE BIGGEST PIECE OF BLU TACK IN THE WORLD. Who's to say I don't? For all I know this is the only piece of Blu Tack in this world, which might make it extremely valuable – after all it is actually more useful than gold in some ways. You can't stick up posters with gold; unless they're in the form of drawing pins, and then they would be too soft to go into the wall."

Even just saying these few things had made her feel bolder, and as she approached the clump of trees she felt almost fearless.

"Sycamores!" she said, with a voice of authority. Actually she had a feeling they were probably oak trees but she liked the sound of the word *sycamore*, and in this place if she wanted to call a tree a sycamore then a sycamore it would be.

"I think if I find this animal I shall give it a name as well."

"Hello," she called into the trees. "Are you there?"

There was a scuffling noise and an angry growl as of someone who really does not wish to be disturbed, but Alma was in no mood to be ignored.

"Come out here where I can see you," she called. "Come on, I won't hurt you."

A protesting snort came from a low hedge to the right of the clump of trees.

"Where are you?" she said more softly. "I won't hurt you, it's all right." She picked up a stick that was lying close by just in case whatever-it-was turned out to be aggressive. A few yards further on she saw a dark brown thing the size of a labrador hunched in a hole in the hedge. The face was hidden and the thing had curled up like a hedgehog. The fur or hair on the back of its head was thick and wiry. It didn't look very clean, so rather than touch it she reached out with the stick and gave it a poke.

"BOG OFF!!" screamed the creature. "JUST BOGGIN' WELL BOG OFF BACK TO WHERE YOU CAME FROM!"

Alma was staring into the hairiest and most furious face she had ever seen. It seemed to be the face of an ancient little man, but it was more like a monkey than a man, with small black glinting eyes and a red mouth with sharp yellow teeth. She could see no bare skin on the face at all, just the red lips and the red rims of the eyes and a black curly beard which covered the cheeks and the chin and the forehead. It was breathing heavily and showing its teeth in a snarl that was supposed to be frightening, but the creature was so small and strange looking that she felt more like laughing than running away.

"DON'T LAUGH!!" it screamed. "DON'T BOGGIN' WELL LAUGH!!"

"You can speak," she said.

"OF COURSE I CAN BOGGIN' WELL SPEAK!"

"Did you send me the messages?"

"NO!! NOW BOG OFF, CAN'T YOU SEE I'M BUSY!?"

"What is the matter with you?"

"NOTHING! NOTHING IS THE MATTER, NOW..."

"BOG OFFF!!" screamed Alma, and it is hard to say who was more surprised, Alma or the creature. It opened its mouth and stared at her.

"I'm sorry," she said, "I don't know why I did that."

"Well I..." began the creature, but it was clearly not used to being shouted at, and it settled down into its place in the hedge and started to rub one of its legs. She watched it for a moment, then realised it was in pain.

"Is your leg all right?"

The creature didn't answer but continued to scratch painfully around a patch an inch across which was red and raw.

"Have you been bitten?" asked Alma.

"Nibbled," said the creature.

"By what?"

At first it didn't answer, then it mumbled, "It was a hard winter..."

"But what was it, rats?"

"Rats? I eat rats, they don't eat me."

"Then what?"

"Got a bit peckish..."

"What did?"

"I DID! OKAY? I DID! IT WAS A HARD WINTER...
KEPT ME GOING!"

"You ate part of your own leg?"

"Well, what of it? Kept me going."

As she watched, it stuffed a filthy, hairy little hand up to its mouth and began feverishly chewing the skin around the fingernails, then it poked the little finger into its nose, fished around and then slipped the finger quickly into its mouth.

"Oh how disgusting!" protested Alma.

"What of it?" said the creature. "You pick your own scabs and eat them, don't you."

"NO!"

"You do! Seen you!"

"You've seen me? Have you been watching me? Did you send the messages?"

"Might of..." said the creature. "Wish I hadn't now."

Alma was almost wishing it hadn't as well. She had hoped for someone or something a bit more glamorous than this offensive person, and she was beginning to realise that the unpleasant smell was not all coming from the piles of rubbish.

The creature was fumbling in the hedge now and pulled out a little tin. This contained some scraps of thin card similar to the one which had been pushed through with the message on it. It took a pinch of what looked like damp tobacco, sprinkled it onto the card, rolled it, expertly licked the edge and twisted the ends.

"What are you doing?" she asked

"Rolling me own," it said. Then it took a lighter out of the tin, and lit the end of the cigarette. The smell was terrible.

"What is it?"

"Leaves, skin, pickings, ear-poke, hair..."

"Thank you!" said Alma. "Is everyone in this country like you?"

"No one in this country is like me," said the creature proudly, "I am unique!"

Just as well, she thought, but she was too polite to say it out loud.

"Are you a he, a she or an it?" she said. "And do you have a name?" She was secretly hoping that it didn't so she could give it one.

"I do," said the creature. "My name is Stinkhorn. And I'm a he. What are you?"

"I am a she," said Alma, "and my name is Veronica Small, but I call myself Alma."

Stinkhorn took a long drag on his cigarette and putting his head on one side, stared at her for perhaps half a minute, then he suddenly stuck out a hand.

"How d'you do?" he said.

She took the paw between finger and thumb and shook it up and down.

"Pleased to meet you," she said, then wiped her hand on the leg of her jeans.

Stinkhorn appeared not to notice and continued to smoke in silence. Alma wondered whether the interview was now at an end. There were more things she wanted to know however, so she said:

"Do you mind my asking, what are...?"

"Yes," said Stinkhorn.

"Yes what?" asked Alma.

"Yes, I do mind you asking."

"Oh, well in that case could you tell me where..."

"No," said Stinkhorn firmly.

"Oh," said Alma. "Well is there anything you can?"

"'P'raps," said Stinkhorn.

"Such as...?"

"These are good!" he said holding up a withered thing that looked like a fat mushroom.

"What are they?"

"Devil's Bolete. Very tasty, better than scabs." He paused and seemed to think for a while, "Hey, come 'ere," he beckoned to her to come closer.

"The information you're after," he whispered, looking furtively to left and right, "the information what thou requirest, lieth on the other side of the sea." He looked her in the eye and winked.

"Probably," he added.

"You mean the things I wrote about?"

He winked again, then whispered, "*Over the Wall.*"

"The Wall? Is that where the Wall is?"

"Who knows?" said Stinkhorn, waving a hand mysteriously. She looked around.

"You were right about one thing," she said.

"What's that?"

"The Garbage. Where does it come from?"

"Always been here," he said, "and more keeps coming up through that bloody trap door."

"What, from my house?"

"If that's where you live."

"You know where I live," she said.

"Well then, that must be where it comes from."

He took a last drag on his cigarette and stubbed it on a little hard patch on the palm of his hand.

"Ooh, doesn't that hurt?" she said.

"Used to; not any more. Besides it makes a nice scab."

"Is this where you live?" she asked, hoping to steer the conversation away from the harvesting of scabs.

"Most of the year," he said. "A good pitch this: doesn't flood and the rent's low."

"You pay rent for this? Rent for a hole in a hedge?"

"Pay the Lawyers," he said casually. "They come and collect."

"The Lawyers? What Lawyers?"

"Lawyers in the village, when they bother to come."

"There's a village?"

"Oh yes. What did you expect?"

"Well, I didn't expect any of this, so I don't really know."

"We're quite civilised you know," said Stinkhorn. "Just because we live in the Wastelands doesn't mean..." He stopped.

"Is that what this place is called?" she asked.

"Couldn't say." He folded his arms, looked away from her and began to hum tunelessly.

Alma looked at her watch. It still said 4.25.

"I think it's stopped." She shook her wrist and listened to the watch but it didn't seem to be ticking. She looked over towards the east; the sun still hadn't risen.

"Are you going?" he said.

"I've got plenty of time," she said, "it isn't even dawn yet."

"Isn't what?"

"Dawn. The sun hasn't come up."

He stared at her blankly.

"The sun!" she said. "When the sun comes up I'd better be going. I have to go to school you know, but even at The Grange they don't expect us to be there before sunrise at this time of year."

"Sunrise?" he repeated.

"Yes, sunrise."

"But there's no sunrise here."

"What d'you mean?"

"I mean," he said with exaggerated patience, "that it is like this all the time, it never changes. The sun doesn't go up, the sun, if there is such a thing, doesn't go down; it is always like this. It's lighter over there," he added, pointing in the direction of the distant sea, "except when it comes on to rain, which it will soon, probably." He looked up at the sky. Alma saw that the clouds were gathering above their heads, and even as she looked large drops of rain began to fall.

"I should be getting back," she said.

"What's the rush?" he said.

"Well if I stay here too long I'll be missed and then I'll get into deep trouble."

"Nah, nah," said Stinkhorn reassuringly. "You're forgetting the time differential. We run on dreamtime here."

"What is dreamtime?"

"Well it's like when you have a five minute snooze during which you have a dream that seems to last for days."

"I don't know that I have dreams like that," she said.

"Or," he said, "you go to sleep and dream that you're defusing a bomb and you see the numbers counting down to zero and when they reach zero, instead of an explosion, you hear this buzzing noise and you wake up and it's the alarm going off."

"Yes, I've never quite understood how that happens."

"Time differential," said Stinkhorn confidently. "An hour in one world might correspond to a minute or even a second in another. I've read up on the subject. So, you've plenty of time. Why don't we go down to the village?"

"To the village? Is it safe?"

"'Course it's safe. We can call on the Lawyers."

Alma thought for a moment. In spite of the gloomy surroundings and the strangeness of her companion, she was enjoying the adventure and she really wanted to believe the bit about time passing slowly. If Stinkhorn was telling the truth then she could stay here and put off the start of school for days – even weeks.

"I can see what you're thinking," said Stinkhorn, and he had to speak quite loudly now as the rain was falling heavily, drumming on the leaves above their heads. "You can stay as long as you like, but mind it doesn't wear you out."

"How do you mean?"

He tapped the side of his head.

"Blow a fuse."

"I won't blow a fuse," she said.

"Oh well, if you think you know," he said. "Don't say I didn't warn you."

He scrabbled out of the hedge and got painfully to his feet. The place where he had been sitting was hollowed out like a nest. Now that he was standing she saw he was about the size of a six-year-old child. He was wearing a long coat of animal skin and his body seemed to be covered all over in thick black fur, like a wiry poodle.

He limped badly due to his leg. When she offered him her hand he just snorted. They set off down the slope towards the village, the sea and the light of the sun, which apparently never rose.

CHAPTER SEVEN

Offal's Circus of Renown

THE BOOK OF SLIGHTS

Mum told me I should make more of an effort to
be liked, so I had this idea that I would tell a joke,
and it would have to be a really good joke, and it
would make everyone laugh, and the dinner table
would be the best place to tell it. Jamie told a
joke once and Mr Smith told him to come and see
him after the meal and he put him in the school
play, just on the strength of telling a joke. So my
cousins told me a joke, and they said that everyone thought it was funny, and if I didn't think it
was funny then I didn't have a sense of humour,
and then they told it to me and I didn't really
think it was that funny, but then I often don't
get jokes so maybe (I thought) this one really is
funny and jokes aren't always the ones you think
are funny, because often the things that I find
funny other people don't. So I picked my moment
carefully, and there was a silence and I was sitting
quite close to Mr Smith, and he is a really kind
person. Once in class he was trying to explain the
phrase 'still waters run deep' and he looked at
me and said, "Like Veronica," and though I hate

my name it didn't sound so bad when he said it. So anyway I just started because I wasn't sure how to start telling a joke, whether you're meant to say, "I have a joke," or just start. I can never remember how most people start jokes, they just seem to be telling them or they come one after another in which case you say, "I've got one! I've got one!" But no one had said very much that day so I just began. I said, "What do you get if you cross a chicken?" I wanted to tell it to Mr Smith but just as I was starting to tell it he looked away, so I had to sort of redirect it to the people on the other side of the table, and Martin heard and looked at me a little surprised, and then everyone seemed to be listening and he said, "I don't know, what do you get if you cross a chicken?" And I said, "Pecked." And then they were all looking at me, and from the far end of the table Paula said, "It speaks!" And everyone burst out laughing, including Mr Smith. She just timed it so perfectly, everyone was laughing and laughing, only I wasn't laughing.

"It's the way I tell 'em," says Paula.

She wants to be a stand-up comedian when she grows up and everyone says she would be very good at it.

They made slow progress. The rain had abated, but the rubbish heaps were slithery and it was clearly some time since Stinkhorn had attempted a journey of this distance; he was limping and he whimpered every so often. When Alma asked him if he was all right he grunted and said he thought he could walk a lot better than *she* could. She tried asking him more questions about himself and the place where they were, but he either shrugged or pretended not to hear.

They walked for half an hour or so and then came in sight of a shabby looking encampment of tents and caravans, in the window of one of which a dim light was burning. A faded sign on the side of the largest tent proclaimed:

OFFAL'S CIRCUS OF RENOWN

"What a dreadful name for a circus," said Alma.

"It's a dreadful circus," said Stinkhorn.

"Have you been?"

"Once – and believe me, once is enough."

"But we're not in any hurry..." She was going to add, "And you could do with the rest," but thought better of it.

"They might have candy floss," she suggested.

"If they do it'll be expensive and disgusting."

"Well, I'd like to stop anyway, if you don't mind."

Stinkhorn said he supposed they could have a quick look if she insisted. They walked in between two caravans and saw a hut with a sign saying:

TICKEST

A skinny dog was sniffing at the side of it. He turned at their approach, gave a woof of alarm and hurried off towards one of the caravans.

"Do you think they're open?" asked Alma.

"They open whenever they can get an audience," said Stinkhorn. "They'll be very pleased to see you. Got any money?"

She felt in her pocket.

"Only twenty pence," she said, "and some Blu Tack."

Stinkhorn looked at the coin and the little blue lump in the palm of her hand. He took the coin and bit into it, murmuring appreciatively, "The Real McCoy!" He gave it back, took the lump of Blu Tack and popped it into his mouth. He chewed briefly, then swallowed.

"Chewing gum?" he asked

"Not really. It's a type of glue."

"Not bad though. Got any more?"

"I'm afraid not."

"Oh well, the coin should get us in," he said.

Alma went up to the hut and knocked on the window.

"Is there anyone there?" she called.

The hut shifted slightly and a mop of peroxide blonde hair rose into view, followed by a wide forehead and two piggy eyes.

"Yus?" said a deep voice.

"Excuse me, when is the next show?" asked Alma politely.

The eyes stared at her for a moment, then the head once again sank out of view.

She waited, and finally the hut trembled again and the eyes reappeared.

"Any conceshuns?"

"Concessions?" asked Alma, looking down at Stinkhorn.

He shook his head and murmured something about not needing any boggin' charity. Alma thought this odd, since she was the one who was paying.

"Well I'm a child," she said, "and my friend... isn't."

The head disappeared again, then a little mirror on a stick appeared, angled down towards Stinkhorn. Alma sniffed; there was a smell of drains coming from somewhere nearby.

"Twenty pence," said the voice.

"That's perfect," said Alma.

"Nothing left for candy floss though," murmured Stinkhorn. "Can't be expected to go to the circus and not have candy floss..."

Alma slipped the twenty pence piece through the little window and received two soiled, much re-used tickets in return.

"When does it start?"

"They're waiting for you," said the voice. "You can go in when you're ready."

Clutching the tickets they headed for the tent, from where an unenthusiastic voice had begun to proclaim: "This way, this way, step right up, step right up. Behold the Seven Wonders of the World! See a man who can saw himself in half without the aid of a safety net; be amazed by our amazing re-enactment of *The Charge of The Light Brigade*; split your sides when you hear the *FUNNIEST CLOWN IN THE LEFT-HAND HEMISPHERE...*"

At mention of the clown there were some whoops of appreciation and applause from the ticket hut. Alma and Stinkhorn pulled back the flap and stepped into the tent. It smelled of paraffin, which wasn't surprising as the place was lit by half a dozen smoking paraffin lamps placed precariously around a foot-high wooden circus ring. Beyond the ring were red velvet curtains. There were just two chairs, which seemed to have been deliberately positioned to provide the worst possible view, right behind a tent pole.

A man in a clown costume took their tickets and pointed to the chairs. He was holding a megaphone and appeared to be the one who had been making the announcement.

"Restricted view only I'm afraid," he said. "Should have got here earlier, we're just about to go up."

Before they could say anything he hurried off through the curtains. Alma and Stinkhorn went over to the chairs, moved them round to the front of the ring and settled down to watch the show.

Nothing happened for a few minutes, except that one of the paraffin lamps expired.

An out-of-tune trumpet began to play a dirge and a man in a red coat and top hat stepped out into the ring. He was tall and thin with a pale face and a black moustache, which looked as though it had been hastily stuck on. The left side of his face was contorted due to the effort of holding a monocle in his eye socket. The monocle was attached to a ribbon that hung around his neck.

"LADIES AND... and..." His voice trailed off as he surveyed the audience and the monocle fell out. He put it back and continued. "Welcome to *Offal's Circus of Renown*. Tonight for your de-lectation we have – a man who will saw a fellow member of the audience in half without the use of anaesthetics, a savage beast who has been tamed by the will of man, and a clown so funny he can make himself cry with laughter."

"That's not what they said before," whispered Alma

to Stinkhorn.

"I told you," he said, "I warned you..."

"Well, I'm not being sawn in half!"

"You young lady, perhaps you would like to come here into the ring?" said the Ringmaster.

"Not really," said Alma.

"Oh!" he seemed surprised. "Oh, that's a pity, and I suppose you sir, don't want to cut her in half?"

Stinkhorn shook his head.

"Oh, well I suppose you'll be wanting to see the other acts then?"

"That's what we've paid for," said Stinkhorn.

The Ringmaster's shoulders slumped and his monocle fell out again. He went through the curtain and there was some heated discussion, after which the young clown was shoved into the ring.

He stood there for a moment without moving, then gave a deep sigh and produced some juggling balls from a deep pocket. Without any sort of build-up he proceeded to juggle first three, then four, then five, sending the multi-coloured balls higher and higher above his head. Sometimes they formed a perfect cascade; sometimes, by crossing hands, he managed to create a figure of eight; then he began catching them behind his back; then with one arm through his legs. Alma had never in her life seen anything so skilful or so beautiful. The act continued in absolute silence, the clown's face registering no emotion. Then suddenly, with all five balls sailing through the air, he thrust his hands into his pockets and walked off through the curtain, leaving the balls to thud one by one onto the dusty floor.

Alma stood to her feet and began to clap and shout, "Encore!"

But the clown did not reappear. Instead the trumpet squeaked again and the curtains opened to reveal the dog they had seen earlier by the ticket office. He was wearing a ruff around his neck in the manner of a Toby Dog, and indeed there was a suggestion of Jack Russell about him, though he was too lanky to be purebred. He walked into the ring, stepping softly as if his feet were sore. At one point he turned and tried to slink back into the shadows, but someone hissed at him and he turned again, his tail thrust so far between his legs that it was brushing the floor in front of him. He sat down among the juggling balls and looked over his shoulder, licking his lips and showing his teeth in a grin. Again an order was given from offstage. The dog looked at Alma and Stinkhorn, then stood once more to his feet.

From behind the curtain there came a funereal drum roll. It sounded like the drum had burst and been repaired badly with Sellotape. The dog leant forward onto its front paws and lifted itself to a handstand position, then tucking in its back legs, it set off around the ring. At the same time someone began to recite in a breathless voice:

Half a league, half a league, half a league onward
Into the valley of death rode the six hundred...

Alma recognised the poem. It was one their history teacher had read to the class, and she knew it had to do with a disastrous cavalry charge. She was trying to work out who was doing the recitation, which didn't seem to be coming from beyond the curtain.

Cannons to right of them, cannons to left of them
Cannons in front of them volleyed and thundered

The dog's mouth was moving in a very un-doglike way.

Into the valley of death rode the six hundred...

Alma leant across to Stinkhorn and whispered, "I do believe it's the dog that's reciting the poetry!"

"Yes," said Stinkhorn, "but he's making a real mess of the acrobatics."

Indeed the dog was finding the task increasingly difficult; he kept nearly tripping over the juggling balls.

Forward the light brigade
Was there a man dismayed?
Whoops! Was there a man dismayed?
Not though... Whoa...! not though the soldier knew
Oh no...

He just managed to keep his balance as he dodged the final ball and reached the edge of the ring. Here he paused, did a pirouette, then began to walk back towards the curtain, while the angry someone whispered:

"Keep reciting!"

Perhaps because the end was in sight, the dog seemed to get a second wind:

Not though the soldier knew
Someone had blundered
Theirs not to make reply
Theirs not to reason why
theirs but to do and die...

He made a dash for the curtain saying very quickly:

Intothejawsofdeathintothemouthofhellrodethesixhundred.

As he plunged off stage the curtain was drawn behind him.

Alma stood to her feet again and applauded even more loudly than she had for the juggling clown. Stinkhorn muttered that it had been better the last time he was there.

There was another argument going on behind the curtains. Eventually the clown reappeared, his expression even gloomier than before. He stared at them.

"There's no pleasing some people," he said.

Alma assumed he was talking about the Ringmaster or whoever it was making a fuss behind the curtain.

"They don't like juggling, they don't like the bloody dog... All right then, I'll give you what you've come for!"

He fished a piece of paper out of his pocket and began to read: "What-do-you-get-if-you-confuse-a-herd-of-cows-udder-chaos." He read this so quickly that it was a few seconds before Alma realised it was meant to be a joke. Giving them another angry stare the clown pressed on with his list of jokes, which seemed to make less and less sense.

"What's the difference between a daisy and a dredger? One's a flower and the other isn't. What's the difference between butter and bitter? U and I. Why don't chickens cross the road anymore? The Council Bantam..."

Suddenly he screwed up the piece of paper, hurled it on the floor and shouted, "Oh what's the point? I give it my best shot. I wrench the life from my very soul, and look at them!" He pointed at Alma and Stinkhorn and screamed, "Look at them! THEY JUST SIT THERE!" Then he burst into tears.

"I think it's time we left," said Stinkhorn, getting up.

The Ringmaster had come through the curtains and placed a stiff arm round the heaving shoulders of the clown.

Alma called out, "Thank you. It was a very good show. We particularly liked the juggling and the dog."

"Philistines!" screamed the clown. "What's the matter with you? Had a sense of humour bypass or what?"

"We'll be on our way," said Stinkhorn.

They made for the exit but their way was barred by a rectangular shape, which came swaying towards them from the shadows.

"My child!" wailed a muffled voice. "What have you done to my little boy?"

The ticket office, complete with occupant, was bearing down upon them. Two fat legs stuck out from the bottom of it; two enormous arms had been thrust through the sides and were carrying it like a wooden petticoat. Alma and Stinkhorn backed towards the ring.

"It's all right mother!" howled the clown.

"My baby, what have they done to you? Oh my heart, my breaking heart!"

For a moment Alma wondered if this wasn't part of the show. She grabbed Stinkhorn and steered him back towards the seats. The ticket office swayed past them into the ring and came to a halt in front of the clown and Ringmaster. Then it dropped to the ground with a crash, and the arms stretched out to embrace the fallen clown. This was an impossibility, but the gesture was understood and the clown went and leant against the front of the hut.

"There, there mother," he said, "it's all right now."

"My little precious one..."

Alma and Stinkhorn noticed that the Ringmaster was looking at them again.

"This is all your fault," he said.

"Let's leave," said Stinkhorn tugging at Alma's sleeve.

"What do you mean, 'our fault'?" said Alma. Something in the tone of her voice silenced both sobbing clown and wailing ticket lady.

With much scraping and puffing the hut turned through 90 degrees and faced them. The occupant lifted her head slightly to look out of the window. The light from the paraffin lamp played on the blonde hair, the piggy eyes and, to their great surprise, a thick blonde beard.

"She's going to take him away from us, she's going to steal our baby away from us with her flashing eyes and her fine speech," she said. The Ringmaster took out a handkerchief and put it in her hand. "Don't upset yourself," he said.

"Upset myself? Upset myself? She's the one who's doing the upsetting. And not for the first time."

"What do you mean?" said Alma, who was getting more and more fed up with being blamed for everything. "I've never been here before in my life, so how can you say not for the *first time*? And what am I even supposed to have done?"

"They're always coming round – the floozies, trying to tempt our lovely boys away from home and hearth, poor mites. One by one my little childer have been lured away from the straight and narrow into paths of wickedness."

The Ringmaster patted the back of the hut. "There, there. It's all right my dear, Sidney isn't going anywhere." He turned to Alma and Stinkhorn, and spoke more softly.

"I think it might be best if you left now."

"We really did enjoy the show you know," Alma said, "and we're very sorry if we've offended anybody."

"It shall not signify," said the Ringmaster magnanimously.

The clown, Sidney, was now sitting quietly in the middle of the ring. There was no sign of the dog.

"Just before we go," said Alma, "can I ask you something?"

The Ringmaster looked at her sadly.

"If you must."

"Do the three of you do everything in this circus? "

"The four of us," said a voice from behind the curtain, and the dog poked his head into view again.

"Oh, yes of course. You were very good," she added.

"Thank you!" said the dog and disappeared again.

The atmosphere seemed to have calmed down now and Alma was reluctant to leave without finding out a bit more about *Offal's Circus of Renown.*

"So are you all one family?" she began.

"We are," said the Ringmaster. "I am Septimus Offal the Seventh, this is my seventh son Sidney and this lady," he indicated the ticket office, "is my wife, Lenore."

"Oh well it's nice to meet you!" said Alma, and nudged Stinkhorn who said that he couldn't see anything particularly nice about it.

The Ringmaster gave a little bow of acknowledgement, Sidney looked up and gave a reluctant nod and between sniffles the gruff voice from the ticket office said, "Charmed!"

"How long have you been in the circus?" asked Alma.

"All our lives," said the Ringmaster. "We have been

performing since before we could even walk or talk or think, and we have trained up our sons in the same way. Sadly one by one they have... moved on, but Sidney has remained. As for myself, in my younger days I was an acrobat and strongman."

"And what did your wife do?" asked Alma.

"Yes, was she the fat lady or the bearded lady or both?" added Stinkhorn.

There were looks of horror on the faces of the ringmaster and his son, and a deep moan issued from the ticket office.

"She," bellowed the Ringmaster, drawing himself up to his full height, "was LOVELY LENORE THE TIGHT-ROPE WALKER!"

"Thank you, we'll be off now," said Alma and pushed Stinkhorn towards the exit.

"What did you have to go and say that for?" she hissed.

"I wanted to know!" he said. "Tightrope walker my foot, she'd have snapped a ship's cable."

"Well perhaps she has only put on weight recently."

At the tent flap Alma looked back at the family huddled in the middle of the ring, and felt guilty for the suffering that her presence had caused. Just outside the tent they found the dog waiting for them.

"Where are you going?" he asked.

"Into the village," said Stinkhorn.

"Mind if I tag along?" he said.

"Won't you be needed for the next performance?" asked Alma.

"Don't care if I am," he said. "They're all barking mad. And they treat me like dirt. I've been meaning to leave for ages, just couldn't think of anywhere to go."

So the three of them made their way out of the circle of caravans and headed off once again in the direction of the village.

CHAPTER EIGHT

The Leprechaun Lawyers

THE BOOK OF SLIGHTS

There is one time I think about more than any other and my face still goes red and I hide under the sheets. We are in the village hall, I am eight years old and we are to go out and sing 'We Three Kings or Orient Are' in front of the whole school plus parents. (I used to think it was 'Ory and Tar' before I found out what 'Orient' meant). We have been rehearsing and rehearsing and I know the words, 'Myrrh is mine its bitter perfume, spreads a life of gathering gloom,' and I feel okay about it because while I am not the best singer I am not the worst either. There are three of us and I'm the second best, or second worst depending on how you look at it, and Mrs Highgate says we'll be fine and not to worry, and I'm really not worrying too much, though it is the first thing I have ever done on my own in front of an audience. And we're waiting behind the curtain and we can hear all the parents arriving and someone says my mother wants me, and I think, this is not right, they are meant to take us home afterwards but they aren't meant to come and see us before, but I have to go and see her, and anyway she has her head round the curtain and she's looking for me, and Granny is there with her, and they straighten my cloak and the crown on my head, and Granny says, "Good luck my dear, oh no I'm not supposed to say that am I? You break a leg!" And at that age I didn't have the first idea what she was talking about. Then I saw my mother looking at me and she said, "Are you sure you want to do this?" and I said "I don't know," and she took my face in her hands and said, "Just be yourself and it'll be fine," but actually I knew that she was more worried than I was. Then I thought, why is she so worried? Does she know something about me that I don't know? And then Granny said, "That's it, you do your best, no one can ask for more than that." But I was thinking: how can I be myself? What are you supposed to do in order to be yourself? And I didn't really want to be myself and Mrs Highgate had said we should imagine that we really were Kings and that would make us sing better and I liked the idea of being a King, of being the mysterious one who brought the Myrrh. I liked the sound of the word Myrrh, it seemed so strange and foreign and unlike any English word. Frankincense is like incense and gold is gold but Myrrh - it's like a person snoring, or a baby asleep. And in my crown and my red cloak I could forget who I was and be a King and go out and sing, and now she said I had to be me. I hate being me. I would rather be anyone but me. I don't even like the word 'me'. I hate saying the word. 'Me - myself - mine' - they are whiny sort of words, words we shouldn't be saying all the time, always going on and on about ourselves.

So when our turn came the others sang their solos first and then it came my turn, and the piano started and I croaked out, 'Myrrh is mine its bitter perfume...' And I knew it was so out of tune, and then I found that the next line wasn't there when I needed it, though it had always been there in rehearsal. So the piano just kept playing, and everyone was looking at me, and I could see them out there in the audience, and Granny put her hand to her mouth, but my mother didn't, she tried to smile. Then the whole of the school joined in with the chorus, 'Star of wonder star of night, star with royal beauty bright, westward leading still proceeding, guide us to thy heavenly light.'

And after the carol service no one spoke to me at all, and I was glad that they didn't. I just wanted to be left alone and I took off the stupid cloak and the even stupider cardboard crown and I swore inside that I would never ever sing in public again, not ever, ever again, or act or think that I could sing or act because I realised what my mother had obviously known, that I was useless at performing, just useless. I will never perform for anyone ever again. From now on I will just stay in the background and eventually I will have grown up and I won't have to be a stupid little child any more and make all these mistakes and always be making a fool of myself the whole time.

"What's your name?" Alma asked the dog as they walked through yet another rubbish-strewn field.

"Oh blimey," said the dog, "I knew you were going to ask me that. What am I supposed to say again?"

"Well I don't know, what's your name?"

The dog thought about this for a while. "Sorry," he said, "I'm not quite clear about this, what do you want me to say exactly?"

"Your name!" said Stinkhorn impatiently.

"Okay, and do you want me to go up on the front legs?"

"No, we just wanted to know your name. Our names are Alma and Stinkhorn."

The dog still seemed confused. "I'm sorry," he said, "I haven't quite got the gist, how does it go?"

"Well normally," explained Alma, "someone says hello my name is – as it might be in my case Veronica Small or Alma for short – and you say how do you do, my name is... Spot or whatever your name is."

"Is it Spot?" he said.

"Well, I don't know."

"And up on the front or the back?"

"No, you can just walk normally and tell us your name."

"And you think they'll applaud?"

"Who'll applaud?"

"The audience."

"What audience?"

"The audience at the next show."

Alma and Stinkhorn looked at each other.

"I think we should just give him a name," she said, secretly pleased because she had been dying to start naming things ever since she had come through the trap door.

"Okay," she said to the dog, "now we are going to give

you a name which is yours to keep and be called by and you don't have to perform it or stand on your front or back legs to say it, it will be yours and yours alone – well, that is, it may belong to other people as well but..."

The dog's expression told her that she was making things overly complicated, so she put a hand on his shoulder and said, "I name you... *Alfred Lord Tennyson.*"

"Strewth!" said Stinkhorn.

"That's who wrote the *half a league* poem," she said.

The dog was looking rather pleased.

"Say it again," he said.

"Alfred Lord Tennyson, but we can call you Alfred or Tennyson for short."

"Or Lord," said Stinkhorn.

"Well that wouldn't be quite right, technically it's a title."

The dog considered for a moment. "Tennyson," he said at length. "I like the sound of that."

"Okay," she said, "Tennyson it is."

They continued walking. Every so often the dog would get up on his front or hind legs for a while. At first Alma laughed and applauded each time he did this, but then she decided this was just his natural way of walking, so she began to ignore it. The dog Tennyson was muttering under his breath and at last he said with great deliberation, "I will call you Bucket and Docket!"

The other two stopped and looked at him.

"You really haven't got the hang of this whole name thing yet, have you?" said Stinkhorn.

"You see you don't need to give us names because we already have names; we were only giving you a name because you didn't have one," explained Alma.

"You're not that bright, are you," said Stinkhorn.

But now the dog was trembling, looking anxiously from one to the other.

"Oh dear," said Alma, "now you've frightened him."

The dog had his tail between his legs again and was stammering snatches of verses – presumably things he had been forced to recite.

"*The boy stood on the burning deck...?* No wait, *If I should die think only this of me...?*"

"It's all right," said Alma soothingly, and she sat down beside him on the ground and put her arms round his neck. "You don't have to do any more reciting or balancing or anything you don't want to do. In fact," a thought suddenly occurred to her, "you don't have to speak any more if you don't want to."

She looked into the tired and frightened eyes, which were now filled with tears.

"Really?" he said, with such longing in his voice that even Stinkhorn seemed to be moved.

"They shouldn't do that you know," he said. "It isn't right. It isn't natural."

"I wonder what they've done to him to make him like this."

"Trained him since he was a puppy I shouldn't wonder."

The dog seemed suddenly too weary to move. He was leaning all his weight against Alma. She tried to pick him up and found that he was incredibly light.

"They can't have fed him much," she said, "he's just a bag of bones."

"Maybe we can find something for him in the village," said Stinkhorn. They were very close to it now; through the trees they could see roofs and a smoking chimney.

"Where shall we go first?" asked Alma.

"The Lawyers is the only place open at this hour."

"What hour is that?"

"Well to be exact it's the only place in the village that's ever open," Stinkhorn explained. "In fact," he continued, "it's the only place in the village that's even inhabited."

They had reached the main street, such as it was: a few shabby houses either side of a dirt track, their windows dark and lifeless, but there was one house that had lights burning in the windows and seemed to be in a reasonable state of repair. This was the house with the smoking chimney that they had spotted through the trees. The wood smoke made Alma think of Christmas, though Christmas was still a long way off.

They pushed open the door and a bell tinkled somewhere in a distant part of the house. Bearing the exhausted Tennyson, Alma followed Stinkhorn into an office furnished with filing cabinets, desks and brass lamps with green shades. The walls, which were a pale green colour, were covered with diplomas and photographs of men in stiff collars. From the back of the office, beyond a glass partition, they could see a flight of stairs leading to the upper floor. Stinkhorn went to the bottom of the stairs and called, "Shop!"

Instantly they heard a disturbance upstairs: chairs scraped across the floor, voices were raised in surprise and there was such a rumbling and crashing that Alma expected to see a dozen people come pouring down the stairs. Instead they were joined by just three men, all wearing tailcoats, tight grey trousers and black shoes. Two of them were elderly, but the third, though dressed the same, was young, being perhaps in his late teens. Alma would normally have felt quite shy about walking unannounced into the home of some total strangers, but the expressions of the two older men were kindly, and none of them were more than a few inches taller than her.

"Look at the poor Doggie," said one of the old men.

"Poor Doggie not well?" asked the other, whose features were so similar to the first that Alma was sure they must be brothers. The younger man hung back and said nothing, but wrung his hands.

"Bring Doggie close to the fire," said one of the brothers.

"Find a blanket," said the other.

"And some warm milk," said the first.

"And a juicy bone."

These commands were addressed to the younger man who had set off in one direction when they had asked for a blanket, and in another when they had asked for milk, and had headed for the door when they mentioned a bone, but now seemed unable to make up his mind which of the three was the most important and so was just hopping from one foot to the other. The elderly gentlemen took Tennyson from Alma's arms, laid him on the rug in front of the fire and began rubbing his paws.

Without looking up, one of the old men said, "Got the rent?"

"Bring it next month," mumbled Stinkhorn.

"Fair enough!" said both old men together, their squeaky

voices hitting slightly different but harmonious notes. Alma thought they seemed nice, but she didn't know what to make of the youth, who was still trying to make up his mind what to do.

"Get them ourselves shall we?" suggested one old man.

"Best had," agreed the other.

They got up, went through to the back of the house and returned with a blanket and a bowl of bread and milk; they didn't seem to have any bones to hand. When they put the bowl down Tennyson raised his head and began to eat, at first tentatively, but then with enthusiasm.

"There, that'll do him some good," said one brother.

"Now come and have a sit. We're neglecting you – sheer neglect! Coffee? Coffee?"

Chairs were brought and cups of coffee were served.

"There," said one of the brothers, "you must be tired and hungry and bored and needy. What can we do you for, what can we do you for?"

"If you ever need a lawyer..." said the other, looking at Alma over the top of his half moon glasses, and slipping a card into her hand. The two men began speaking quickly.

"Now where to begin?"

"What's the brief?"

"What is our strategy?"

"Do you think we should settle out of court, Mr Beezly?"

"Mr Hay, I think we should plead guilty!"

"Will there be time off for good behaviour?"

This last remark was directed to Alma, who was by now completely confused.

"I think we should start again," she said. "We haven't

come here for legal advice."

"Oh!" said both gentlemen in surprise, harmonising once again.

"And we haven't come to pay the rent," added Stinkhorn.

"So you mentioned," they said, with a hint of disapproval.

"So you're not a stolen child then?" said the one who had been referred to as Mr Beezly.

"Me?" asked Alma.

"I!" he corrected.

"I mean, I? No."

"Are you sure?"

"Quite sure."

"This Elf hasn't stolen you then? He doesn't want us to negotiate a fee with your parents?"

"Oh, he isn't an Elf... Is he?" she looked at Stinkhorn questioningly. He pointed to the side of his head and made a circular motion with his finger.

"No I don't think he's an Elf, and he certainly hasn't stolen me."

"Not an Elf, but could be a Pixie, or a Leprechaun, or some such? One of our specialities you know; they used to call us the Leprechaun Lawyers. We did a good trade once upon a time, but it's all gone out of fashion now, all these fillums and war-games; the children can zap 'em now see, so they're not afraid anymore. We used to deal with Bogarts and all sorts – very lucrative."

"Yes we hoped our nephew would join us in the partnership..." Both old men turned to look at the agitated youth who was now hovering near the bottom of the stairs, biting his lip.

"Come and sit down Nephew, you're making us all nervous." He hurried over to one of the desks, and lifting the tails of his jacket, sat down and began rearranging pencils.

"So are you brothers?" asked Alma. "I thought you were at first, but you called each other by different names."

"Cousins, Miss...?"

"Small, Veronica Small. Or Alma for short."

"I am Mr Hay and this is Mr Beezly and we are cousins, Miss Small."

"Twice removed!" said Mr Beezly.

"At least!" said Mr Hay. "And our Nephew," he gestured towards the youth.

"Say hello Nephew."

The boy looked at the ceiling and said, "Hellooo," in a quavering voice. He was breathing heavily and rubbing his hands together.

"Is he all right?" asked Stinkhorn. "He doesn't look normal to me."

"NO!" said Mr Beezly vehemently. "No, Mr Stinkhorn, he is not all right. We are saddened, are we not Mr Hay?"

"We are saddened Mr Beezly, for we had such high hopes."

They both drew their chairs closer to the visitors and lowered their voices.

"We had such high hopes, Miss Small..."

"He was such an exceptionally bright child..."

"Could read at the age of two..."

"Sooner, before he was fully two..."

"Before he was fully two, his parents – our dear cousins, found him reading the telephone directory."

"Of course they wanted the best for him..."

"And they themselves were simple folk, so they sent him to us..."

"And we had such high hopes..."

"Hay, Beezly and Nephew... You didn't see the sign outside?"

"I'm sorry, I didn't look," said Alma.

"Doesn't matter!" said Mr Beezly. "Doesn't matter! You wouldn't have seen it no matter how much you'd looked, because it isn't there!"

"It isn't there!" echoed his cousin.

"All our hopes dashed..."

"And by what?"

They paused, both leaning back in their chairs with their eyebrows raised. Alma waited for them to go on, then realised that they were waiting for her to say something.

"Erm, by what?"

"We'll tell you! By the Creeping Wordslip!"

"The Creeping Wordslip? What is that?"

"Congenital lunacy," murmured Stinkhorn.

They gave him a severe look. "Libellous words, Mr Stinkhorn," said Mr Hay, "but under the circumstances we will overlook them. As we were saying, the Creeping Wordslip..."

"Let us demonstrate!" said Mr Beezly.

"Nephew!" he called. "Come over here and deliver the speech you prepared for the case of Porter versus O'Riley."

"Now you'll see something," he said and winked at Alma and Stinkhorn.

The youth took a deep breath and composed himself, then he looked through some papers on the desk and selected a single sheet. They all turned their chairs towards him.

The two cousins folded their arms and settled back to listen. On the rug by the fire Tennyson was now sleeping peacefully. The youth stood to his feet, put the thumb of his left hand into his waistcoat pocket and struck a confident pose, completely at odds with his previous manner. He looked round at his audience and smiled reassuringly.

"Ladies and Gentlemen of the Jury," he began, "in addressing you this afternoon, I am well aware that my words will arouse in you emotions which you may find... uncomfortable. For the last seventeen days we have been discussing matters that any rational human being would find distasteful, not to say harrowing; but there comes a time in the life of the man or woman who wishes to be a truly useful member of society, when their eyes must be opened to behold the inner workings of the human heart."

He stepped out from behind the desk and began to pace the floor. His voice, far from quavering, was now strong and resonant and Alma had the feeling that whatever he said she would be bound to agree with him.

"The Human Heart, ladies and gentleman, what can we say about the Human Heart?"

He lifted a hand heavenwards.

"That it is the fount of love, the seat of joy and affection?"

He looked down, frowning and dropping his voice to a dramatic whisper.

"That the heart is deceitful and desperately wicked?"

He paused, and looked each one of them in the eye.

"And who shall know just *how* wicked?"

They sat in silence, and he held them there for a few seconds. Alma heard the fire crackling in the fireplace, and he held them still; he held them perhaps just a fraction too long, and then he held them a little longer and Alma realised that he had no idea what he was going to say next. The youth referred once again to the sheet of paper, but it seemed he couldn't find the place. He tugged at his collar.

"Ah," he said, "ah yes..." and he began to read, but the quavering note had come back into his voice.

"The... the... the consequences of our actions may at times be slow to find us out... but... but..."

His confidence had disappeared, and he even seemed to be having trouble reading the words off the page. He went back to the desk and held the sheet under the light, but he had lost his momentum.

"Well," he said, sadly, "it is nows downs to Naples and I to supply the world with noodles." Alma and Stinkhorn looked at each other.

"This brain-fag of hardened lip-salve, this little thinking cap, this leaky funnel... I ache for maximum peaches, post haste, post haste! Sit on your hands ladies and gentlemen, after all is said and done we are chumps and plutocrats, rumbustious and well couched. Gracious is that the date? I feel condensed. Your eyes, my dear, are like two limpid pools, and what, I may well ask...?"

They waited to find out what he might well ask, but that seemed to be it for now.

"A postscript! A postscript!" cried Mr Beezly and clapped his hands encouragingly. They waited, but no postscript was forthcoming. The speech seemed to have taken a lot out of the youth, who slumped onto the desk and lay there, moaning.

"It is sad," said Mr Hay. "The meaninglessness has him in

its grip – he hardly comes out with anything at all these days, except when visitors arrive. The meaninglessness encroaches, and everything else diminishes, nothing is quite how it once was." He sat back in his chair and put his hands into his pockets.

"But there is no work anyway," he went on. "We have been forced to take on tasks that in former days we would never have touched. Obviously in the legal profession one is obliged to deal with the baser elements, but recently we have had to sink so very low..." His voice trailed off, and a dark look passed across his face.

"As to our Nephew, well, we shall have to let him go, but to where? The whole region is in recession." He turned to Alma. "The tourists you see, we just don't get the tourists any more, nobody comes to visit us – apart from your good selves of course." He took hold of her hand and gripped it tightly.

"What does it all mean, Miss Small? What does life mean?"

Alma could feel things becoming unstable. She tried to remember what the first note had said.

"It means we must try to... We must try to give... life... meaning?"

Her words met with no response. They all sat in silence and listened to the crackling of the fire. Alma found the atmosphere suddenly oppressive. The blood was thumping in her temples and she was beginning to feel dizzy. She looked at the cup in her lap and doubts began to creep into her mind. What was she doing here with these strange people? She didn't really know any of them. What if Stinkhorn *was* an Elf who had tempted her to come through the trap door;

what if he was in league with the Leprechaun Lawyers and they were going to hold her to ransom, or worse still, slit her throat and bury her under the floorboards? What were these *baser elements* they had been forced to begin working for? As the terror began to take hold of her, she noticed that the two old men were looking at something behind her. She thought, "Someone is creeping up on me... There is a fourth partner in this firm, the one who is going to tie me up or stab me, and he is standing right behind me... This whole speech thing was just an elaborate distraction."

There was still a little coffee left in her cup, and an idea occurred to her. She knew she would have to move very quickly if she was going to evade capture and make it to the door. Once outside she was pretty sure she could outrun them. Out of the corner of her eye she thought she saw a dark shadow move along the wall. It was behind Stinkhorn now, but in a few seconds it would reach her. With a sudden cry she leapt to her feet, spun around and hurled the cup, contents and all, at the looming shadow. The cup hit the wall and smashed into a hundred pieces; the two old men fell backwards in their chairs and crashed onto the floor; Stinkhorn shouted, "What the Biggin Hill...?" Tennyson woke up and struggled to get to his feet; only the youth made no movement.

Alma was trembling and staring at the dark coffee stain that was trickling down the wall.

"I'm so sorry..." she said. "There was a shadow..."

"Do not fret my dear," said Mr Beezly picking himself up. "Our house is not well appointed. There are so many shadows – we often alarm ourselves. Come and warm yourself. Why, you're trembling like a leaf!"

She was brought to the fire, and Tennyson stood to make room for her on the mat, licking her hand reassuringly. The Nephew was sent into the kitchen to make some soup.

"You all right, Al?" asked Stinkhorn.

"Yes, I'm okay. "

"A bit of a turn, eh?" said Mr Hay.

"Why don't I put on a record," said Mr Beezly. He went over to the gramophone and cranked it up. As he was lining up the needle, just before the crackly music filled the room, Alma thought she heard the click of the front door closing.

Beds were made up in the spare rooms in the upper part of the house and despite the fact that the sun still hadn't risen, it was agreed that they should all call it a day and sleep until they woke. Tennyson was left by the fire to act as guard dog, though he was obviously exhausted enough to sleep through the clumsiest burglary. Alma too was feeling tired; she was given a room with thick curtains, and the Cousins insisted she have first use of the bathroom. When she emerged they had put fresh sheets and an eiderdown on her bed. She checked her watch, and saw that it had clicked on to 4.26.

"So it *is* still working," she thought, "and time is passing very slowly. At this rate I won't have to be back in school for weeks. It's like a whole extra holiday."

She switched off her bedside light, snuggled her head into the pillows and slept as she hadn't slept in years.

CHAPTER NINE

Three's Company

She had been walking through a green valley in the early morning, under clear skies, the ground wet with dew, the moss cool and springy beneath her bare feet. In an orchard of cherry trees there were birds with long tails, chattering and chasing one another among the branches. The sides of the valley sloped steeply but did not rise to any great height; everything seemed to be on a reduced scale. From somewhere nearby came the sound of music, a beautiful lilting melody carried by the breeze, growing louder and louder. Suddenly a flatbed railway wagon with bright red wheels came hurtling into view at the end of the valley. On it was seated a string orchestra of about a dozen musicians in evening dress with violins, violas, cellos and a double bass. For the few seconds that the wagon remained in view the music filled the valley, then as suddenly as it had come, it disappeared into the mouth of a tunnel. The music faded and the stillness returned.

Alma opened her eyes and realised she was smiling. She stretched and looked around and then, remembering where she was, sat up in bed. The curtains were still drawn but the daylight was peeping in at their edges. She could hear people moving around downstairs; the clink of plates and the delicious smell told her that breakfast was served.

When she arrived in the dining room Stinkhorn was devouring a plate of eggs and bacon. He had managed to smear yoke on his beard and when she pointed this out he mumbled something about saving it for later. The dog Tennyson was in a corner of the kitchen eating a bowl of scraps and one of the Cousins was unwrapping a paper parcel full of bones.

"The butcher's van has just been," he explained.

They sat Alma down and placed a plate in front of her. The baker's van had apparently also paid them a visit and there was sweet sticky brown bread with butter and honeycomb. After breakfast they all took mugs of coffee into the office and sat around the fire again. The atmosphere was much clearer. Outside the clouds had begun to blow away and though the sun still didn't seem to be any closer to rising, the sky was much lighter, and there was a hopeful, morning feel to everything. A journey was definitely in the air, but Alma wasn't sure where she was going or who would be coming with her. When she looked up Mr Beezly was staring at her.

"The road is calling Miss Small. Am I right?"

"You are right, Mr Beezly," she said.

"When the road calls..." said Mr Hay. "But who will be going with you today?"

"I don't know," said Alma, looking at Stinkhorn – he had his feet up in front of the fire and was wiggling his toes comfortably. The raw patch on his leg looked less angry.

"I think perhaps all this walking is doing me some good," he said.

"Does this mean you won't be returning to your pitch in the hedge?" asked Mr Hay.

"Well not for the time being," he said, "but don't you go renting it out to anyone else. I'm not going away for ever you know!"

Messrs Hay and Beezly exchanged glances.

"You'll get your rent," said Stinkhorn.

"And what of Tennyson?" asked Mr Hay. The dog was curled up on the rug now, and looked quite at home.

"He's welcome to come with us of course," said Alma, "but he does seem to be very happy here. I don't suppose you might consider..."

"Keeping him? Oh I don't know if we could do that. What do you think Mr Beezly?"

"Another mouth to feed Mr Hay! A most welcome one of course, and we do love having visitors, but in the long term..."

"In the long term, there are already more of us than the business can comfortably support." They turned as their Nephew entered the room. He came in quietly and went to his desk without looking at anyone.

"Good morning Nephew," said Mr Beezly.

The Nephew inclined his head but said nothing. On a sudden impulse Alma said, "Perhaps you would like to come with us."

She had directed this remark to the Nephew, but he kept staring at the desk.

"Well, Nephew?" said Mr Beezly. The youth looked up questioningly.

"This young lady was just asking you if you would like

to accompany them on their journey." He stared blankly for a moment, then placed a finger to his chest and raised his eyebrows.

"Yes, Nephew! Yes!" said Mr Hay, nodding enthusiastically. "A call to adventure!" Then he spoke to his cousin, "I think it could be the making of him Mr Beezly. A quest! A challenge!"

"Well, I'm not sure we're going to do anything very exciting," said Alma. "I mean, we're not slaying dragons or anything, just going to have a look around. We thought we might see if we could get to the sea."

"Or across it," suggested Stinkhorn.

"Well I don't know about that," said Alma.

The Nephew was rearranging papers on the desk, even though they were already in perfect order, then he began to sharpen a pencil that was already needle-sharp.

"Speak Nephew! Would you rather stay or go? Speak!"

The youth laid down his pencil, making sure it was exactly parallel to the edge of the pile of papers. Then he cleared his throat and rose to his feet, rather as he had done before his great speech to the jury the previous evening.

"Uncles of mine," he began, and once more his voice was full of confidence. "My very dear Uncles, since I was a lad of five you have cared for me as your own son, you have fed and clothed and cared for me, you have taught me everything I know. I fear that I have been a great disappointment to you. I have tried not to be a nuisance, but I am aware that the more I have tried to be good and diligent and to honour the trust you have put in me, the more the Creeping Wordslip has encroached upon my... Has eaten into... Has taken over..."

Once again, he was losing control.

"I have tried so hard... But the butter has melted... The blubber has wobbled..."

"You have tried too hard," said Mr Beezly kindly, "and it has been entirely our fault. We never allowed you to be a child. We were foolish and greedy; we thought you would make us our fortune. We never saw you as a little boy who needed to have fun and enjoy himself. Too soon we loaded you with the cares of this world..."

"It is time for you to move on," said Mr Hay, going to his nephew and putting his arms around him. Mr Beezly joined them and they said their tearful goodbyes. Alma and Stinkhorn rose and went to the door to allow them some privacy. Outside the clouds were gone and the sky was clear, though the smell of the rubbish from the fields and hills all around was, if anything, more powerful than it had been before. After a few minutes the Nephew came to the door carrying a small suitcase. The Dog Tennyson stood with the two old men in the doorway.

"He can stay with us," said Mr Hay, stroking Tennyson's head, "he seems like a nice little doggy."

"Perhaps not the most intelligent," said Mr Beezly, "but a nice dog nonetheless."

Alma was about to say something about Tennyson's remarkable skill as an acrobatic declaimer of poetry, but he caught her eye and gave a tiny shake of his head. They all shook hands with the Cousins and patted Tennyson. Alma said they would probably be back soon, and the Cousins said they would always be welcome, then the trio set off down the road in the direction of the sea.

They hadn't gone a hundred yards before Alma was regretting her impulsiveness, for the youth was so incredibly shy that they could get nothing out of him at all. Not only would he not reply to any of their questions, he wouldn't even acknowledge that he had heard them speak, and when Stinkhorn waved a hand in front of his face he didn't blink. He walked a yard behind them; when they stopped he stopped, and whichever way they turned, he followed them. Though she didn't like to say it, Alma was thinking that they had done a very poor swap for Tennyson, who was socially way ahead of this poor creature.

"There must be some way of getting him to speak," said Stinkhorn. "We know that he can speak, and speak very well when he wants to."

"Perhaps if we gave him something to read out," said Alma, but they had nothing with them to read apart from the notes that Alma had pushed through the hole in the wall. She tried showing these to him, but he wouldn't even reach out his hand to take them. She tried putting them into his hand, but his fingers wouldn't grip. So after a while they gave up and ignored him, and Alma thought this might be a good opportunity to try to get some more information out of Stinkhorn.

"How did you answer my notes?" she asked.

"Very cunningly," said Stinkhorn with a satisfied laugh. "Took me ages to copy your handwriting on the second one."

"But how did you get the letter out of the envelope without breaking the seal?"

"Envelopes is easy."

"What do you mean?"

"More than one seam."

"What, you steamed it open?"

"Sort of."

"And how did you seal it again; with glue?

"Slug."

"So how did you come to be in the Wastelands?" said Alma, hastily changing the subject.

She waited for an answer, but none came. She could feel her patience wearing thin.

"What is it with this place? Everyone is so uptight! Talking to you two is like trying to get blood out of two slabs of concrete!"

Stinkhorn pulled out his tobacco tin and proceeded to roll himself a cigarette. He did this quite expertly as they walked along, but when he stopped to light it Alma just kept walking. "If they can sulk, then so can I," she said to herself.

The Nephew was now thrown into terrible confusion, being unsure whether to stay with Stinkhorn or follow Alma. Stinkhorn's lighter wouldn't catch so by the time he had got his cigarette going she was about fifty yards ahead and the youth was moving back and forth between them, hopping around in distress. Stinkhorn looked up and saw Alma disappearing over a hillock.

"Women!" he said and sat down on a stone.

"Fag break!" he called.

Alma walked faster. "I don't need these morons," she thought. She would have kept walking, had she not heard a wail of anguish behind her. She stopped and looked: the Nephew had put down his suitcase at the halfway point between her and Stinkhorn and was walking round and round it in circles, rubbing his hands. As she watched he put his head back once again and let out the same awful cry.

Alma was running back towards him. She took him by the arm and tried to get him to look at her, but he kept his head down. The fact that he had stopped rubbing his hands together and seemed content to stand still showed her that he was pleased she had come back. Stinkhorn had joined them, still smoking but looking slightly ashamed.

"You're too bossy," he said.

"I like that! You are one of the stubbornest creatures I have ever come across."

"*I'm* stubborn? Didn't I just walk down here, despite having called a fag break?"

"Well, didn't I come back when the Nephew yelled?"

"Yes, 'cos you're soft!" said Stinkhorn.

"Hang on. How can I be both stubborn and soft at the same time?"

"You're a woman!"

"Right!" said Alma. "I'll tell you how it's going to be: either you treat me like a human being and tell me something about yourself, or I will leave you two here and go straight back through the trap door into my own world and NEVER COME HERE AGAIN!!"

And now the Nephew did look at her; Stinkhorn too seemed shaken.

"All right," said Stinkhorn. "All right, I'll tell you what you want to know." He dropped his cigarette end and walked on. The Nephew picked up his suitcase and followed him. Alma was almost disappointed. A part of her was beginning to wonder whether the going back through the trap door option might not have been the best plan, but she had committed herself now. She took a deep breath.

"Better than school," she said, and set off after them.

When they fell into step Stinkhorn began to tell his story: "I was abandoned as a child, at least I think that's what happened; I may have just got lost; I don't really remember it too well. There was a big city and crowds of people. It was night-time and raining and the streets were slippery, people rushing everywhere and I was in a carriage of some sort, a thing with wheels – now I come to think of it I suppose it was a pram – and I was being pushed along by someone who would speak to me every so often, though it was in a language that I couldn't really understand, but I have an idea they were meant to be kind words. I was rather frightened because all the people were so much bigger than me, but I knew that even if I didn't know where I was, this person did, and if I didn't know where we were going it didn't matter because this person knew where we were going. And then we came to a street and there were coloured lights and the red one meant that we had to stop and wait for the green one; and I was watching the lights and they changed and all the people who had been standing waiting with us, they all moved off across the street, but we didn't move, and I thought, well it doesn't matter, because even if I don't know the reason why we're not moving the person who is pushing me knows the reason. But we waited for a long time, and I couldn't feel the strength from the hands that had been pushing me, but I could feel the other people who kept bumping into the pram, and it would roll wherever it was pushed, and then it rolled into the street, and there were a lot of lights and loud noises."

He stopped and pulled out his tin again. Alma was going to ask him if he really needed another cigarette, but then she saw how his hands were shaking and said nothing. She and the Nephew stopped and they all sat down.

"Fag break," she said.

When he had got the cigarette going Stinkhorn went on: "Then someone else started pushing me; I could tell it was someone else because of the way they were pushing, they were doing it half-heartedly, and they kept calling to other people, but they never spoke to me at all. Then I was seeing the ceiling of a corridor, with very bright lights flashing past and we were going through doors that had to be unlocked and which slammed behind us, and we came into a dark room and the person gave the pram a shove and it crashed into a wall, and then the lights were turned out."

"And you were alone in the darkness?"

Stinkhorn looked at Alma. "That's right," he said.

"And when you called out they didn't come?"

"They never came," he said.

"Someone must have come eventually," said a voice.

Alma and Stinkhorn looked up in surprise. It was the Nephew who had spoken, but now he was looking down again.

"Someone always comes..." he continued. "Take away the empties... Whistling..."

They waited for him to say something else, but he didn't.

"They must have come in the end," said Stinkhorn, "but I think that was after many, many years."

"It couldn't have been years," said Alma, "you would have died."

"I'm not very good on time," he said. "It could have been years or those other things..."

"Hours?"

"No, the other things."

"Days?"

"That's the one. It could have been some of those, I don't know really; it was always dark you see, pitch dark; couldn't really tell if my eyes were open or shut. I may have gone to sleep. I don't remember going to sleep, but I may have done."

"And what happened next?"

"The next thing I remember is the Wastelands," he said, "and finding out what was good to eat."

Alma waited for him to go on.

"And?" she said, encouragingly.

"And what wasn't."

"But... but... didn't you go to school? I mean, how did you learn to write and to speak."

"I found some little trapdoors," he said. "I found that there were people, not people like me, but not so very different. I found that I could watch them through chinks in walls, through holes in floorboards, and that I could listen. Their rubbish found its way into my place and I learned to read a bit from old newspapers and food wrappers and what have you. I picked things up... the way you do, you know."

He was trying to sound cheerful, but there were tears flowing down Alma's cheeks.

"What a terrible life," she said. "How could you bear it?"

"Didn't have much choice, did I?" he said bitterly.

"Ladies and Gentlemens..." said the Nephew, shaking his head. "Geordies and Gentlehens..."

Alma went over to Stinkhorn who was sitting with chin in his hands and put her arm around his little bony shoulder.

"Stinkhorn," she said. He looked at her. "Thank you for telling us your story. I can see now why you didn't want to and I'm sorry if I pushed you too much."

"Oh, don't feel too bad for me," he said casually. "I made most of it up."

He jumped up and tested his bad leg, which seemed to have grown even stronger.

"Now if you two have quite finished moping, perhaps we could continue with our journey: I feel the need to be beside the seaside!"

CHAPTER TEN

Back to School

THE BOOK OF SLIGHTS

"Veronica Small, I want to have a word with you." This was shouted across the changing room. Everything went quiet and they were all staring at me again. In my head there is someone very tired who turns slowly and says, "What have I done now?" But in reality I don't speak at all, I just go up to the Headmaster's wife – we call her Janet because she isn't a real teacher and when you first arrive she pretends to be friendly, but you soon find out what she's really like, unless you're one of her favourites. I am not one of anybody's favourites, except perhaps Mr Smith's. I go up to her and she says in a really loud voice so that everyone can hear, "I saw what you were doing today you dirty little girl."

I didn't know what she was talking about. I think I managed to say, "What?" before she blurted it out to the whole room.

"Picking your nose and eating it!"

Everyone went, "Eughh!"

"I didn't..." I was going to say, I didn't eat it, and I hadn't. I may have picked my nose without thinking, and I do sometimes eat it when no one can see me, but I knew I hadn't done it today; I wouldn't - not in public.

"Don't you deny it!"

"But I didn't..."

Her eyes flashed. "Do you dare..? Do you dare to call me a liar?"

And instead of saying, "Yes, you are a liar," I floated up into the corner of the room and watched the scene unfolding.

(This really happened, only not to me. This happened to James Carew. But it's the sort of thing that might happen to me. My mother is always talking about dirty habits. In our house no one is allowed to fart or burp or pick their nose, and if you go to the toilet and make a bad smell you have to spray the room with Glade Air Freshener. And when I get shouted at I do float up into the corner of the room. It's usually easier that way).

Their path now led along the side of a polluted river, whose banks were strewn with shreds of plastic and corroded oil drums. The water was brown and a frothy scum eddied in the backwaters. There was little evidence of wildlife in this country; occasionally they saw a scraggy bird flapping listlessly across the sky, but nothing else. The plants and trees looked undernourished and Alma didn't think anything would be able to live in the river. Stinkhorn went down and scooped up some of the water, but even he wasn't willing to risk drinking it.

"How much further do you think it is to the sea?" she asked him.

"I don't know, but there's not much to eat or drink around here. I've always got my tobacco to fall back on of course, and I dare say I could find some toadstools or such like, but I don't know what you two could eat."

"Are there any more villages?"

"Don't think so. Once we reach the sea we'll be all right; we can maybe get a boat across to one of the islands; some of them are inhabited so I've heard."

"Are there boats?"

"I've seen a few," he said.

Just then the Nephew gave a little cry. They turned and saw that he was pointing at something. At a bend in the river a couple of hundred yards away there was what looked like the corner of a garden wall and beyond that an area of mown grass.

They picked their way between rocks and rubbish and in a few minutes came in sight of a fine mansion, complete with turrets and battlements. Lawns swept up to it from the river, and there were herbaceous borders and a rose garden whose scent wafted across the air, masking the smell of the polluted river. They walked along the wall until they came to some wrought iron gates. A sign on one of the gateposts read:

SUNNY TOWERS ACADEMY

"They won't want the likes of us in there," said Stinkhorn.

"Nonsense," said Alma, "they will be kind and charming to strangers. They will treat us as honoured guests," and she pushed open the gate and walked confidently up the path towards the front door. Aware that the others were hanging back she turned and beckoned to them.

"Come on," she said, "I know these sort of places. I promise you it'll be all right."

Reluctantly Stinkhorn and the Nephew came through the gate and followed Alma up the steps to the front door. She was just reaching out for the brass bell-pull, when the door swung open and a round-faced child came running out. She stopped when she saw them and burst into tears.

"I should have known," she said in a whining voice. "I should have known. I'm sorry; I promise I won't do it again. I'll go back now and be good. I swear it." Before they could say anything she had run back into the hallway leaving the door open.

"What do you think?" said Alma, feeling less assured. "Should we ring the bell or what?"

"We should go away," said Stinkhorn. "I have a strong feeling we should get out of here." They looked at the Nephew but he was as non-committal as ever and stood staring at his feet and clutching his suitcase. Alma ventured a look through the door. The school was less cheery inside than it was outside. There seemed to be a lot of flaking blue paint, pitch pine and the usual school smells of floor polish, disinfectant and child-sweat.

"WHY are you three not in your LESSONS?" A middle-aged woman in a blue nurse's uniform was standing behind them with her hands on her hips. She wore a nurse's cap and sharply pointed glasses, and she had one of those upside down watches pinned to the front of her dress.

"You, my girl!" she snapped, pointing at Alma. "What class are you in?"

Without quite knowing why she stammered, "I'm in 4A..."

"I'm in 4A *SISTER!*" bellowed the woman. "And you?" she turned to the Nephew. He shuffled his feet and tried to look away.

"LOOK AT ME!" she said, making even Stinkhorn jump. When the Nephew still failed to respond she grabbed him by the chin and turned his face towards her. He still averted his eyes, so she brought her face right up close to his and yelled again, "You will ANSWER me, RIGHT now!"

The poor Nephew let out a stream of nonsensical words.

"What did you say? Did you say *Kettle*? How dare you say *Kettle* to me when I ask you a civilised question? You are on detention! What is your name?"

"Oi! Blabbermouth!" shouted Stinkhorn. "Why don't you leave him alone, you old crone?"

The woman looked down at Stinkhorn in surprise. Her eyes narrowed and she hissed, "What is this?"

"I am not a what, I am a whom!" he said.

The Sister opened a pocket in the side of her dress, drew out a silver whistle, placed it to her thin lips and blew a loud blast. There were shouts and a scratching, scampering sound from within the building. Alma was the only one who was standing in a direct line with the open door and consequently she was the first to see what was coming.

"Stinkhorn, run!" she screamed. She would have run

herself but the Sister had got hold of her arm. The poor Nephew was crouching down and attempting to pull his jacket up over his head, but Stinkhorn was leaping down the steps and making for the front gate; his little legs pumping as hard as they could, he tumbled and scrambled along the gravel path. Alma stood and watched helplessly as a huge black dog bounded down the steps in pursuit of the fugitive. There was no real contest, the dog had caught up with Stinkhorn before he reached the gate, grabbing him by the coat and dragging him to the ground.

"Call it off! Call it off!" shouted Alma at the top of her voice, but a sharp slap on the side of the head stunned her into silence. Two men in blue overalls came out of the school and went down to where the dog had Stinkhorn pinned to the ground. One of them clipped a leather strap onto the dog's collar while the other picked Stinkhorn up by the scruff of the neck.

"What shall we do with 'im Sister?"

"Take it to the pavilion and lock it away. It will have to be... de-loused."

Stinkhorn struggled, but the man was powerfully built, and the dog set up such a ferocious barking that he soon gave up resisting and allowed himself to be marched off towards a building on the far side of the lawn.

"Now you two will come with me directly," said the Sister. Alma's arm was being pinched and she was frightened and confused and had no idea what to do. Apart from that one time at the Leprechaun Lawyers she had felt almost fearless since coming through the trap door, but now she was her old timid self again.

"Perhaps if I don't make a fuss," she thought, "these people will leave me alone and I can find a way to escape."

The Nephew was whimpering as he shuffled along behind them.

"And will you both stop snivelling!" shouted the Sister, giving Alma's arm a violent shake.

They came to a flight of stone stairs. On each cold step sat a child with its head through the banisters. Their faces were pale and expressionless. One or two of them looked up as they passed, but none of them moved.

"You two will be joining them on detention if you don't stop your noise!" shouted the Sister. She marched them along another corridor and into a sparsely furnished room. At last she let go of Alma's arm.

"Now, would you mind telling me where your uniforms are?"

"We don't have any uniforms," said Alma weakly, "because we don't go to this school."

"We'll see about THAT!" bellowed the Sister, and she went over to a cupboard and began pulling out pieces of clothing. She found shirts, socks and underpants in a drawer, a grey dress for Alma and shorts and a jacket for the nephew. Brand new ties sealed in plastic came out of another drawer.

"Your parents will be charged for these of course," said the Sister as she handed a pile of clothing to each of them. "You, my girl, can stay in here and change and you, boy, can change in the surgery. And I'll take that thank you very much!" She yanked the suitcase out of the Nephew's hand and dragged him out of the room.

The door slammed and Alma was left alone. She began

to put on the uniform. It actually felt quite nice to be putting on some clean clothes and when she was finished she looked at herself in the mirror it didn't look too bad. The uniform was not very different from the one she had to wear at The Grange. She looked at her watch: it was 4.27.

"Oh well," she thought, "turns out I've had to go to school even earlier than usual."

But the whole thing seemed somehow normal, and she was already doing her old detachment trick; she felt like she was floating out of her body, simply watching herself going through the motions.

"If we're quite finished daydreaming," snapped the Sister, who obviously had experience of opening doors soundlessly, "you two have wasted quite enough of my time, and you are late for assembly!"

The Nephew was out in the corridor; somehow the Sister had got him into his new clothes. He looked much younger now without his dark tailcoat and narrow trousers. The two of them followed the starched uniform down corridor after corridor until they could hear the murmur of voices. They came to some double doors with glass panels.

"Right!" said the Sister standing to one side and pushing open one of the doors. "In you go and explain why you are late."

As they stepped into the hall three hundred heads turned to look at them. A man in a black academic gown was standing on a raised dais at the far end of the hall. Behind him other men and women, also in black gowns, were seated in a row. The assembly was just about to get under way.

"Ah! Latecomers," said the man, whom Alma took to be

the Headmaster.

"Well? What do you have to say for yourselves?"

"We're... we're very sorry we're late Sir."

"I should think so too. Dock three house points." There were groans from many of the children.

"Now get into your places."

Alma looked around at the hostile faces, but there didn't seem to be a place to sit down anywhere. She hated being this exposed, and hated more than anything to have everyone stare at her. She had no idea where to go or what to do. For the moment she forgot all about the Nephew and Stinkhorn, she forgot her other life, it was just her – alone in a strange place facing an impossible situation. Then just to make things even worse, someone started laughing.

"Be QUIET!" shouted the Headmaster. "Will you two please SIT DOWN!"

Alma sat down.

"Not there, for goodness sake!"

She stood up again and stumbled towards the back.

"Now where are you going?" The laughter erupted again. "I said SIT DOWN!"

She sat down again.

"NOT THERE!" roared the Headmaster in utter disbelief.

He left the dais and came striding through the hall. Alma was close to tears; looking round she saw that the Nephew had been pulled down by some of the boys, so now she was the focus of everyone's attention. The Headmaster clamped his hand around the back of her neck and marched her through the hall towards the dais. When he got there he pushed her down, about a yard ahead of the front row, which was made up of the very youngest children.

"Now you sit there where I can keep my eye on you," he said.

One of the other teachers stood and addressed the school.

"Every head bowed and every eye closed. God grant us the wisdom to speak when we are spoken to, to look before we leap, and to doff our caps respectfully. Amen."

"Amen!" came the response.

The Headmaster was pointing at Alma again. "Are you deaf as well as stupid? What did Mr Hilditch say?"

"Erm, look before you leap..."

"Every head bowed and every eye closed! You didn't bow your head."

Before she could stop herself Alma said, "How do you know?"

There were gasps from around the hall.

"OUT!!!" screamed the Headmaster. Behind him, some of the staff had stood to their feet. "GET OUT AND WAIT IN MY STUDY!"

So she had to walk out in front of the whole school. She kept her head down, and went the wrong way at first and that caused even more hilarity. Finally she was through the double doors again and breathing in the relatively cool air of the corridor. Once out of the hall she began to walk as fast as she could, and by chance managed to find her way to the front door. She turned the handle and it opened: there was the path and the gates where they had come in.

CHAPTER ELEVEN

Scapegoats

When the children around him got up at the end of the assembly, the Nephew thought he had better follow them. He couldn't see Alma anywhere, so he attached himself instead to a girl who had been sitting close to him and who was approximately Alma's age. A few children looked at him strangely and asked if he was a new boy, but he avoided their gaze and didn't answer their questions. Once out of the hall they didn't go into class but filed into one of the long corridors where they formed two lines and stood to attention with their backs to the walls. On the side where he was standing there were grey flannel coats hanging on hooks; he tried to get in behind them so that as little as possible of him could be seen. A hush descended as the Headmaster came along the corridor, his gown flowing out impressively behind him. When he reached the end he turned and stood to face them all. He produced a clipboard and began to read out names.

"Sprage!" he called. A little way down the corridor a small sandy haired boy stood out from the wall. All eyes turned to look at him.

"Sprage, you horrible child come and collect your sheets

and take them to Matron."

Sprage walked the length of the corridor. There was a wicker laundry basket against the wall near where the Headmaster was standing. Sprage reached into it a pulled out a bundle of damp sheets, then he had to walk all the way down the corridor as the other children booed and hissed and pulled faces at him. A few stuck out their feet and tried to trip him up; when one succeeded and sent him sprawling, a great cheer went up. The Nephew, cowering behind the overcoat, was terrified that it would be his turn next and pressed himself flatter against the wall. As the boy passed him their eyes met for a moment.

The Headmaster was consulting his clipboard, making no attempt to control the increasingly brutal atmosphere. When Sprage had reached the end of the corridor and trudged up the stairs, the Head looked up again and once more called for quiet.

"Jessica Coverdale!" he shouted.

The Nephew peeped out from behind the coat and saw the round-faced girl who had been trying to escape when they first arrived. She was shaking her head and weeping. The other children did not shout or jeer this time, instead there was silence.

"Jessica Coverdale," said the Headmaster with great solemnity, "venite ad sacrificio."

The Nephew understood immediately what was about to happen. He watched as she staggered up the corridor; several times she tried to turn back, but whenever she did the other children stepped out and barred her way, cruel hands pushing her on when she flagged. Eventually she stood trembling before the Headmaster. He had taken a black cap from his pocket and was placing it on his head. There was a movement beneath his gown and a small boy stepped out. He was dressed in a uniform that was much too tight; in fact it was so tight that the Nephew wondered how he had ever managed to get into it. There were red marks around his wrists and legs where the fabric of the sleeves and short trouser legs bit into the flesh; his face was grimy. As soon as he came into view the children roared. The boy's back was bent under the burden of an ancient, tattered rucksack.

"Coverdale, remove the burden," continued the Headmaster. Still weeping, Jessica reached forward and began to undo the buckles that held the rucksack in place. This took some time because they were so tight and the boy was too weak to help her. He staggered while she was pulling at them and held onto the headmaster's gown to steady himself.

When the last buckle was undone the burden fell from his back and crashed to the floor. To judge from the sound it made as it fell it contained something unimaginably heavy. The boy turned and shuffled away down the corridor. Jessica was now standing with the rucksack at her feet holding onto the straps. Two of the senior children stepped forward and lifted it onto her back. She staggered as she took the weight and almost fell. They held her up while they pulled the straps tight and fastened the buckles. Once the burden was in place they stood back and the Headmaster boomed out the words: "Members of the School, I give you *Jessica Coverdale!*" The children began to scream as loudly as they could. As Jessica staggered down the corridor some of them produced shoelaces and bits of string from their pockets and flicked at her legs. They were excellent shots and by the time she reached the cowering Nephew her legs were covered in welts and cuts. She staggered on and disappeared into the shadows.

"Coverdale will bear the burden for one year," said the Headmaster when quiet had returned. "As for the Foul Boy Jenkins..." At the mention of this name the booing recommenced. "The Foul Boy Jenkins has now been banished from the school forever, and no record of his name shall remain in the archives or in our memories. He shall never be invited to join the Association of Former Pupils."

"Hear, hear!" cried the children.

There was a noise at the end of the corridor. The Nephew peeped out and saw the Sister come striding towards the Headmaster, shushing the children as she came and ordering those that had moved to go back to their places. She went up to the Headmaster and handed him a note. They held a whispered conversation, then the Sister stood to one side and the Head addressed the school once again.

"Children," he said, "there appears to be one further item of business." He cleared his throat and looked at the note the Sister had given him. "There is a new pupil in our midst. Indeed it appears we have two new pupils..." At this the Nephew wished he could unpick the lining of one of the coats and crawl into it.

"Where is Veronica Small?" called the Head. There was no movement in the corridor.

"Veronica Small!" he called out again. Still there was no answer.

"The girl who lost her house points this morning – where is she? Very well, if she does not come forward, the next exeat will be cancelled." The children moaned and began looking around for the cause of their misery.

"I've got her! She was trying to get into the pavilion."

One of the men in blue overalls was dragging Alma down the corridor. The booing began again.

"Trying to get into the pavilion?" queried the Headmaster in surprise. "Why was she trying to do that?"

"Some creature she brought with her. Sister told us to shut him up in there and give him the old, you know... *de-louse*."

"Is it er... human?" asked the Headmaster in a worried voice.

"Nah, it's some sort of animal."

"Oh well then..."

"He is human!" protested Alma.

"Silence!" said the Headmaster.

"I will not be silent! What are you going to do to my friend?"

"How dare you speak to me in that insolent tone!" he roared. "Sister! Mr Hargreaves!" Immediately the Sister and the man in overalls stepped forward. The Sister tore a strip of Elastoplast from a large roll and covered Alma's mouth; then her wrists were taped together and when she tried to kick, her ankles were held by the man while the Sister bound them. The Headmaster grasped Alma roughly by the shoulders and turned her towards the children.

"Now," he said, "look carefully children. If you thought the Foul Boy Jenkins was bad, if you thought the accursed Coverdale was evil, behold the venomous SMALL!" He gave Alma a shove and she toppled forward onto the floor. Her head smacked against it and as she looked up at the savage faces, a trickle of blood flowed down into her eye.

"I think I would like to wake up now," she thought. The

faces danced before her and she felt that at any moment they might descend upon her and rip her to shreds. But suddenly a voice rose above the chaos.

"PEACE!" it cried. "PEACE! BE STILL!"

And instantly all was silent. Twisting round Alma saw the Nephew, once again standing tall, his face purposeful as he stepped out from behind the coats and walked towards her.

"My Friends..." he continued, and at the word *friends* some of the charge seemed to leave the atmosphere. The Nephew now had the same bearing Alma had witnessed during his impressive speech at his Uncles' house, but she wondered how long it would be before the *Creeping Wordslip* caught up with him.

"My friends... What... is... this?"

He had reached Alma now, and bending down he lifted her to her feet.

"What the...?" began the astonished Headmaster. "Who the hell do you think you are?"

"I," said the Nephew, "represent Hay, Beezly and Nephew, Solicitors at law!" He bent down again and began to unbind Alma's ankles.

"Ah, I see," said the Headmaster, nervously rubbing his hands. "Well, we want no trouble, no difficulties. If there has been a complaint from one of the parents I'm sure we can straighten things out..."

Now the two prefects who had helped to put the burden on Jessica's back stepped forward to help the Nephew, unbinding Alma's wrists and gently removing the tape from her mouth.

"Thank you," she breathed when they had peeled it off. When she was free one of the other children stepped forward and offered her a handkerchief for her bleeding forehead.

"It's all just a bit of harmless fun you see," the Headmaster continued. "The children like it."

"And now," said the Nephew, ignoring the Headmaster and addressing Mr Hargreaves, "I believe our friend has been locked in your gas chamber."

There were little gasps from the children as the truth began to dawn on them. From the pocket in the front of his overalls the man produced a large key, which he handed to the Nephew. There were murmured apologies from the children, some of whom were now crying openly. Behind them the Headmaster had turned on the Sister and Mr Hargreaves.

"You said it was an animal! I have been given bad information here Sister. How can I be expected to run a school if you give me unreliable information?" The Nephew suddenly turned on him, his face reddening with anger.

"THOU SHALT NOT!" he said. The Headmaster seemed to shrink, and clutched at his chest.

"Sorry!" said the Headmaster. "Sorry. You're right. My fault. All my fault. The buck stops here. I have let things get out of hand. I have not been firm enough with the children or with my staff. It shall not happen again, you can be sure of that. We want no trouble with the law." He slowly bowed his head.

As Alma and the Nephew headed for the front door, no one tried to stop them; the Sister and Hargreaves had disappeared. At the end of the corridor Jessica, still with the burden on her back, was sitting at the bottom of the stairs. They went up to her and began to undo the straps, but when the Headmaster saw this he began shaking his head.

"I say!" he called out. "I say, you can't do that! I mean, I'll admit we may have gone a little too far just now, but we can't go unpicking the whole fabric of school life. Everything in moderation. The children like this way of doing things! It was their idea: by the children, for the children. The children know best."

By the time he reached them they had undone the buckles and were lifting the burden off Jessica's back.

"I'm sorry, but you'll have to replace it." he said. "It is a cherished tradition of the school."

With a huge effort Alma and the Nephew picked up the burden and advanced towards him. Sensing what was in their minds he backed away; his left eye was beginning to twitch.

"I say now, steady on..."

Some of the children had come up behind the Headmaster, and hands were fastening themselves to his arms and legs.

"Now then children! Isn't it time for you to go to your classes?" he protested, but they held him tightly now, and they were turning him round.

"Sister! Mr Hargreaves! Help me!" he wailed, his voice cracking. The prefects helped Alma and the Nephew lift the burden onto the Headmaster's back, then smaller hands grabbed the straps and began to pull them tighter and tighter.

"Yes, yes! A bit of fun!" he said. "I can take a joke as well as the next man, but I think this has gone far enough. A little too tight for my liking! Too tight!" He staggered off in the direction of the main hall, with the littlest children chasing after him and laughing, flicking at his legs with shoelaces. He stumbled and fell and the last they saw of him he was rolling on his back, kicking his legs in the air like an upturned woodlouse, while the children took it in turns to jump on his stomach. Leaving him to his fate, Alma and the Nephew walked out of the front door into the daylight.

Some of the children came out onto the steps to see them off; they were waving and calling their thanks, but they looked as if they were just waking up from a dream. Round the back of the pavilion they found a rusty steel door. The Nephew fitted the key into the lock, and when they pushed the door open they saw Stinkhorn curled up in the corner of a small room with metal walls like a walk-in freezer. He looked up as they entered.

"Ah," he said, "I was just having a little doze. Are we off then?"

"Yes," said Alma, going up to him and giving him a hug.

"What's that for?" he said, pushing her away in embarrassment.

"For being alive, and for being right. It was a horrid place."

"Well they were quite nice to me," he said. "Good pitch this. What happened to your forehead?"

"I fell," she said, "but I'm okay now."

The Nephew appeared at the door holding a large tin.

"Ah! Got some food did you?" asked Stinkhorn. The Nephew turned the side of the tin towards Alma for her to read.

"CYANIDE," she said. "That's what they were going to feed you Stinkhorn."

"Ah well," he said, "I dare say I've had worse."

"I doubt it very much," said Alma.

"So how's cheerful Charlie been then?" he said, nodding in the direction of the Nephew.

Alma looked at him proudly.

"He has been amazing," she said. Stinkhorn didn't seem that interested.

"Don't suppose you got any food, did you?" he went on.

"No, but I think we should probably look elsewhere; I don't think I could go back in there for anything right now."

There was a shout from the direction of the house, and they saw one of the children come struggling across the lawn, carrying a bag. It was Jessica Coverdale; her legs were a little red and still flecked with blood, but she was smiling.

"Wait up!" she shouted. As she came closer they saw that she had the Nephew's suitcase, and that she had a rucksack on her back. She swung it to the ground and they saw that it was full of bottles and fruit and sandwiches. There was another bag in it that contained their old clothes.

"I thought we might need these," she said.

"We?" queried Alma.

"If you don't mind," said Jessica, "I thought you might let me come with you. I can't stay in this place, even though I don't have to carry the burden anymore. I can't face them, not after the way they treated me."

"Well, I've no objection," said Alma. "We don't really have the first idea where we're going though, other than that we're heading down to the sea."

"Sounds good to me," said Jessica, and that seemed to be the end of the discussion. They took it in turns to change back into their old clothes in the shed, then they wandered down to the gate and with a final wave to the children, who were now sitting around relaxing on the steps or wandering in the rose gardens, they set off along the polluted river.

CHAPTER TWELVE

Sanderby Coriander

THE BOOK OF SLIGHTS

There are some injustices which simply cannot go
unrecorded. On Tuesday morning when I arrived
at school Julia was suddenly best friends with me,
which should have made me suspicious. Then she
started going on about the English homework
and how she never wrote down what we were
supposed to do, which was to write a poem; so I
told her this and she said, "But what sort of a
poem?" So in the end to speed things up I showed
her my book and she said, "Thanks a million, I'll
give it back to you at break time." Which she did,
and she was with Jane and Paula and she gave it
back to me and looked me straight in the eye and
said, "We've misjudged you." Then in the English
class Mrs Benson said, "We are going to go round
the class and read out our poems; who would
like to start?" And Julia put up her hand, so Mrs
Benson said, "Yes, thank you dear." Well, I could
not believe it because Julia began to read out MY
poem, almost word for word, and when she had
finished everyone clapped and I didn't know what
to do. I looked at Julia and she just smiled back

at me like nothing was the matter. And meanwhile other people were reading out their poems and I could hardly hear them because I was feeling sick, and then Mrs Benson was calling my name, and saying, "And last but <u>not</u> least, Veronica Small!" And I looked at my book and at the words which I had written and they began to look like a foreign language and for a moment I wasn't even sure I had written them.

"Yes Veronica? You have done your homework?"

"Yes Mrs Benson, but..."

"But what?"

And somehow I missed the chance to tell the truth about what had happened – there was a moment when the truth could have come out, though really I should have interrupted Julia as soon as she began to read, or said something immediately afterwards but now I'd left it so long, but there was still a little window for the truth to be told, but I held back and instead of saying in a loud voice, "Julia Crowden has stolen my poem!" I said, "But it's not very good." And I was hoping and hoping that she wouldn't make me read it out at all, or that by a miracle the bell would go early.

"Read your poem please Veronica."

"But..."

"READ your poem, we shall be the judges of what is good or not good."

So I began to read, and I stammered, and there

were gasps and I heard Julia saying, "Well of all the cheek!"

And Mrs Benson made me read the whole thing out. And it was not exactly the same, Julia had changed a few words, but it was almost exactly the same.

And Mrs Benson said, "When did you write this Veronica?" And I said, "Last night." And she said quickly "You did NOT write it last night," and I said, "I did."

"DO NOT CONTRADICT! You did not write it last night you wrote it today."

"No I didn't ..."

"You wrote it today, RIGHT HERE DURING THIS CLASS! Not only do you have the NERVE to arrive in my class not having done your homework - not for the first time I might add - you are also so stupid that you think I will not notice that you have copied word for word the work of one of the brightest students in the year!"

Then the bell did go and everyone left the room.

I lie awake at night and go over all these things, though I don't want to. I wish I could forget about them, so sometimes I make up other endings. Like this time I should have told on Julia straight away, and let them take me to the headmaster if they wanted, or to the police, we could have hired a lawyer, gone to the International Court of Justice, and still I would have stuck to my story.

The four of them walked in single file along the path. Alma and Jessica were in front followed by Stinkhorn with the Nephew bringing up the rear. The latter had lapsed back into silence, but he seemed more at peace with himself now. Alma offered to take it in turns with Jessica to carry the rucksack, but she refused, saying that compared to what they had made her carry at the school it was light as a feather. After they had walked for about an hour they found a nice spot at a bend in the river where there was a sandy beach. They stopped for a rest and a picnic.

"How long were you at the school?" Alma said to Jessica as they sat around waiting for Stinkhorn to finish his roll-up; Jessica wrinkled her nose at the smell.

"I'm not too sure," she said. "We never seemed to have any holidays or exeats. I can hardly remember what my parents look like. The exeats were always cancelled because someone did something wrong. Once we all had to stay over the Christmas holidays because a window got smashed and no one owned up. I think it's been about fifty years or so."

"But you can't have been there that long," said Alma. "You can't be that much older than me."

"Can't I?" said Jessica, looking up. Alma looked at her properly for the first time. There was something so deeply sad in Jessica's eyes that Alma had to look away, and they were both silent for a while.

A little later, feeling better for the school sandwiches, they got up and continued the journey. The path led away from the river for a while and they had to climb up a steep wooded slope. The foliage was so thick that even at the top of the rise they still couldn't get a glimpse of the sea. When the path brought them back down to the river about half a mile further on they were surprised to see that it was now a lot cleaner.

They walked in silence most of the time. Jessica seemed absorbed in her thoughts and Stinkhorn was busy picking bits of sandwich out of his beard. Alma was staring at the river, and wondering how it could have changed so suddenly. Then she cried out to them all to stop.

"Wait a minute," she said, "I think we're going the wrong way."

"What d'you mean?" said Stinkhorn.

"Well if we're going to the sea, then we should be going downstream; but look, we're going upstream." They all looked at the river and sure enough it was flowing through the valley back in the direction of the school.

"Maybe this is another river," said Jessica. "In which case we should follow it downstream."

"Well, all rivers flow to the sea," Alma responded, "so I suppose we should; but if we follow the path we'll just end up back at the school."

In the end they went back the way they had come until they reached the place where the path sloped upwards away from the river. There was no path along the riverbank at this point, but the undergrowth was not very thick so they decided to see if they could hack their way through it and see where the river led to. They all broke sticks off trees and laid into the nettles and brambles. It was tough going and in half an hour they hadn't gone more than a hundred yards. Then, around a bend in the river they saw a strange sight: a little way further upstream the river formed a slowly turning pool: it looked like the siphon bathwater makes when it goes down the plughole. On either bank at this point were large piles of sand and silt and rubbish. They struggled on until they reached the pool.

"I get it," said Alma. "For some reason this part of the river flows inland from the sea until it meets the other part of the river flowing downstream, and it all gets mixed up here in this pool and all the rubbish gets washed up on the banks."

"But where does the water go?" asked Jessica.

"It must go underground somehow – perhaps there's an underground lake or something."

"Make sure you don't fall in," said Stinkhorn, and they all took a couple of steps back from the edge of the pool, each imagining themselves turning slowly round and round before disappearing into who knew where.

Stinkhorn was now clambering over one of the mounds, sorting through some interesting looking bits of garbage. Every so often he would take an experimental bite out of something; a couple of times he chewed thoughtfully, making little satisfied noises; another time he spat quickly.

"Dead cat," he said authoritatively. "Been there just a bit too long. I mean, I like 'em ripe but... there's a limit."

Alma had found something which looked oddly familiar. It was a small glass bottle covered in fancy blue and yellow leather with a stopper attached to the neck of the bottle by a woven thong.

"I've got one of these at home," she said, "only it's different: mine is red and green." She sat down suddenly.

"That is really strange," she said.

"What's strange?" said Jessica, who had also been picking up interesting items.

"Well, when I was younger the couple who lived opposite went abroad to Portugal or somewhere, and when they came back the old lady had brought me a present. And I remember she came to the garden gate and I was playing there while my mother was gardening, and I remember her leaning over the gate and saying, 'Now Veronica, which one would you like?' And she had these two leather covered bottles, one was red and green and the other..." She paused and turned the bottle around in her hands. "The other was exactly like this. And I couldn't make up my mind, but my mother was rushing me and saying, 'Isn't that kind of Mrs Holt. Now come on, which one would you like?' And I took the red and green one, but as soon as I took it I knew that I really wanted the other one, but I didn't like to make a fuss and change my mind, and my mother said, 'Now what do you say?' And I wanted to say, 'Could I have the other one instead?' because now it looked so much nicer, but I said, 'Thank you very much Mrs Holt.' And then she went away, and presumably she gave the other bottle to one of the other children in the street. I never saw it again, but it was just like this. I could almost believe that this was it."

"Well if you'd chosen the blue and yellow one you would always have wanted the red and green one," said Jessica sensibly.

"Yes, you're probably right," said Alma. But she put the bottle in her pocket.

"Oh, oh, oh, oh!" Someone was crying out in alarm. She looked up and saw the Nephew standing at the foot of one of the sandhills; he was jumping up and down and pointing at something. Jessica and Alma hurried over to him and presently Stinkhorn joined them, alternately chewing and spitting.

The Nephew was trembling. At his feet were some plastic bags full of sheets of paper, but as they went closer they realised that he was not pointing at the plastic bags. A sleeve was sticking out from the bottom of the sandhill, a black sleeve, at the end of which was a white cuff and a pale, limp human hand.

"Oh no! Oh no!" said Alma rushing up to it. In her mind she knew that what they had found was a dead body in a sandhill, but still her instinct was to try to get the person out just in case there was a chance that they might still be alive. The Nephew held her back. Looking up she saw that there were tears in his eyes. Jessica too was tearful; Stinkhorn on the other hand had quite a different expression on his face.

"Oh Stinkhorn!" shouted Alma. "How could you be thinking that?"

"Thinking what?" protested Stinkhorn, spreading his arms. "What did I do?"

He wandered off, muttering to himself. Jessica and the Nephew both sat down. Alma looked at the sad little arm, then without quite knowing what she hoped for, she touched it. Instantly she leapt back, for not only did the hand feel warm, but when she touched it, it moved.

"IT'S ALIVE!" she shrieked. "It's still alive!"

For a moment they just stood and stared. Then they all ran to the sandhill and began trying to dig the "body" out.

"Gently!" said Alma. "We don't want to hurt him." She

felt sure it was a him, for even though the hand was slender and sensitive it was definitely a man's hand. But no sooner had they begun to dig around the arm than it came to life and began slapping at them with surprising strength.

"Wait!" said Alma. "Wait, perhaps we're hurting him. Let's wait a minute."

They fell back and watched the hand for a moment. It was now pointing upwards at something. They tried to see what it might mean.

"Look!" said Jessica. "Look, there's a tube sticking out of the sandhill, do you see?"

They did see: about five feet above the arm a piece of white plastic pipe was sticking out of the sand. Alma went over to the side of the sandhill, but when she tried to climb up towards the pipe the hand waved her away urgently, so she stayed on the ground and called, "Hello, can you hear us in there?"

The hand instantly gave the thumbs up sign.

"Are you all right?"

The hand paused for a moment, considering its reply, then it flattened itself, palm down and waggled a couple of times, making a so-so sort of gesture.

"How did you come to be under a sandhill?" asked Jessica.

The hand paused again, this time rubbing the tips of its fingers together. Then it began to feel around in the plastic bags. It opened them expertly, and took out a pen and a blank piece of paper. It smoothed out the paper on the ground, took up the pen and began to write.

They all went closer and gathered round to see what it would say.

"I'm better off in here... by and large," it said.

"Why is that?" asked Alma.

"Well, it's long story," it wrote.

"We don't mind," said Stinkhorn, and turning to Jessica he said, "Any more sandwiches left, girlie?"

"My name is not Girlie, it's Jessica. And yes there are some more, but perhaps our friend here is hungry – we could break some bits off and drop them down the pipe. Are – you – hungry?" she said slowly and clearly.

"I can hear you quite well," the hand wrote, rather testily, "and I am not stupid."

"Oh, sorry," she said. "Well, would you like us to try to drop some sandwich down to you, or might we crush you if we climb up the sandhill?"

"I have food," the hand wrote. "It's mostly tinned stuff but I'm used to it."

Jessica passed around the sandwiches and they took it in turns to ask questions.

"Would you like us to dig you out?" they asked.

"No thank you VERY much!" came the reply.

"Why not?" was the obvious rejoinder.

"Have you tried living out there?" it wrote. "It's a cruel, cruel world. Why don't you come and join me under here?"

"Oh we couldn't do that," said Alma. "Well I couldn't at any rate. I get claustrophobia."

"Oh you'd soon get used to it," wrote the hand. "It's quite comfortable and quiet and you can sleep whenever you like. I was just having my afternoon nap when you lot came by."

"What's your name?" asked Stinkhorn.

"I," wrote the hand, and there was a bit more of a flourish to the letters now, "am Sanderby Coriander, the Poet."

"Sanderby Coriander?" roared Alma. "That's what my mother is always saying when she prays in tongues."

"A <u>plagiarist</u>!" wrote the hand with several underlinings. "This has been the bane of my life."

"Does that mean there's something wrong with his wrist?" asked Stinkhorn, squinting at the unfamiliar word.

"No you moron," wrote the hand angrily. "There's nothing wrong with my blasted wrist. A plagiarist is someone who copies other people's ideas."

"I know what it means," said Alma sadly. "I was accused of plagiarism once."

"What, only once?" wrote the hand. "I have been accused more times than I care to remember – people have stolen my ideas, published them, and then when I have shown my work, I am the one who is accused of plagiarism!"

"That is just what happened to me!" said Alma, bouncing up and down.

"With the greatest respect," wrote the hand, "to judge from your voice you are just a little girl, whereas I am a poet with an international reputation. I hardly think the two can be compared."

Stinkhorn put his finger to his nose and pushed his head back. "He's a bit full of himself," he whispered.

"I heard that!" wrote the hand. "Perhaps you doubt my talent? Okay then, have a look at this lot!"

The hand of Sanderby Coriander, the internationally renowned poet, picked up a bag of papers and began sorting through the sheets. He ran his delicate fingertips across the writing and seemed to be able to tell what he'd written on each one. Eventually he found the sheet he was looking for and tossed it towards them. Alma picked it up and began to read.

Platterbills

I pondered, lonely as a sot
Who's on his fifteenth Holsten Pils,
When all at once I saw a lot
Of hungry Duck-pussed Platterbills:
Two dozen saw I at a glance,
And all regarding me askance.

Audacious as a bossy aunt
They ate my supper off the tray,
Consumed my flatmate's Bonsai plant,
Then set about a Milky Way,
That I'd been saving up to eat
For afters, as a special treat.

I crept towards the door, but one
Reached out a claw to touch my knee:
It seemed a wise thing not to run
From such voracious company.
I stood quite still and hoped that they
Would eat my food and go away.

But oft, when in my bath I lie
To bask in blissful solitude,
They come and nibble at my thigh
Which resurrects my anxious mood.

They've even scoffed my espadrilles,
Those fiendish Duck-pussed Platterbills.

They all clapped politely when it was over and the hand made little circular motions by way of acknowledgement. Then it began to write again.

"They had the cheek to tell me that I had based it on someone else's poem; that mine was simply a parody!"

"It does remind me of a poem we did at school," said Alma. "It was called *The Daffodils...*"

"Hah! You see!" wrote the hand with great urgency. "That's it! This other chap has copied my poem and I'm the one who gets accused of plagiarism!!"

"But I think the man who wrote the Daffodil poem lived quite a long time ago," said Alma.

The hand was not in the least phased by this.

"That's what they would have you believe," he said, "but how can you be sure? It's all a plot."

"A plot against you?" said Stinkhorn derisively.

"Yes against me! Just like all these blasted reviewers – they're all in league. Do you know what they said about my first collection?"

Without waiting for a reply the hand began rifling through the papers again. The Nephew, seeing some way that he might make himself useful, went over and began helping to sort out the papers, putting them in neat piles. The hand didn't notice this and pulled out a batch of newspaper cuttings. It selected one and waved it at Alma. She took it and read, *"In his first collection, On the Brink of an Edge, one discerns in Coriander's work the influence of such writers as Carter Meekesh, Django Fleabite and Random Custard..."*

The hand waved for her to stop.

"Enough, enough," it wrote. "When that review came out it was the last straw. Imagine comparing me with those dullards! I could no longer face the world. I bought a lifetime's supply of tuna fish and Coca Cola and came to live here." It gave a wave to indicate the surroundings. "Here where sullied water mingles with the brine. They shall see my face no more, I shall not trouble them again..."

The four travellers had stopped listening and were looking at each other. They all nodded, then going over to the side of the sandhill they began to dig.

"What are you doing?" wrote the hand in dismay, then tossing aside the pen it began to slap blindly to left and right. They heard a very faint voice howling through the breathing tube.

"Leave me alone you idiots! I don't want to come out, I don't want to come out!!"

"We have listened to you," said Alma, "but you really are pathetic – just because you get a review you don't like it's no reason to go and hide for the rest of your life. Besides it's not healthy to live in a pile of rubbish."

"But I like it in here!" he screamed. "Please! They'll tear me to shreds!"

"No one will tear you to shreds," shouted Stinkhorn right down the breathing tube and there was a little howl of pain from the entombed poet. More of his jacket could be seen now as they pulled away sand and sticks and empty tuna fish tins and Coke bottles. He was trying to wriggle deeper into his hiding place, fighting them off like a worm in the beak of a bird. Stinkhorn and the Nephew took hold of the arm and heaved. The whole sandhill collapsed as they dragged him out into the daylight. He knelt there shaking off the sand and shielding his eyes from the sunlight.

"I'm blinded! I'm blinded!" screamed the Poet.

Stinkhorn had found an old pair of sunglasses on one of the rubbish heaps and he brought these and put them into his hand. The Nephew brought him a wide brimmed hat.

The Poet sat on the ground and began rubbing his legs to get the circulation going. From what little they could see of his face beneath the hat and dark glasses he seemed to have a long nose and a straggly beard and moustache.

"Vandals!" he said turning and trying to focus on the ruins of his sandhill. "Look what you've done to my home!"

"It was for the best," said Alma going up to him and taking him by the elbow. She helped him to his feet.

"Who gave you the right to decide what is best for me?" he said. And for the moment she couldn't think of an answer.

"But there was really no need for you to be living underground," said Jessica.

"Need? What do you know of my needs, of my suffering? Were you tossed aside by your parents at the age of seventeen? Do you know how it feels to be rejected by your peers, to be a laughing stock, to be mocked and ridiculed? Well – do you?"

All four were sitting with their heads bowed. Nobody spoke for a long time. The Poet had adopted a dramatic pose and was waiting for them all to wilt before the power of his words. It was the Nephew who spoke first.

"P... p... please accept our humble ap... aperitif. We too are very sore..."

Stinkhorn cut in, "What he's trying to say is, what do you think we are all doing here in the Wastelands? We've *all* been abandoned and rejected and made into scapegoats and what have you. You're not so special mate, so I'd belt up if I were you."

This was not the response the Poet had been expecting.

"Ah yes," he began, "but you see, for the likes of you my friend such treatment is... Well, how shall I put it without wanting to seem unkind? This is what you might expect; you would perhaps not feel the slight in the way that someone of my delicate disposition..."

"Delicate disposition my foot!" said Stinkhorn. "Anyway I haven't the stomach to sit here all day listening to this twaddle. Anyone coming?"

"This... What did you say?"

"I think he said twaddle," repeated Jessica, standing up. They were all getting ready to move on.

"This is exactly what I meant, you see. This is precisely why I asked you not to drag me out of my home. As soon as I come out into the open I get shot down in flames. I am misunderstood; I am slighted... Hey, where are you going?"

"We're off," said Alma. "I'm sure if you want to get back under your sandhill, it isn't so badly damaged that you can't find some way of doing it."

"Yes, just think of all that lovely tuna fish," added Stinkhorn. "Tata!"

"I say," he called after them. "Where are you all going?"

"We must go down to the sea again," called Stinkhorn,

"to the lonely sea and the sky..."

"Hey!" cried the Poet indignantly. "I wrote that! Hey, come back here you plagiarising oik, I'll sue you for every penny you've got."

He scooped some tins of tuna and bottles of Coke into an old raffia bag with one handle and hurried after them.

CHAPTER THIRTEEN

Growth

THE BOOK OF SLIGHTS

When Uncle John came to stay last year he said, "So what are you going to be when you grow up?" He has rings on his fingers and his car is always parked at an angle in front of the house, with the front wheels turned to the left. He pulls up and turns the wheels at the last minute then revs the engine just before he switches it off so that it looks as though he's arrived in a hurry. But then he takes ages to sort things out - putting papers in his briefcase, tidying the inside of the car, which always looks perfect. He comes to stay occasionally without my Auntie, but as soon as he gets here he's itching to leave. "So what are you going to be Veronica?" I said, "A barrister," which is what I always say when people ask me though I really have no idea what I want to do. Uncle John said, "Ooh, at the bar eh?" and made a little noise like he was impressed. Then he grinned and said, "Or perhaps <u>behind</u> the bar?" And he started laughing and my Dad laughed too, and Uncle John leaned back in his chair and drank his drink and crossed one leg over the other and sat there bouncing his foot up and down. I didn't laugh because it was cruel. "No room at your firm, John?" asked my Dad. "Well," said Uncle John, "we're always on the look out for good interns." "I'll bet you are!" said my father, but nobody laughed this time and he looked embarrassed. When Uncle John comes round it is traditional to laugh only at his jokes. Granny looks at him all the time. When my Grandpa died Uncle John took over the family firm. My Mother gets some money every month 'and we all have Uncle John to thank for that'.

"Uncle John," said a loud voice, and I was surprised to find that it was me speaking, "why do you wear those rings?" Uncle John was looking at me over the top of his glass. I felt like he was actually looking at me for the first time; he never normally looks me in the eye, but now suddenly he felt like I was a threat, like I wasn't playing by the rules.

My Father said I shouldn't say things like that, but Uncle John held up his hand for silence, and of course there was silence.

He looked at the rings: there were two of them and one had a coin in it; they were a bright sort of gold, not dull like my mother's rings.

"Why do I wear these rings?" he said slowly, and he leant forward in his chair and eased one of them off.

"On his deathbed..." he said, and he looked around at my Father and Granny and my Mother who had just come in from the kitchen. "Veronica was just asking why I always wear these silly rings." Mum gave me a look.

"I didn't say they were silly," I said, though that was what I thought.

"I was just telling her that on his deathbed..." he looked very sad. "My Grandfather..." he swallowed and I wondered if he was going to cry and I suddenly felt so sorry for what I'd said.

"...Sold me this ring!" Then he threw it up in the air and caught it and everyone laughed and Granny even clapped a little. I didn't laugh, because it was a joke I had heard before on TV, and because Uncle John was giving me a look, and he was smiling but I could tell that I had just got a black mark against my name.

I lie awake trying to think of ways to get my revenge on him, but all I can think of is to let down his tyres the next time he comes. But he would know it was me and then what would happen? He might stop giving us the money.

When the Poet caught up with them they were some five hundred yards along the river bank. They had gathered around a billboard displaying a picture of a smiling family out for a drive on a winding country road. The slogan along the bottom announced:

BAXTER, SUCKLING & TENSLEY ASSOCIATES
BUILDING A BETTER FUTURE FOR US ALL

The family were all happy and good-looking, their car was sleek and expensive, the country road swept them along between forests and fields full of sheep and in the distance were mountains, a waterfall and a lake that reflected white clouds and a blue sky.

"Ha!" said Sanderby Coriander as he came panting up the hill to join them. "Don't you believe a word of it! Building a Better Future indeed."

"Who are Baxter, Suckling and Tensley?" asked Alma.

"Big business – they own most of the land around here. Confounded Capitalists. I'm a Chartist myself..." said the Poet.

"Most of the parents of the children at Sunny Towers work for them," said Jessica.

"Do you go to the Academy?" asked the Poet.

"I did," said Jessica, "but I've just resigned."

"Resigned? Would it were that easy!" said the Poet. "I used to go there myself. I still get some of the *former pupils* literature. They never really let you get away. You carry the mark..."

"I take it you didn't enjoy the experience," said Alma.

At first he made no reply, but she saw a shudder pass through him.

"Is your school not like Sunny Towers then?" asked the Poet.

"Of course it isn't," said Alma. "This is a wretched country, I can't imagine why anyone would want to live here."

"Oh I don't know," said Stinkhorn, "I wouldn't mind living around this part of it. This is the posh end."

And even Alma had to admit that the scenery was improving. There were wild flowers and tall trees with healthy looking leaves and the smell of rubbish had all but faded. The path had widened out and was almost a road, and it looked as though they were approaching some more buildings.

"BSTA offices," said Jessica.

There were three tall office blocks surrounded by lawns crisscrossed by gravel paths. Lights shone in every window and they could see people sitting at desks. There was another, even bigger billboard with the same picture of the happy family and the same slogan, only at the bottom it also said:

HEAD OFFICE

"Have you come for the Open Day?" said a voice. They all turned round. Peering at them through red-rimmed glasses was a woman who looked so very much like a bird it was hard to believe she was quite real. She had a long beak-like nose, she was very thin and knee-length black breeches accentuated her long legs. Her hair was white at the roots and black at the ends and stuck out at strange angles. She wore a jacket with padded shoulders, and somehow managed to look neat and fashionable in spite of her strange appearance.

"Does an Open Day involve a feed?" asked Stinkhorn.

"We provide tea and cakes," said the woman.

"Oh, well in that case, that is precisely why we're here!" said Stinkhorn, and he turned and scowled at the others, daring any of them to contradict him.

"This way please," said the woman, and she led them along one of the paths behind the office blocks into an older building with ivy growing up the outside. The colour of the ivy ranged from vivid green to autumn red-gold, and the panes in the windows reflected the light unevenly. The wooden door had iron studs and a brass doorknob. Once inside their feet sank into the carpets and the walls were covered with rich wallpaper and some expensive looking paintings.

"That is a Van Gogh," said the woman, noticing Alma's interest. "Not many people know it's here." Alma suspected that the light fittings might be made of solid gold; certainly in this building no expense had been spared.

They reached a door with a *do not disturb* sign and a sort of traffic light on the doorpost.

"Actually things have been pretty quiet so far," said the woman, "and the Associates did say they would be pleased to meet the representatives of any of the big companies. Would you like me to see if they are free?"

"Oh yes please," said Alma, thinking it would be wonderful to meet such distinguished and successful people.

"I am their secretary by the way," she said. "Miss Quill. And you are representing...?"

"Erm, Small, Coriander, Coverdale, Stinkhorn and Nephew," said Alma quickly, trying to slur the name Stinkhorn.

"Very good," said the Secretary, "I will introduce you."

She pressed a button underneath the three lights and the red light came on. They waited and the lights turned to yellow, then to green.

There was a hissing sound and the Secretary pushed open the door. She put her head round it and spoke softly. There was some discussion and they heard her say, "Small,

Coverdale, Coriander, Stickall and Nephew." Alma thought it sounded rather good, but at the same time she had a feeling they were already out of their depth. However she was reassured when she heard several deep voices begin to boom appreciatively. The Secretary turned to them.

"The Associates will see you now." She held the door for them to enter.

Alma walked into the room and the others trooped in behind her. Sanderby Coriander removed his hat respectfully to reveal a near bald pate covered with a few wispy hairs; Alma wondered if he counted them like her father. He kept his dark glasses on however, and they made him look quite interesting.

"Gentlemen, Gentlemen!" said one of the booming voices. Around a large, highly polished mahogany table were seated the most extraordinary group of creatures that Alma had ever seen: they resembled nothing so much a huge ticks. Their great grey-yellow bodies were squeezed into armchairs; they had tiny heads and their arms stuck out as if they were wearing jackets that were much too small for them. But they were not wearing jackets; indeed they did not seem to be wearing anything. Several of them had unsightly lumps and goitres on their bodies and arms; these growths were in turn lumpy with growths of their own. There were a lot of tubes that came from under the table and were attached to little sockets around where their waists would have been, had any of them had anything which could be described as a waist. There were six of them in all, seated around the far end of the table, and in front of each was a discreet computer screen. Scattered on the table were a lot of expensive magazines.

"Gentlemen, Gentlemen, come in, come in! And you've brought your charming children with you, how nice! And you've even brought your... one of your pets. Well that is just grand. A family day out – this is exactly what we like to see. Indeed this is the reason why we're in business. Come, come have a sit."

The one who had spoken gestured with a gelatinous arm in the direction of the chairs which the Secretary was hurriedly placing around the end of the table closest to the door.

"Miss Quill," said another of the Ticks, "I wonder if you would mind very much plugging me in to number six – I've just seen a little opportunity."

The Secretary hurried over and extended another tube from under the table. She fitted it onto a spare socket under the creature's left arm and tightened it.

"Thank you, thank you," he said. "Ah yes, that's much better."

Alma wasn't sure if it was her imagination, or just a result of the Tick resettling itself in its chair, but she could have sworn that its stomach expanded by a couple of inches.

"Ah, there we are," he sighed with satisfaction. "That was Horace and Grimbley. I've had my eye on them for the last couple of weeks. As I'm sure you will agree Gentlemen, in our business the most important thing is growth! *Growth, by right means if you can; if not – by any means, Growth!*"

"And not just Growth," chimed in one of the others, "but Rate of Growth!"

"How right you are Mr Suckling."

"And Rate of Rate of Growth!" said another.

"Capital, Capital, Mr Jarvis. Now then: introductions! We

understand you are from... Erm, who was it Miss Quill?"

"Small, Coverdale, Coriander, Stickall and Nephew, Mr Baxter."

"Ah yes, so you Sir must be Mr..."

"Coriander," said the Poet, who being the oldest was the one who had been addressed.

"And you, Sir?" said Mr Baxter turning to the Nephew.

Alma thought she should perhaps interpose, as the Nephew was unlikely to come out with anything that made much sense, but not for the first time he surprised them all.

"Legal Counsel!" he said in his impressive voice.

"Indeed! Indeed!" said all six Associates in respectful tones, and they turned towards each other and murmured for a moment or two.

"Well," said Mr Baxter, "perhaps we should introduce ourselves. I am Mr Baxter, this is Mr Tensely and going round the table: Messrs Suckling, Jarvis, Hope and Trumpet-Bellew."

"It's very nice to meet you!" said Alma, and the Associates all began cooing and chuckling.

"The little girl, the little girl!" they said. "Did you hear her?"

"You have a charming daughter," they said to the Poet. "Absolutely charming."

"Now," said Mr Baxter, "to cut to the chase, just to give us some idea of where we're at, what sort of car do you drive old chap?"

The Poet was a little taken a back by this question.

"What sort of... car?" he queried.

"If it isn't a rude question," said Mr Baxter. "You see

we've just been thinking about upgrading, hence all the mags." He indicated the magazines scattered across the table.

"Been going through the specifications and we like the look of the new Bentley, but I dare say..." he gave the Poet a sideways glance. "I dare say you're a Roller man, what? Eh?"

"Well, I have to admit..." said the Poet, playing along and enjoying the esteem.

"I thought so, you see! I thought so. Why, I had you down as a Roller man the minute you stepped through that door. I can tell, you see. Got a nose for it. Now! Down to business. What volume are we looking at here?"

"Well I..."

"Obviously you'll need to talk things over with your... er... Legal Counsel. Damn fine chap I should say; take good care of him Coriander or we'll be trying to steal him away from you, eh? What? So what shall we say – ball-park figure?"

"Well, I'm not sure..."

"In the first year what shall we say?"

The Poet looked rather fuddled now that the talk had turned to facts and figures.

"Shall we say fifteen?" suggested Mr Tensely.

"Surely eighteen?" countered Mr Suckling. "In the first year."

"At forty-two?" continued Mr Trumpet-Bellew, in the most casual tone.

"Surely that is rather generous T-B?" countered Tensley.

"Ah yes, but I think in this instance, since they have brought along their charming children..."

"Very well," said Mr Tensley, "Eighteen at forty-two. I trust that that will be satisfactory?"

The Poet seemed to have no resistance at all, and was

nodding his head gratefully.

"Miss Quill," called Mr Baxter. "Could you bring in the relevant papers and some coffees for our valued clients."

Alma was staring at Mr Baxter. The goitre on his neck was the size of a rugby ball, and the growths on his goitre were like golf balls, and these had little pimples on them the size of peas. Then as she watched something happened which made her feel quite ill: one of the pea-sized pimples moved. It scuttled across the goitre and took up residence on a different golf ball-sized lump. Suddenly overcome by faintness, she had to look away and start breathing deeply.

"Whoops!" said Mr Baxter. Something on his screen had caught his eye.

"Oh dear, oh dear!" chorused the Associates who had all received the same information.

"Hmm. Perhaps you could turn us down a bit, Miss Quill. I think the market has taken a dive. Sadly, there comes a time," he said with a shrug, "when we must all tighten our belts!"

Miss Quill hurried out of the room and a few seconds later the Associates settled a little in their chairs.

"Excuse me," said Alma, plucking up courage.

"Ah! The little girl, the little girl again!" said Mr Baxter delightedly. "She's a bright one, make a good secretary one day I shouldn't wonder. Yes my dear, what would you like to ask? Ask anything, anything, be it unto half my kingdom!"

"What is it exactly that you make?" she said.

There were grunts and coughs and splutterings of anger and alarm from each of them, and if they could have stood to their feet and begun pounding on the table she felt that they would have done so.

"What did she say?" bellowed Mr Baxter. "Hi! Coriander! You should keep your children under better control man. It's disgraceful."

"Yes, yes. We invite you in here in good faith..." protested Mr Hope, and they all repeated the words, "In good faith!" over and over again.

"Who asked them in here anyway?" queried Mr Trumpet-Bellew, raising his voice above the growing uproar.

"It was that blasted Quill!" screamed Mr Suckling, his little face turning red, and one of his goitres moving indignantly six inches higher up his neck.

"Quill!" they chanted as one. "QUILL!"

Miss Quill came hurrying in with the tray of coffee.

"Here it is gentlemen, I'm sorry it took so long."

"QUILL!" shouted Mr Baxter. "Where on earth did you find these dreadful people?"

"Why, they were outside in the lane Mr Baxter; they came for the Open Day."

"Open Day? Open Day? Since when do we have Open Days?"

"Well, the first one was last month if you remember Mr Baxter. It was agreed to have them monthly, at Mr Jarvis's suggestion."

There was a sudden silence and five of the Associates turned to look at Mr Jarvis, who up till now had contributed little to the negotiations.

"Jarvis?" hissed Mr Baxter.

"Ah... now I will admit," said Mr Jarvis nervously, "I will admit, JB, that I may have suggested, I think during one of our brainstorming sessions, I may have mooted the idea of... erm... of the Open Day as a concept... But it was Hope who implemented it!" and with great relief he pointed a stubby finger at Mr Hope. All eyes now turned on him, and he trembled in his armchair like an enormous blancmange.

"Hope?" barked Mr Baxter menacingly.

"Now... I know what you are all thinking," said Mr Hope,"and I will admit that I was the one who implemented the idea of the Open Day, BUT, and I think the figures will back me up here, I think you will find that *since* the implementation *of* the Open Day, figures have improved by some three and a half percent, am I right T-B?"

"Perhaps you would like to step this way?" Miss Quill had come over to the travellers very quietly and was whispering in Alma's ear. Alma nudged Coriander, who nudged the Nephew who nudged Jessica who nudged Stinkhorn who had fallen asleep and consequently fell off his chair onto the floor.

The Ticks all turned to look at them.

"Wait!" shouted Mr Jarvis. "It's her fault!"

"Oh no, not again," thought Alma. "Why do I get the blame for everything?"

However he was not pointing at her, but at Miss Quill.

"Jarvis," said Mr Baxter, "you are absolutely right."

"She'll have to go," said Mr Hope.

"Forthwith!" said Mr Tensley.

"Clear your desk Miss Quill!" roared Mr Baxter.

"And don't bother asking for a reference," said Mr Suckling.

"Yes, and before you go, ask Miss Lamb from accounts to step in would you, we'll need to show her the ropes," added Mr Baxter.

Miss Quill showed Alma and her friends out of the room. As she closed the door there was a chorus of lewd laughter.

"I'm really sorry about that," said Alma.

"Don't be," said Miss Quill, "I've lasted six months longer than I thought I would, and that's six months too long."

"How long have you been here in all?" asked Stinkhorn.

"Six months."

"But what did I say?" asked Alma.

"You asked them what they made, and the truth is they don't make anything at all."

"Middle men," explained the Poet. "They live by buying and selling things made by the hands of others."

"Not even that," said the Secretary, "BSTA buys and sells things that don't actually exist at all, but which people intend to make."

"And do the things get made eventually?" asked Alma.

The Secretary thought for a while.

"Well I don't actually know because they never keep things for long enough to find out. I have to say though, they are experts in their field; none of the other companies can touch them. Now if you wouldn't mind just hanging on for five minutes while I tidy up in here, I'll show you out. Why don't you have your coffee and biscuits while you wait?"

They sat down in her office and ate and drank while she sorted out her desk. The Nephew immediately stepped in and helped her – he seemed to know instinctively what to do. She explained a couple of things to him and he set about putting papers into filing cabinets and boxes. Meanwhile she went over to a cupboard and opened it to reveal a television monitor. It seemed to be connected to security cameras in the Committee room. The screen was divided into four and showed different views of the table around which the Associates were all rocking back and forth in their chairs, seemingly excited about the prospect of having Miss Lamb from accounts as their new secretary.

"They'll treat her even worse than they treated me," murmured Miss Quill.

"Isn't there something you could do?" asked Alma.

"Oh yes," said Miss Quill, and there was a steeliness in her voice which Alma found alarming.

The Secretary went over to a console on which were laid out a lot of little wheel-shaped knobs like the valves on an old fashioned radiator. She paused and looked at the screen – the Ticks were still celebrating. She reached out for the first knob and turned it slowly clockwise, then looked back to the screen. For a moment or two nothing happened, then Alma noticed that one of the Ticks, she thought it was probably Mr Hope but she couldn't be quite sure, began to expand visibly. At first he seemed to enjoy this. He looked at his screen, gave a little shrug and clapped his soft hands in pleasure. Miss Quill turned the next knob, and now it was Mr Baxter's turn – he too seemed to rise in his chair, laughing even more heartily than before. One by one she turned all the knobs and each of the Associates expanded until they were all at least as big as when they had first met them.

"I think we're all ready Miss Quill," said the Poet putting his coffee cup down on the tray.

"Unless there are some more biscuits?" said Stinkhorn, who had stuffed the ones that hadn't been eaten into his pockets.

"Yes, Mr Stickall," said Miss Quill, "I'll find you some more biscuits, and I'll be with you all in just a couple of minutes." They were standing round her desk now, watching her work at the console. She reached out for the first knob again, and with a flick of her wrist she spun it right round until it was fully open. On the screen Mr Hope had stopped laughing. His arms rose in the air as he began to expand rapidly. Miss Quill's slender hand moved quickly down the console spinning each knob until it stopped with a soft *clunk*.

On the screen they could see the Associates struggling desperately to disconnect the tubes from the sockets, but their arms were too short and their bodies too fat to reach them. Through the door they could hear the screams growing louder and louder. Alma wanted to turn away but there was something irresistibly fascinating about the scene. The arms of Mr Baxter's chair had burst and he had somehow managed to get to his feet. He was waddling towards the door; bits of him appeared to be falling off onto the floor, but it was the parasites abandoning his over-extended body. Now the tubes were stretching and for a moment it seemed that he might actually be able to pull away from them, thereby relieving the pressure, but just as they reached their full extension there was the sound of a soft explosion and one quarter of the screen suddenly became blurred.

"He just burst!" gasped Jessica. "He popped like a balloon!"

There were two more explosions and Messrs Jarvis and Hope expired unpleasantly before their eyes. The remaining three lasted only a couple more seconds. All four sections of the screen were now almost completely obscured.

"Growth, gentlemen," said Miss Quill dryly, "by right

means if you can, if not, by any means."

She switched off the screen, picked up her handbag and turned to the five who were standing behind her looking pale and shaken.

"Well," she said, "that's everything taken care of here. I don't suppose you could offer me a job at your company, seeing as I have just eliminated the opposition?"

"Erm, I'm afraid we don't have a company," said Alma.

"Oh," said the Secretary, her padded shoulders drooping a little.

"But you are welcome to join us – we're heading for the seaside."

"The seaside?" mused Miss Quill. "Well, I must admit I could do with a holiday. Yes, if you're going to the seaside and you have no objection, I will accompany you."

They all said she was most welcome and shook hands with her and Stinkhorn reminded her about the biscuits and filled his pockets, also giving a few packets to Jessica to put in her back pack. They stepped out of the office and went crunching down the path.

CHAPTER FOURTEEN

Customs

Down on the beach the dark-skinned man had just heaved a package out of the water and was beginning to rip the plastic off it. Inside he found a piece of board with a photo stuck to it. He took the photo into the stable and propped it on his workbench against the wall. Something about the face was familiar and significant, but he couldn't remember why.

"I think this means I should be getting ready for another voyage," he said. A chestnut mare looked up from its feeding trough.

"You'll be all right in the pasture till I get back," he said. The horse nodded and went back to its meal.

He went out to the jetty and ran his hands along the side of the ship. He thumped his fist against the rough wooden planks. It was a good ship this one, the best he had ever built.

*

They had only gone a few hundred yards when the Poet began complaining about his legs.

"I'm not used to this. I have been lying down for a hundred and fifty tins."

"Is that how long you were in there?" asked Stinkhorn. "Long enough to get through a hundred and fifty tins of tuna?"

"And approximately the same number of bottles of Coke," he said.

"And did you always have one arm out in the open air?" asked Alma.

"Only when it wasn't raining," he said. "I had some room for movement in the sandhill but not much light. But I found I didn't really need it. I could write quite well without seeing what I had written."

"But what did you write about if you couldn't see or hear anything."

"Oh, I could see and hear a lot inside my head," he explained. Alma thought this didn't sound very healthy and said so.

"You may well be right," he said, "but I wouldn't need to be healthy if you'd left me where I was. This walking is such an unnecessary waste of energy. I mean, where are we going to? Just to some place that we will have to come back from, and which will probably be a disappointment when we get there."

"But don't you want to see things and have experiences? Don't you want answers to your questions?" asked Alma.

"Questions are usually more interesting than answers," he said, "and I can have far greater and deeper experiences within the confines of my own head without leaving my sandhill."

"You'll get used to it," said Stinkhorn. "I lived in my hedge for more than a hundred and fifty tins, more like a hundred and fifty thousand I should say. My legs weren't much use to start with but you'll be surprised how quickly you adapt."

The Secretary and the Nephew were deep in conversation at the back of the line. The Nephew was talking so softly that Alma couldn't hear him, but from what she caught of Miss Quill's words they seemed to be discussing something called the double-entry method of book keeping.

"I must rest, else I swoon!" wailed the Poet, placing the back of his hand to his forehead.

They helped him to a patch of soft grass under a tree and laid him down. Stinkhorn took out his tin and rolled himself a cigarette. The Poet showed some interest at first, but when Stinkhorn described what the tobacco was made of he shook his head, lay back on the grass and went to sleep.

"Stinkhorn," said Alma.

"Yes my dear," he said puffing out a cloud of smoke.

"Where are we going exactly?"

"To the seaside. I thought that's where you wanted to go."

"Yes, but what did you say earlier on about what I was looking for being on the other side of the sea?"

Stinkhorn looked pensive. He took a couple of drags on his cigarette, holding it between two long black fingernails.

"I... I don't quite remember what I said..."

"You said that the thing I was looking for was on the other side of the sea."

"Did I really?"

"You said *over the wall*. Why did you say that?"

"Well perhaps because it's true," he said mysteriously.

"But how do you know it's true?"

"Sometimes," he said, "I overhear things. Or else they just come to me, and when I say them they sound good; they sound like they might be true, but I've really no way of knowing. The only way to find out is to try it, and even then you may not really know for sure."

"So this could all be a wild goose chase?"

"Could be," he admitted. "I could have just made all that *over the sea and over the wall* stuff up, out of me own head."

Alma looked at her watch.

"Do you think they might be missing me?" she said.

"How long have you been here?"

"According to my watch about two minutes."

"Well it's my guess they're both still safely tucked up in bed, and you've got at least a couple of months until you'll be missed. Are you all right?"

Alma was leaning forward with her head between her knees. Stinkhorn quickly stubbed out his cigarette.

"I'm all right," she said, "just a little faint."

After they had rested for a while they woke up the Poet.

"How I wish I was back in my nice warm sandhill," he said, reaching for his dark glasses.

"Well, that is the road that leads back to your nice warm sandhill," said Stinkhorn, pointing back they way they had come.

"Right," said Alma, "I think we should discuss where we're going."

"And why we're going there," interposed Stinkhorn.

"And if we're going there," stressed the Poet. "I'm very much for turning back myself."

"I'm not," said Jessica. "The further away I get from that dreadful school the better I like it. I don't really care where we're going as long as it's not back to Sunny Towers."

"What about you Miss Quill?" said Alma.

"I really need to unwind," she said. "I'm heading for the seaside with or without the rest of you."

"So'm I," said Stinkhorn. "Got to get back to the sea."

"And what about you, Nephew?" said Alma.

He was standing a little apart, looking at the ground.

"Well?" said the Poet, not understanding the youth's reluctance. "Speak up man! Can't you speak?"

The Nephew began swinging his suitcase back and forth; then he swung it up into the air and brought it down with a crash on the ground in front of him. He bent down and undid the catches, then he opened the lid an inch or two and drew out some sheets of paper. He looked at the top page for a moment then turned it round so that they could all see what it said. It was a sort of publicity flier:

White Whale Tours
When you absolutely <u>have</u> to know

Underneath was a token for a free voyage.

"How many do you have?" asked Stinkhorn.

The Nephew counted – there were six identical sheets.

"But where do we get the tour from?" asked Jessica.

"From the seaside of course," said Stinkhorn.

"And where do you think it goes?"

"Who knows?" said Stinkhorn. "We won't know until we get there – which is the whole point of the tour."

"The Earthly Paradise!" said the Poet in a dreamy voice. "I have imagined it, and written of it so many times..."

"To a place where you can relax," said the Secretary, "where you don't have stupid people taking advantage of you and telling you what to do every minute of the day."

"Where no one bullies you," went on Jessica, "where they don't rip up your homework and tell you to do it again *properly this time.*"

"Where you are given all the food you can eat and all the drink you can drink and all the smokes you can smoke..." said Stinkhorn.

"I don't think they allow smoking," said the Secretary, a little sternly.

"Boggin' well do," said Stinkhorn. "Boggin' well better had or I'm going to the other place."

"And what do you hope for?" said Alma to the Nephew, who was still holding the advert out in front of him. He looked in his suitcase again and brought out a sepia photograph. Alma went closer and saw that it was a picture of a child in an old fashioned suit with a high collar.

"Who is it?" she asked.

The tears were welling up in his eyes.

"The brother, alas, I never had; the sad sister, a lass I never knew." he said. He put the photo away quickly and they could get nothing further out of him, though Stinkhorn kept on asking him what he meant.

"Well," said Alma at length, "it seems we all have a reason for going over the sea."

"Wait a minute," said Jessica. "What's your reason?"

Alma thought for a moment.

"I think for me it is that I absolutely have to know..."

"To know what?"

"I'm not sure exactly. I want to know the reasons for things in general... I want to know what is on the other side of the wall at the edge of everything you can imagine."

"Sounds like a good enough reason to me," said Stinkhorn. "Not that you need a reason, but I say we press on and see if we can't get on one of these tours. I dare say they'll have comfortable cabins and decent grub on board. And from the look of those gulls I reckon we're less than a mile from the sea."

As no one disagreed with this plan they moved off into the forest. The path here was less defined and a couple of times they came to places where it wasn't clear which way they were supposed to go. Once they took a left hand fork which petered out after about twenty-five yards. They retraced their steps and took the other fork. After a little while the path widened out until once again it was as wide as a single-track road. In the distance they could see a red and white striped barrier, like a railway crossing, with a blue hut to the side of it. They passed a sign which said:

Customs and Passport Control,
please SLOW DOWN

They slowed down, even though they hadn't been walking very fast in the first place, and at length they reached the barrier. On either side of the road they could see a barbed-wire fence stretching into the distance through the trees.

"Hello?" called Alma.

There was no reply. Then they all tried calling. They looked inside the hut, but it seemed to have been abandoned.

"I vote we just go through," said Stinkhorn. "Nice hut though. Wouldn't mind stopping in there for a while."

"I think we should probably press on," said Alma, not much liking the idea of spending a night, or what passed for a night in this strange country, cooped up with five other people in a tiny shed.

The Nephew seemed quite keen to be the one to raise the barrier. He went and stood by the weighted end and began to lift it into the air, but as soon as the thin end of the barrier left its cradle an alarm began to sound from somewhere inside the shed. Lights flashed and in the distance they heard the roar of a diesel engine starting up. Their first instinct was to freeze; Alma had the feeling that machine guns were probably trained on them, ready to mow them down if they moved. As it turned out, she wasn't far wrong. Beyond the barrier the road rose up to the crest of a hill, and from there they saw a puff of smoke, quickly followed by the sound of a gun firing.

"EVERYBODY DOWN!" yelled Stinkhorn. They flung themselves onto the path, and the Nephew flung himself into the shed. A second later there was a loud explosion and the path twenty yards ahead of them flashed and churned, sending earth and rocks up into the air. They stayed where they were as the debris fell spattering around and on top of them. Then they heard the rumbling, clanking sound of an approaching armoured vehicle. Alma looked up and saw the turret of a tank come into view. It squeaked to a halt about ten feet from where they were lying. A hatch opened and a head in helmet and goggles popped out.

"On your feet!" it shouted in a high-pitched voice. They all stood up and instinctively put their arms in the air.

"And no funny business," said the head. "We've got a

machine gun." A black muzzle sticking out of the front of the tank waggled back and forth.

Alma's first thought was that this wasn't a real tank at all, but a miniature replica of some sort: it was only about three feet wide and perhaps six feet long. If Alma had stood next to it, it would only have reached up to her shoulder. The head withdrew for a moment and there was a discussion inside the tank, presumably with the driver, though it was hard to imagine there being enough room for two people inside such a small vehicle.

"Okay," said the head, popping up through the hatch again, "I'm coming out. Now you keep those hands where I can see them."

The diminutive Tank Commander heaved himself up through the hatch and jumped to the ground. Another hatch opened at the front of the tank and the driver stuck his head out and stared at them menacingly.

The Commander was wearing a leather jacket with a sheep-skin lining, combat trousers and black boots. From a holster at his belt he drew a silver revolver. He was about the same size as Stinkhorn, but so well proportioned that you couldn't help feeling he was just a bit further away than he seemed.

He stopped, raised his goggles to his forehead, and looked at them, waving the pistol back and forth along the line.

"Hey you!" he called to the Nephew who was looking out through the window of the shed. "Get out here and join the line – if I decide to shoot you I don't want to have to ruin my office."

The Nephew came out and stood next to the Secretary with his hands in the air.

"Okay," said the Commander, "now I'm going to put my pistol in my holster, but don't get any ideas, 'cos my man has the machine gun pointing right at you. Understand?"

They all nodded.

"Okay, okay," he said, swaggering towards them, "now let's see some ID. Let's see those passports. Come on lady, we don't have all day."

Miss Quill looked down at him and smiled. "Excuse me," she said, "what is it precisely that you want?"

"Come on lady, let's see that ID."

"I was not aware that one needed any *ID* to go to the seaside."

"If you want to pass this checkpoint then I need to see me some ID and check through your bags."

"We have some tokens," said Alma. The Nephew opened his case and handed the papers to the Commander. He took them and began trying to find a place where the light came more strongly through the trees. Eventually he took out a cigarette lighter, which he lit and held close to one of the tokens.

"As I thought," he said. "Forgeries the lot of them." He held them above the flame. Instantly the pages caught light and before the team could do anything the tokens were twisting and blackening on the ground.

"You had no right to do that!" shouted Alma.

"No right?" queried the Commander. "That's what you say. What I say is, he who has the biggest gun has the biggest right, and seeing as none of you seem to be armed that makes me about as right as it is possible to be."

"Oh, what is wrong with this country?" said Alma, raising her fists in frustration.

"What is wrong with this country?" repeated the Commander in his squeaky voice. "I'll tell you what's wrong with it, it's full of *garbage*, that's what's wrong with it. What can you expect from a country full of rejects and failures? Now I suggest that you all turn right round and head back where you came from, because one thing is absolutely for certain, and that is there is no way that a lot of low-down, good for nothing, non-entities like you are going to come through here and spoil the lands across the sea like you've spoiled the place you're in now."

"But we insist..." began Miss Quill.

"Listen lady, I'm going to count up to five and if you aren't running back the way you came, me and my friend here are going to open up on you like the Fourth of July!"

"We absolutely refuse to move!" declared Miss Quill.

"It's all the same to me!" said the Commander, cocking his pistol. "ONE..."

"You can't just send us back," moaned Jessica.

"Oh yes I can, TWO..."

He turned and signalled to the driver who swung the tank's main canon in their direction.

"THREE..."

The Poet was the first to dive for cover, quickly followed by Stinkhorn and Jessica. Miss Quill stood a couple of seconds longer.

"FOUR..."

For no discernible reason the Nephew started crooning, "*Oh for the wings, for the wings of a dove...*" Miss Quill grabbed him and Alma by the arm and tried to pull them away.

"NO!" said Alma. "I will not be pushed around by this little..."

"FOUR AND A HALF...!" yelled the Commander, coming right up to her and pointing the pistol at her nose.

"Oh go on then you horrible little man," said Alma. "Go on then, I don't care."

"FOUR AND THREE QUARTERS...!"

Miss Quill and the Nephew sprinted for cover behind the nearest tree.

"I am warning you, kid!" shouted the Commander.

Alma could feel the blood begin to thump in her temples again. "They're coming for me," she thought. "This is it. The footsteps have nearly reached the top of the stairs, but I don't care, I can't go on living like this; I have to break through into a better place, where people will stop ignoring me or treating me like an idiot and start explaining to me what this is all about, and if that means I have to get shot then so be it, but I HAVE TO KNOW!!"

"FIRE!" said the Commander and stood back. As in a dream Alma watched the little tank buck and heave. A puff of smoke rose into the air and something wobbly came flying towards her and whacked her in the face. She was flung to the ground and red lumps of semi-congealed liquid sprayed everywhere, splattering the trees and the sides of the hut and falling onto the backs of her friends as they cowered behind rocks and trees.

When all was once again silent Jessica looked out from behind the tree stump where she had been hiding at the sickening mess on the ground.

"Oh Alma!" she cried.

The others came slowly out into the open. All were blubbering, Stinkhorn was snarling with rage and advancing on the Commander who was standing there with his feet apart unloading his pistol.

"You will regret what you have done!" shouted Miss Quill.

The Nephew went straight over to where Alma's body was lying and knelt beside her.

"Now you will have to kill us all!" said Miss Quill, her voice rising in fury.

"Well perhaps not all," said the Poet backing away.

"Not any of us!" said the Nephew in such a calm and matter of fact way that they all turned to look at him. He wiped something from Alma's face, then put his finger into his mouth and tasted it.

"Hmm. Raspberry."

"Raspberry?" said the Poet in disbelief.

Stinkhorn had joined him. "He's quite right," he said. "Raspberry jelly."

Alma was now trying to get up, but her mouth and throat were so full of jelly that all she could do for a full minute was cough and splutter and spit and occasionally swallow.

"You... you..." she spluttered. "You stupid idiot! That could have killed me!"

"A little jelly never hurt anyone," said the Commander, grinning.

"It jolly well did hurt!" protested Alma. "It was a horrible thing to do. I could have died of shock."

"I know. Look I'm sorry about that, but you see we have to put everyone through some kind of test before we let them through. Sorts out the sheep from the goats, if you know what I mean. You have to really *want* it."

"So does this mean we can all go through?" asked Jessica.

"Well, it depends on your leader," he said. "She can take anyone she wants. But I must warn you that although you have earned the right to pass, you would be much better advised to all turn back and go home."

"We're not doing that," said Alma.

"Have you lost someone?" asked the little man in a kindlier tone.

"Not exactly..."

"Hmm... It's unusual," he said. "Unusual, but not unheard of. Normally though, your type don't get very far. If you want my advice, which you probably don't, you'll just go back home. Believe me, answers are nearly always a disappointment."

"How far is it to the sea?" Alma asked.

"The sea is just on the far side of those sandhills beyond the trees."

"Are there boats?"

"If you're looking for answers across the sea," he said, "you have another major problem: no matter how many answers you find, by the time you've made your way back here, you'll have forgotten every single one of them."

"Some of us," began the Poet, grandly, "have excellent memories."

"That's not the point. Do any of you happen to know the name of the sea that lies on the far side of that sandhill?"

"Lanty Canocean?" Stinkhorn called out hopefully.

"No... No it isn't called that..." the Commander seemed momentarily thrown by this bizarre guess. "Most people call it *The Sea of Unknowing*, because when you come back from the other side you forget everything you knew when you were there. We get a few people like you coming through here from time to time; mostly they've lost someone they loved and they want to go over and check that they're okay, or else they want to know the answers to the mystery of life, and they find their way in here and maybe they hitch a lift across the sea, but the few who come back can never remember a thing about where they've been."

The little Commander came over to Alma and reaching up, touched her temple.

"Let's have a look here," he said. "Hmm, how long have you been in the Wastelands?"

"I don't know, only a few minutes by my watch, but by your time about two or three days I should think."

"Two or three *days*? I'm afraid you're about to leave us then."

"What do you mean?"

"You're going to blow a fuse any minute. It's different for your friends because they live here all the time, but for in-comers like you, well, quite a few don't last more than a day and the most I've ever heard of anyone lasting is three days. You're running out of air."

"But I've only been here a few minutes."

"No, three days of *our* time. Then they blank out and find themselves right back where they came in. Mostly the people who get this far haven't been travelling for more than a few hours. Any more than that and they won't have time to get across the sea. That's why so few make it. Have you experienced a ringing in your ears recently?"

"A drumming and thumping..." admitted Alma.

"That's it. Well you could go any time."

"But what if I do blank out? Can't I just come straight back?"

"Well the problem is if you blank out the whole thing gets wiped. You won't remember a thing, just the same as if you'd come back across the sea."

"What if I go back home now and then come again another time?"

"If you made it back to whatever doorway you came in by without blanking out then you would probably remember some of it, but then you'd have to find your way back here again, and even then you wouldn't have much time to get across the sea unless you came really fast and didn't stop at all on the way. It's like you've dived into a swimming pool and you're swimming under water. You don't really belong here you see. You need to breathe the air of your own world; that's why it's drawing you back."

"But I'm breathing, I'm breathing."

"Yes but our air, you need to breathe your own air."

"I'll have to go back and take a really deep breath and then come here again..."

"You're not going to make it," he said looking at her closely. "You're going to blank out any minute, I've seen it before."

"Oh no, what are we going to do now?" said Jessica, looking very miserable. "I'll have to go grovelling back to Sunny sodding Towers."

"And I'll have to go back to my accursed sandhill," said the Poet.

"Hang on," said Stinkhorn, "I thought you loved your sandhill?"

"Not when there's the prospect of journeying to a land where all our questions can be answered," said the Poet, his voice shaking with emotion. "To a man of my disposition that is the ultimate goal of existence!"

Everyone agreed that now they'd heard about this place across the sea they really didn't want to have to go back to their former lives, but there seemed to be no answer.

"Why don't you all just go on without me," said Alma sadly.

"Oh no," said the Commander. "They haven't been through the test. And in all the time I've been on duty here no resident of the Wastelands has even got as far as this checkpoint without an in-comer to spur them on, and not one has passed the test for themselves."

Alma could feel the blood thumping in her temples again. A chair was brought from the hut and she sat down. They all gathered around her, and the driver came over from the tank.

"There was a kid who came through here a while ago," he said. "He made it all the way across the sea and all the way back and never blanked out once. Not that he remembered much about what it was like, but he was gone for a while so we figured he must have been across."

"How did he manage it?" asked Alma.

"When he stumbled into the Wastelands he'd been playing football and he happened to have the ball under his arm, so when he ran out of breath he made a hole in the football and breathed in a bit, then he was right for another couple of days."

"Damn and blast!" said Alma. "I could have brought one if I'd thought of it. Stinkhorn why didn't you tell me about this?"

"I warned you about blowing a fuse," protested Stinkhorn, "but I didn't know all the details of how it worked and you seemed to be doing fine."

"Wait," said the Secretary. "What if we write a note and

put it in your pocket?"

"Won't work," said the Commander. "If she blanks out she will be right back where she started in exactly the same state as when she came in. It will seem like none of this ever happened."

"But I could post her a note through," said Stinkhorn, "like I did before."

"No, you don't understand," said the Commander. "*You* won't remember it either."

"Couldn't you remind us?" said Jessica.

"Sorry, it's against regulations. It's all to do with customs law." He pulled a little green book out of his pocket and waved it at them. "Besides, if I tried to explain, you probably wouldn't believe me."

Alma had her head between her knees and was taking very shallow breaths.

"What is the Nephew doing?" said the Secretary suddenly. She was staring at the youth who had slunk off into the Customs hut and was sitting on the floor in a trance-like state. His eyes were closed and he seemed to be pretending to drink something. They watched him for a while. He kept on miming putting something to his lips and drinking.

"I think I'm going," said Alma. The trees multiplied then merged together and she felt light-headed.

"Alma," said the Secretary urgently, "did you bring anything with you from the other side? Anything that might contain air?"

"No, I didn't bring anything."

She looked at the Nephew whose mime seemed to have become more insistent: he was going through it over and over again in exactly the same way.

"A bottle!" shouted Stinkhorn. "He's miming a bottle!"

Alma saw their faces coming and going in a sort of fog. They seemed to be asking her something but she couldn't hear what they were saying. Then she saw Stinkhorn come up close to her and start searching through her pockets.

"That's nice," she thought. "I'm leaving and he's going to see if there's anything he can nick before I go."

Then he was waving something in front of her face, something blue and yellow. She felt the neck of the bottle in her mouth, then she was drinking in the sweet refreshing air of her own world. Instantly her mind began to clear, the dizziness and the thumping disappeared and she felt herself coming back to them. She opened her eyes fully and looked around.

"I'm okay," she said. "I feel fine."

They all started clapping their hands and bellowing for joy and slapping each other on the back.

"Why didn't you tell us you'd brought a bottle of air with you?" asked the Secretary.

"I didn't bring it with me," she said, "I found it here, on the Poet's sandhill. It must have got through from my world with the garbage. That must be a really good stopper for the air to have stayed in it all this time."

The Commander was looking at the bottle, tipping it backwards and forwards.

"Your air is much heavier than ours," he said. "You can feel it swilling around – there's still half a bottle here, enough for another breath or two. Should keep you going for a few more days yet."

"So what do we do now?" asked Alma.

"You proceed on your way with our blessing," said the Commander. "The sea is just over the crest of the hill – listen."

They listened and heard the sound of waves breaking on a shore and the cry of the gulls.

"And how will we cross it?"

"Well for obvious reasons you can't get one of the regular sailings. But there's a few people who run charter cruises."

"Hey, wait a minute," said Jessica indignantly. "I've just remembered something – what about our tokens!"

"Yes, White Whale Tours!" said the Poet.

"Ah, yes. Look, I'm sorry about that," said the Commander, "I think I may have got a little carried away. Thing is, I never thought you'd actually pass the test, so it all seemed rather academic. Look, I'll write you a note." He scribbled on a pad, tore off a sheet and handed it to the Poet.

"That should be good enough. It just says that you all had free passes but that they were accidentally destroyed by a clerical oversight. Now come along, I can't stand around all day wasting time. Off you go – sooner you're gone the sooner you'll be back, and that air won't last forever you know."

"Quite right," said Alma. "We'd better hurry if we're going to get across the sea. Where's the Nephew?"

They found him in the hut still miming drinking from the bottle.

"How did he know about that?" said Stinkhorn as they helped him through the barrier.

"He just seems to know things," said Alma. "It's like he has just a few really important things in his mind, and he knows them so well that there isn't much room for anything else."

They waved goodbye to the Commander and the Driver and walked up to the top of the hill. From there they looked down on a rocky bay where a ship was tied to a wooden jetty. In the distance stretched a shimmering, silver-blue ocean. The light was all coming from beyond the horizon, and it was so bright that it was hard to believe that there could be so much light in the sky and yet the sun still not have risen.

"I suppose the sun will rise eventually," said Alma after they had gazed in silence at the scene for a minute or two.

"Unless it's already set," said Stinkhorn.

CHAPTER FIFTEEN

The Ship

The dark-skinned man was gathering shells and placing them in spirals on the sand, pressing them in so that they made a satisfying scrunching sound. He noticed that he had made a shape which matched the shape of each individual shell. In his mind he was going through an inventory of all the things he was supposed to have done. The horse was taken care of, the provisions were all on board. It was hard to say how long the voyage would take, or how many passengers he would have. He listened to the call of the gulls. They seemed to be saying that all would be well.

Just then he heard human voices and looking up he saw a group of people come slip-sliding down the sandhills towards him.

*

"I'm sorry to trouble you," said Alma. "We were wondering if you were White Whale Tours?"

"I don't think so," said the dark-skinned man.

"So you didn't send out the tokens then?"

"The tokens?"

"Yes, we all had free passes for a White Whale Tours cruise."

"I don't think that was me," he said, "but let's have a look, it might jog my memory."

"I'm afraid they were burned by a clerical oversight, but we have this note from the Customs Official."

Alma showed him the note. He looked at it for a while, turning it first this way, then that.

"How many are you?" he asked.

"We are six," said the Poet. "Six wandering souls, seeking answers beyond the sea."

"Can you take us across?" asked Alma. "We can pay you something..."

"There is no need for payment," said the man. "I was going anyway. Whenever I'm getting ready to go across the sea myself someone always turns up."

"What is it like across the sea?" asked Jessica.

"It is different to how it is here," he said.

"Will we remember anything when we come back?"

"I really couldn't say what will happen or what won't happen."

There was a loud thud as the ship bumped against the jetty. The waves seemed to have grown larger in the last few minutes.

"The tide is turning," he said. "We must go on board."

"Is there food on board, by any chance?" asked Stinkhorn.

"Everything is ready," he said. "We should have enough to last the journey. Your cabins have all been prepared."

He led the way up the gangplank. The ship was a high-waisted vessel made of rough timber covered with dark brown pitch. It had no sails, but looked a bit like the sort of sturdy but rather dull Noah's Ark sold in craft shops. The only thing that didn't quite fit with this image was a rickety looking funnel from which there rose a plume of grey smoke.

In contrast to the plain exterior, the inside of the ship was surprisingly luxurious. They each had a small but comfortable cabin with a bunk bed, a table, a chair and a washbasin. There were two beautifully tiled bathrooms with cast iron baths with lion's paw feet. The toilets had wooden seats and chains with porcelain handles with the word *pull* in blue writing. They had names emblazoned across the cisterns: one was called *The Thunderer*, the other *Standard Niagara*. At the end of the corridor they went up some steps to a saloon with sofas and armchairs. Beyond this was a dining area and beyond that the galley from which came the smell of fish and baked bread.

"Chowder and crusty loaves," said the man. "It should be ready quite soon. Why don't you get settled in? I'll get us under way and then we can eat in about an hour."

"Where is the rest of the crew?" asked Alma.

"There's only me," he said as he went down the gang-plank onto the jetty.

They each chose a cabin and those that had belongings stowed them away in the cupboards and drawers. Alma put her leather-covered bottle behind her pillow, making sure that it was propped upright so that it shouldn't fall over and allow any of its precious contents to leak out. In her wardrobe she found a towelling dressing gown, a pair of slippers and a supply of clean socks and changes of underwear in different sizes; also pyjamas, thick woolly jumpers and denim jeans. She undressed, put on the dressing gown and slippers and went into one of the bathrooms where she turned on the taps. There were bottles of bath salts and oil and soon she was lowering herself into water that was just that little bit hotter than was absolutely comfortable, but which she knew would feel just right once she was in. She settled contentedly with her chin just above the water. There was even a foam pad on the back of the bath at just the right height for her head.

"Ahh!" she murmured, closing her eyes. "This is the best... thing... ever."

Supper, if indeed it was supper, it could just as well have been lunch, was probably the best meal that Alma had ever tasted. They were all incredibly hungry and Stinkhorn seemed to have an endless capacity for seafood chowder which he declared had always been his favourite food. The man kept bringing round the pan and scooping out extra helpings to whoever wanted them, and there were loaves and salty butter and ice-cold spring water to drink. Whenever they tried to thank him he just said it would have gone to waste if they hadn't been there.

Everyone helped to clean up and then they went into the saloon and ate chunks of chocolate and some kind of hot, spiced drink. They lounged on the sofas and drank and nibbled and one by one began to yawn and make their excuses and head off to bed. Alma was the last to get up. She had been curled up in an armchair wearing her furry dressing gown and had got so comfortable she could hardly bear to move. Eventually she managed to drag herself to her feet and stagger towards her cabin. As she passed one of the large windows she looked out at the silver sea gliding past. The ship was slicing through the water with surprising speed. The dark-skinned man came and stood next to her and they watched together in silence for a while.

"Wait a minute," said Alma, "if you're down here, who's steering the ship?"

"It's a sort of auto-pilot," he said. "Not to worry, there isn't very much to bump into out here."

They looked for a while longer.

"How long will it take us to reach the other side?" asked Alma. In the back of her mind there was the sense of an impending deadline.

"You have time to sleep," he said. "There's no rush you know – you'll have plenty of time to get to where you're going."

Though she didn't really understand what he meant, his words made her feel better. She realised that her shoulders had been tense. She relaxed and let out an enormous yawn. Just before she drifted off to her cabin she said, "Should we call you Captain or what?"

"You can call me whatever you like, but my name is Ahab."

"Goodnight, Captain Ahab," she said.

CHAPTER SIXTEEN

The Island

THE BOOK OF SLIGHTS

Paul asked Mrs Conroy a really good question in Sunday School. He said, "What about the people who've never heard of Jesus? Will they go to hell like the bad people?" And Mrs Conroy laughed and said God didn't send people to hell for being bad but for not believing in his Son. "We're all bad," she said, "but we have put our faith in Jesus and therefore we will be saved."

Paul said, "But what about the people who've never heard of Jesus? Will they go to hell?"

She said she didn't know exactly but she was sure God would treat them fairly. She said that if someone had never heard of Jesus, God couldn't very well send them to hell for not believing in him, could he? And that seemed fair enough. But then she finished the lesson by reading us a story about David Livingston, who was a missionary in Africa in the nineteenth century, and he preached for years and in all that time he only made one convert to Christianity. And I could feel this question drop into my mind, and I looked around at the others to see if they were thinking it too, and they didn't seem bothered at all, but to me it just seemed so obvious that I couldn't believe everyone wasn't thinking it, and I couldn't believe that Mrs Conroy hadn't seen it herself. And then I thought, well perhaps she has, perhaps she is waiting for one of us to ask this question and she will have a really clever answer for it.

And she closed the book about David Livingston and she looked at her watch, and then she said, "Well, we still have a few minutes. Does anyone have any questions?" And nobody did; even Paul didn't seem to want to ask it, so I put up my hand and she said, "Yes Veronica?" And I said, "Mrs Conroy, if God doesn't send people to hell if they haven't heard of Jesus, why do we send missionaries to places where people don't know about Jesus?"

"We send them so that they can know about Jesus and find eternal life," and she smiled very kindly, but then she turned away and wouldn't look at me, and I sensed that she was afraid of what I was saying, but I just couldn't stop and I said, "But you said that David Livingston preached to thousands and only converted one, so that means he got one soul into heaven but sent thousands to hell, because when they got to heaven they wouldn't have the excuse of not having heard of Jesus."

Then there was a noise in the corridor and the parents were coming out of the service and Mrs Conroy didn't even try to answer my question, she just pretended I hadn't spoken and she said, "Right, I'll see you all next week."

And then I saw her go out into the corridor and talk to my mother, and when we got in the car she said, "Mrs Conroy told me you have been disrupting the class."

And I said, "I just asked her a question."

And she said, "Is this something your father told you to ask?"

And I said, "No."

We drove home in silence and she got out of the car in an angry way and when we got inside she turned to me and said, "You are a very rude girl and you will apologise to Mrs Conroy next week."

But I think she should apologise to me.

When Alma awoke she sensed that the ship was no longer moving: that is to say, it was rocking gently from side to side, but the forward motion had ceased. There was a knock on her door.

"Come in!" she called.

Jessica's head appeared. "Come on, Alma," she said, "we're here."

Alma leapt out of bed, pulled on her clothes, splashed some water onto her face and dashed out into the passageway. The rest of the group were gathered on the quarterdeck leaning over the side. They were looking out onto a stone quay that jutted out from a long sandy beach. Beyond the beach were fields sloping up to what her mother would have called a *Stately Home*. It was surrounded by pine trees, and scattered around it were cottages, barns and greenhouses. A few people were wandering around carrying gardening tools and baskets. There was a flagpole on the quayside from which a red and white flag was flapping in the breeze. It had a coat of arms involving a Unicorn and a Lion.

"I sense that we have reached our *Earthly Paradise*!" whispered the Poet.

Alma dashed back into the ship, along the passageway and out through the door that led to the gangplank. From the quay she looked up at the others who were still gazing over the side.

"Come on!" she shouted. "We haven't got long and there's so much to ask."

"Look!" called the Secretary. "There's someone coming."

She pointed to the field where a bearded man was striding towards them. He was wearing a beige smock made of a coarse material and an old pair of wellington boots. His hair had been unevenly cropped, but the most curious thing about him was that he appeared to have some sort of animal clinging around his neck. He was shouting at them, but it was a while before they could work out what he was saying. Alma got it first.

"He says we must hurry or we'll miss the gathering on the beach – sounds like it might be quite nice," she said.

"Sounds religious," said Stinkhorn, but Jessica said she was used to assemblies and an outdoor one might be fun. The Poet and the Secretary both said they had no objection to attending a service. The Nephew as usual stuck with the majority, and in a couple of minutes only Stinkhorn was left on deck. Ahab had disappeared, but whether he was below decks or on shore no one quite knew. Finally, with much grumbling and complaining, Stinkhorn followed them ashore. The man in wellington boots had headed off along the beach to where a group of people were taking their seats on benches arranged in a semi-circle in front of a lectern and a small harmonium.

When the man reached the lectern, the animal climbed down his body and swung itself very slowly towards the harmonium. Alma had assumed that it was a monkey or a lemur, but now that she got closer she saw it was a sloth. It heaved itself onto the stool and sat at the keys of the harmonium. Reaching down a foot it began to pump the pedal which drew the air into the bellows, then it placed its claws on the keyboard and began to play a mournful tune. Apart from the lack of speed it played surprisingly well, and Alma was reminded for a moment of Tennyson reciting his poems while walking on his front paws.

"Have a seat dear ones, have a seat!" called the man as they approached. They found an unoccupied bench and nodded to the other members of the congregation, which was mostly made up of elderly people.

"I wonder if we should be in the Sunday School?" whispered Alma to Jessica, who had sat down next to her.

"I don't see any Sunday School, and I think he would have told us if we were in the wrong place."

"And now, I shall lead you in song," said the man, who seemed to be a minister or preacher of some sort. The organ wheezed out the tune at approximately one quarter speed and the man, who had a rather sweet voice, led the singing in such a way that they found they could join in quite well, even though the hymn was unfamiliar. What with the sound of the sea and the meadow smell of the grass and flowers, they all felt their spirits being lifted.

The last verse ended with the words,

"...*And soon his face we'll see.*"

And then there was silence. Everyone sat down and bowed their heads. Now the Preacher began to speak.

"Dearly beloved brethren, once again we have gathered together in His sight. Though we may not see Him, we know that He sees us. He knows we are here, and He looks into our very hearts. He knows the thoughts and longings of our inmost souls." He paused briefly and turned to look at Alma and her friends.

"I see that we have some visitors with us today, and we want to say that you are most welcome here, all of you, both men and women and little children and... All of you are welcome." There was a chorus of *Amens* from the rest of the congregation.

He continued, "Let us make them welcome in our midst and hope that they will choose to stay with us here in His mighty presence."

They waited for a moment in silence and then the harmonium started up again as the Sloth began to play a sprightlier tune. This was the sign that the gathering was ended and people began to drift back towards the house, some of them shaking hands with the Preacher before they went. Alma and the others waited until the last.

"Welcome, wandering souls," he said. "Welcome, and well done for having finally reached us. It will have been a long and perilous journey. Now come, come with me."

He led the way along the beach and as he passed the harmonium he reached out and scooped up the Sloth, which placed its arms around his neck and stared at the group over the preacher's shoulder. The animal had the saddest face Alma had ever seen, but she decided this was probably not because of its disposition, but because the black markings around its eyes made it look like it had been crying for a week. The shorter members of the team had to trot to keep up with the striding man.

He turned to them and said, "By the way, my name is Songspinner."

"Oh, nice to meet you," said Alma. "We are..."

"There is no need to tell me your names," he said.

"Why?" asked Alma.

"Because very soon you will be receiving new ones."

"New names?" said the Poet.

"New, and yet old. Your own ancient, forgotten names."

They were following him now up the steps and into the main house. A lady in a white dress stepped from behind a desk as they entered.

"Yes, Songspinner?" she said.

He took her to one side and spoke softly, then beckoned to the group to follow him up the stairs.

"Your rooms will be made ready directly," he said, "but first you are to meet *Him*."

"Him?" queried Alma.

"That is correct," said Songspinner in a voice of awe, "HIM!"

"I knew it," said the Poet. "This is the end of our quest, the reward for all our hardships!"

Songspinner led them to a door at the end of a corridor. "You will have many questions," he whispered, his hand on the doorknob, "but it is better to listen than to speak. There will be more opportunities to be in His presence. This, my friends, is only the beginning."

"And to whom are we speaking to?" said Stinkhorn.

Songspinner smiled at him.

"You are about to meet your Maker!" he said, and with a flourish he opened the door and stood aside to let them pass.

They stepped into a simple, book-lined study, at the far end of which was a white marble desk. A man was sitting behind the desk, silhouetted against the light from a stained glass window. It was hard to see his face. He raised a hand and beckoned to them to come closer. Once they were all in Songspinner closed the door.

"Come, gather on the floor," said he, scattering cushions.

Alma stared at the man behind the desk. She found it almost impossible to say how old he was. Her first impression was that he was about the same age as her father, but then he smiled at her, and she thought he was much younger. He was extremely handsome, but there was something strange about his eyes – they were a milky blue. He turned his head from side to side but didn't look at them directly; rather he seemed to be *sensing* their presence. With a shock, Alma realised that he was blind.

She looked at the others. They were all staring in wonder at the man behind the desk; even Stinkhorn seemed to be impressed. When the man spoke, any tension they might have felt in coming into his presence disappeared.

"You have travelled far," he said.

They all said that yes, they had come quite a long way, but a couple of them mentioned that Alma had actually travelled further than any of them.

"Where is she?" he asked.

"I'm here," said Alma.

He turned towards her.

"They call you Alma," he said.

"That is what I call myself," she said.

"But you had another name."

"That is true."

"And I shall give you yet another: I shall call you *Serena.*"

"A beautiful name," said Songspinner.

"Thank you." He looked back to Alma. "It means the *Lady of Peace.* But tell me why have you travelled all this way, and overcome such obstacles in order to meet me?"

"Well, I had a few questions and I couldn't seem to wait for the answers."

"Tell me."

"Well sir, I wanted to know... all sorts of things, like the meaning of life and, and why I was born and what I'm supposed to do with my life... If it's not a foolish question."

"No my dear, no. It is not a foolish question. I made you, in order for you to be with me."

"You mean to be with you here?"

"Exactly."

"But in that case why did you put me on earth?"

"I put you on earth to see if you would pass the tests and earn the right to be with me forever."

"But what if I don't pass the tests?"

"You must remember that many are called, but few are

chosen. Thus far you have made the right choices. You have found your way into my presence, but you have not yet made the final commitment. Therefore it remains to be seen whether or not you will end up with us here or go... elsewhere."

"So – do you actually send people away from your presence?"

She was beginning to feel the same frustration she felt in Sunday School, but then – those wonderful eyes!

"Serena," he said, "my dear Serena, you are troubled about many things, but it is not for you to carry such burdens. Let me worry about the souls who have not been chosen."

"But I can't see..."

"There are so many things you cannot see. It is not that I have not chosen them but that they have not chosen me. Every man and woman I create has a free will. They make their choices and reap the rewards or suffer the consequences. And no matter how much I love them, I cannot change that."

"But how many will be saved?" she asked.

"You see how few are with us here in my country," he said, dropping his eyes. "It is a source of great suffering to me."

"Suffering to *you*? What about *them*?" interjected Stinkhorn. The man looked up quickly, and though the calmness never left his eyes, there was something about the eyebrows which hinted at annoyance.

"And who are you that speaks now?"

"I am Stinkhorn!" said Stinkhorn, proudly.

"Aha!" said the man with a laugh. "And I think we shall give you a new name as well, for you are bold indeed. Therefore

I will call you *Bravissimo*. What think you?"

"Stinkhorn will do fine," said Stinkhorn.

"As you wish," said the man, nodding his head. He turned back to Alma.

"As I was saying before our friend here chose to interrupt, it is not that I choose or do not choose, it is that I am accepted or refused. I cannot force anyone to join me; they choose their own punishment. I trust that answers your question."

"I think it answers it brilliantly," said the Poet. "I too had been wanting to ask just such a question and now I feel quite satisfied in my mind."

"Good, I am glad. And what is your name?"

"Sanderby Coriander the Poet," he said. "You may perhaps know some of my work?"

"Of course," said the man. "I know all of your work, but I will give you a new name. Let me think. You are *Naphtali* – a deer set free, the one who gives beautiful words."

The poet beamed.

"Naphtali!" he breathed. "Oh yes, it is in itself a beautiful word."

But Alma could not quell the nagging voice in the back of her mind.

"But why..."

The man held up his hand.

"My dear Serena, I have answered several of your questions, and now I think it would be only fair if I moved on and answered the questions of some of your friends."

"But you haven't really answered my questions," she said, surprised by her own insistence.

"No, you have not," came a voice from the end of the sofa. It was the Nephew.

"I was taught by my Uncles that the punishment should always fit the crime."

The man rested his chin on his hands and peered into the air above the Nephew's head.

"I shall call you... *Sagittas*, the bringer of wise words. Now are there more questioners? Who is next?"

The Poet nudged Jessica, who was sitting next to him.

"I don't really have a question," she said.

"And this is the deepest wisdom of all. I shall call you *Zairian*, the beautiful, daughter of the Most High."

Jessica bowed her head to hide the fact that she was blushing.

"And there is one who has so far remained silent."

They all turned to look at Miss Quill.

"What is it that you would like to ask?"

"I would like to ask you to stop giving us all these ridiculous names," said the Secretary.

"Right!" said the man behind the desk, standing to his feet. "I have tried to be reasonable with you, but you are obviously reprobates and time-wasters. Songspinner, show these people out."

"Oh no," thought Alma, "why does this keep on happening?"

"We're very sorry if we've offended you," she said.

"You haven't offended me, my dear. Not in the least. Why should I be offended? You have only offended yourselves. Songspinner, thank you!" He had come out from behind the desk and was following them down the room with his arms spread out before him; his calm demeanour had evaporated and now he looked quite menacing.

"We only wanted some answers..."

He glared at her, and Alma realised with another shock that he was not blind after all.

"Yes my dear, you wanted answers but you did not want *The Truth*."

"I really wanted to make sure I wasn't a complete mistake."

"Well there's no point my saying anything further, is there? You haven't accepted my answers up till now so why should I give you any more? Good day!" Songspinner had shoved most of them out of the room and was tugging at Alma, who was hanging onto the doorpost. She looked pleadingly at the man.

"Please," she said. "Please, I'm so desperate..."

"Off you go now." He began to prise her fingers loose.

"So do you mean I have to go back home to live out the rest of my life without any idea of what I'm supposed to be doing in the world?"

"Well, what did you expect? We can't all have important lives you know. There are plenty of people a lot worse off than you are. If there's one thing that really gets on my nerves it's spoiled, middle-class children like you who come here whinging and moaning about their lot. Perhaps you'd rather be starving in a refugee camp? And as to what happens in the afterlife, well that's really down to you, isn't it. I'm not about to change the whole system just because you don't happen to agree with it. Do you think everything should be organised according to what you think is best?"

"Well no..."

"WELL NO! Well in that case I'll thank you to get back to your pathetic little life and stop wasting my time!"

He had her fingers free now and Songspinner was pulling her out into the corridor.

"I know that my life isn't that hard but I still have questions about it. I would just like to know..."

"To know what?"

"To know why I was born."

"That's classified information..."

"But..."

"THERE'S NO *BUT* ABOUT IT!" he screamed, and slammed the door so hard that some plaster fell off the wall.

They were all standing panting in the corridor.

"Oh that is great!" said Songspinner who was pacing up and down, tugging at his beard. "That is great! You lot have really done it now. He was getting so much better, he was starting to relax a bit, he was smiling at people, a few more weeks and we'd have had him coming back to the gatherings. But you infidels have to come sneaking in here and set us back years."

He pointed an accusing finger at Alma. "You're the ringleader, aren't you. You with your duplicitous questions. Who sent you here?"

"Nobody sent us," protested Alma, "we came of our own accord."

"Begone!" he shouted pointing down the corridor. They all turned and hurried along it. They almost ran down the stairs and out of the front door.

"Begone, ere I drive you out with a whip!" He followed them to the top of the steps and continued to shout and stamp his foot. People were streaming towards them from all over the island with worried looks on their faces.

"Has it happened again?" said a large man with a pitchfork.

Alma was relieved to see that the ship was still moored to the quayside.

"This was not a good idea," muttered Stinkhorn. "I never liked this place."

They set off towards the ship.

"Wait!" called a voice.

It was Jessica. She was standing at the foot of the steps, with tears in her eyes. Alma and Stinkhorn turned back towards her.

"Why did you have to say that?" she wailed. "He called me beautiful!"

"We have to get out of here," said Stinkhorn. "Believe me, things are about to get a lot worse." They each took an arm and led Jessica, crying and struggling, towards the ship.

"I fear we have made a dreadful mistake," said the Poet as they hurried up the gangplank. "We shall live to regret today's doings. There are people whom it is not wise to cross; people who make good friends but very bad enemies. He would have been such a wonderful Patron. The verses I could have written for him! Those wonderful eyes – like deep pools of liquid calm."

"Well they weren't so jolly calm towards the end, were they." said Stinkhorn.

Ahab was now on the jetty slipping the cables off the bollards.

"Come back!" shouted Songspinner, who was now running towards them. "I need to explain to you."

"That's all right," called Stinkhorn, "no explanation required."

Ahab pulled up the gangplank as Songspinner came panting onto the jetty.

"He'd been so much better," pleaded Songspinner, gasping for breath. "We hadn't had an incident in months."

Alma looked down at him from the deck.

"Well, we're very sorry if we caused any distress," she said.

"What?" said Songspinner. "What did you say?"

"She said we're very sorry if..." Stinkhorn paused when he saw the look in Songspinner's eyes.

"I heard what she said."

"Well, least said, soonest mended," said Stinkhorn. Then he whispered to Alma, "We need to get out of here, now!"

"I heard what she said!" repeated Songspinner, now with real menace in his voice.

To Alma's relief she felt the ship begin to move away from the jetty, but for some reason she couldn't free herself from Songspinner's gaze. Some of the other islanders had joined him. They were all staring at Alma.

"Who sent you here?" said Songspinner.

"Nobody sent us," said Alma. "Honestly."

The ship was clear of the jetty now. Stinkhorn came back and stood next to Alma.

"Begone!" called Songspinner.

"We be-going," said Stinkhorn. "G'bye."

"Begone, ere I curse you all!"

The ship was now sailing along the coast of the island,

leaving Songspinner and the crowd shouting and shaking their fists from the jetty. Alma turned away so as not to have to look at them and imagine what dreadful curses they might be uttering. Further down the beach she saw the little semi-circle of benches and the harmonium, and midway between it and jetty a dark shape was lolloping slowly across the sand.

"It's the Sloth," she thought. It seemed to see her and paused and waved a paw in her direction. Uncertainly she waved back. It waved again.

"What do you think it wants?" said Miss Quill, who had just joined her.

"I don't know. Perhaps it's cursing us as well."

"I think it wants to come with us," said Miss Quill.

"It's too late," said Alma. "Unless we turn back."

"I don't think we want to do that," said Stinkhorn.

Ahab had just come up onto the quarterdeck.

"Can we turn back?" asked Alma.

"Not easily," he said.

She looked back at the shore, but the Sloth was no longer on the beach.

"Where can it be?" she wailed.

"There! Look, in the water!" shouted Miss Quill. The Sloth was swimming towards them with surprisingly powerful strokes. Ahab came and stood beside them.

"A sloth," he said. "Good swimmers, sloths. Better in the water than on land. I'll get the rope-ladder."

"I fear our troubles are not yet at an end," said the Poet, pointing to the jetty. Songspinner had jumped into a canoe and was paddling towards the Sloth, shouting at them as he came.

"I curse you!" he said. "I curse you all! You can't take my Sloth away. I trained it up! Have you any idea how long it takes to train a Sloth to play the harmonium?"

Ahab dropped the rope ladder just as the Sloth reached the side of the ship. It hooked two long claws over the bottom rung and they heaved it up, just before Songspinner came clattering alongside. He whacked the gunwale with his paddle, splintering it in the process.

"I knew this would happen!" he roared in despair. "I knew I never should have taken on an assistant named after a mortal sin!"

As they pulled the dripping animal aboard Songspinner stood up in the canoe and tried to scramble up the side of the ship, but he couldn't get a grip.

"I curse you!" he shouted, pointing up at them. "And this is my curse upon you all – hear me well! Because you have belittled The Great One, the Powers of Heaven shall belittle you. You shall all shrink! When half your journey is over, you shall shrink to half your size, and when half of what remains is gone, you shall have shrunk by yet another half. And then you'll wish you could return. You will seek repentance but find none. You've made your choice. You've had your chance – your only chance! I call down the powers of the elements upon you, the powers of wind and wave. You shall be tempest tossed! Tempest tossed and ever shrinking, EVER SHRINKING!!"

They watched him grow smaller and smaller, and though they could no longer hear him, they could see him standing in the canoe waving his arms, pulling down wrath from the sky. Without a word they all went below decks and hid away in their cabins.

CHAPTER SEVENTEEN

The Curse and the Sloth

In spite of Songspinner's curses, the day remained fine and the sea calm. Gradually the travellers left their cabins and came up on deck or sat in the saloon. Ahab served another wonderful meal, and they began to feel more cheerful, all except for Alma who went out on deck by herself and leant over the side. After she had been there for a while Ahab came and stood beside her.

"So I suppose we'll be back in a few hours," she said.

"Back?" he queried.

"Yes, back at the beach. You know, where we met you."

"It's possible," he said, "but I think it unlikely."

"What, you mean because of the curse?"

He looked up at the sky, which was perfectly blue.

"Look over there," he said, pointing back to where the outline of the island was disappearing from view. Above it Alma could just make out a little black cloud.

"A cloud the size of a man's hand," he said.

"What does it mean?"

"A storm," said Ahab. "We don't have them often, but there's one coming now."

Alma looked ahead towards the brightness beyond the

horizon, then back towards the dark cloud.

"Wait a minute," she said. "We're not going back to the beach, are we. When we set off we were heading towards the brightness, and we're still heading towards it now. If we were heading back, then the light would be behind us."

"You did ask to be taken across the sea," said Ahab.

"So that place was never our final destination?"

"It could have been. For some it is, but obviously not for you."

"But are we going to a better place or a worse place?"

He stared into the distance. She followed his gaze and saw a dark outline on the horizon.

"Both better and worse," he said. "We are going to Aeonia, the place where things are made whole again."

"Well if things are made whole, then surely it's a good place."

"Not everything wishes to be made whole," he said. Alma was about to ask what he meant by this when something in the sea caught her eye. There was a dark shape coming towards them under the water on the starboard bow. At first she thought they must be going more quickly than she had imagined, and that they were passing over a bank of seaweed, but then she saw the shape change direction and she shuddered as she realised that it was a huge sea creature many times larger than the ship.

She looked at Ahab.

"What was that?" she whispered.

He smiled.

"It's been following us since we set out," he said, "though it seems to have got a bit bigger recently."

"Got bigger? But how can a thing suddenly get bigger?"

"I shouldn't worry," he said. "It is only following us out of interest. It means us no harm. The storm on the other hand..." His voice trailed off and he looked once again at the clouds that were now massing behind them.

"I had better go and make things fast," he said.

He went below decks leaving Alma, with her back to the rail, trying to make sense of what was happening. The blood was once again pounding in her temples. She looked at her watch and saw that it was 4.29. The prospect of being back at home had suddenly begun to seem warm and safe. But then she remembered that if she did go home she would be in assembly within four and a half hours and in a maths lesson within five and wondered whether she shouldn't go and have another little draught of air from the bottle. "No," she thought, "I don't feel anything like as bad as I did in the forest, and I don't want to waste what I've got left. I'll wait until I see what this Aeonia place is like before I decide what to do."

The ship gave a lurch and Alma felt her stomach wobble. Looking back along the wake she could see that the storm clouds were definitely catching up with them. They made angry shapes in the sky. The wind was also getting stronger, and she went down to her cabin to get another pullover.

The ship was rolling now and once in the cabin she lay down on her bunk. With her eyes closed she could feel the queasiness begin to subside, and the motion of the ship seemed almost pleasant. She found herself drifting off to sleep again.

There was a knock at the door and Miss Quill came in holding a piece of paper.

"Alma, are you all right?"

"I'm okay as long as I'm lying down."

"Are you well enough to have a look at something?"

"I think so." She sat up in bed.

"The Nephew and I have been doing some calculations," said Miss Quill, "and... Well to be honest it doesn't look like we're going to make it."

"To land you mean? But we're not very far away. You can see it over to the east. Ahab says it's called Aeonia, and that it is a place where things are made whole."

Miss Quill shook her head.

"Have you seen the birds?" she said.

"What birds?"

"The seabirds. One landed on the rail just now."

"What about it?"

"It was huge."

"So? Perhaps the birds are really big in this part of the world."

"Perhaps," she said, "but the storm is getting worse. And after all, if one thing comes true then perhaps the other will too."

Alma saw what she was getting at.

"You mean the curse?"

Miss Quill nodded. Alma shivered.

"There was a shape under the water," she said. "When I mentioned it to Ahab he said it had been following us for ages, but that it seemed to be getting bigger."

The Secretary showed her the sheet of paper with its pencilled calculations.

"This is what the Nephew and I have worked out. I

haven't told the others because I didn't want to alarm them, but look: if by some chance what that dreadful man said is happening and we are shrinking then we will never reach our destination, no matter how close it is."

Alma stared at the figures on the paper. She couldn't quite grasp what Miss Quill was trying to say.

"Shrinking?" she said. "What's shrinking? You mean the ship?"

"The ship is shrinking, and we are shrinking too. That's why everything else seems to be getting bigger."

"But even if we are, it will be all right. If what Ahab says is true and in this place things become whole again, then no matter how small we are when we get there, we will be okay... Won't we?"

"You don't understand what I'm trying to say. Do you remember what the curse was? *When half your journey is over, you shall shrink to half your size, and when half of what remains is gone, you shall have shrunk by yet another half.* Look here." She pointed to the calculations. "If we cover half the distance to our destination, then we shrink to half our original size. So if, let's say, the ship is a hundred feet long when we set out, then by the time we have gone half way to Aeonia then the ship is fifty feet long. Let's say we are then ten miles from land, over the next five miles we will shrink to twenty-five feet, over the next two and a half miles we shrink to twelve and a half feet. Over the next mile and three quarters we shrink to just over six feet..."

"But it's going to take us ages. I'll have run out of air long before we get there. And what will happen to you? You'll be absolutely tiny by the time you get there."

"But it's worse than that," said the Secretary, her normally calm voice constricted, "if our calculations are right – and I'm sure they are – we'll simply never get there at all."

Alma looked at the two long columns of figures. The size of the ship and its distance from land got smaller and smaller as they stretched down the page, each time being divided in half. But she could see that no matter how far you took the calculation, the distance remaining would never reach zero.

"Even if we could stay afloat, which of course we won't once the ship has become very tiny, but even if we could, we would never, ever reach land. You see there is no number so small that it can't be divided into two, just the same as there is no number so large that you can't double it. Our destination will always be just out of reach."

Alma let the full horror of their situation sink in. The Secretary just kept staring at the figures. The sea air had made her black and white hair hang limply against her face.

"Have you told Ahab?" asked Alma.

"Not yet."

"We should go and speak to him. Perhaps there's somewhere else we can go which is closer, somewhere we can reach before we get too tiny. Or else maybe he can increase our speed or something."

The Secretary rolled up the paper.

"I don't think it will make any difference. No matter how fast you travel or how short the distance, it always works out the same. We'll never make it."

They went upstairs to Ahab's cabin. There was no answer when they knocked, so they opened the door and looked in. He was fast asleep in his bunk. The Sloth, now dried out, was curled up on a blanket at his feet.

"Shouldn't you be at the wheel?" asked the Secretary.

"The wheel?" he said, squinting at them sleepily.

"Yes, shouldn't you be steering the ship?" said Alma.

"Steering? Well it's a nice idea but there really isn't any way of steering this ship."

"What do you mean?"

"Well, for a start it doesn't have a rudder."

"Doesn't have a rudder? Then how does it get to where you want it to go?"

"It doesn't," he said. "I don't want it to go anywhere, and even if I did it wouldn't make any difference. It gets to where it wants to go and there's nothing I can do about it."

"Well it's not going to get anywhere this time," said Alma. "Miss Quill and the Nephew have done some calculations and it isn't going to get to Aeonia or to anywhere else."

The Captain was wide awake now and rubbing his chin.

"How d'you mean?" he said.

They spread out the sheet of calculations and explained it all to him. He didn't seem very concerned.

"Ah yes, but you see there's always a certain amount of shrinkage when you're going to Aeonia. Once you're there you'll find you start to fill out. We'll be fine."

"But that's the point, we aren't ever going to get there. Haven't you understood what we've been trying to say? We've been cursed and we're shrinking at such a rate that we will never reach our destination no matter how long we keep going."

"How do you know we've been cursed?" he said.

"Well didn't you hear that man's curses?" said Miss Quill.

"Songspinster or whatever his name was."

"Yes I did, but there's a lot of difference between someone firing a curse at you and having it actually land."

"But what about the storm? He said we would be tempest-tossed."

"There are storms from time to time," he said. "The ship is built to withstand much worse than this."

"But the storm came just when he said it would, and now we've started shrinking..."

"Oh we'll be fine," he said. "You worry too much. I never started out on a journey that didn't reach its destination." He lay down again and pulled the blanket over his shoulders.

"Yes but just because it hasn't happened in the past, doesn't mean it isn't going to happen in the future. Could you at least see if we can't speed up a bit?" she said.

"Speed up?" he said sleepily, still with his back to them.

"Yes, you know, all engines full speed ahead?"

"Engines?" he murmured. "What engines?"

"There must be an engine. What about the funnel?"

"Generator," he said. And that was all they could get out of him apart from some gentle snoring.

Alma and the Secretary went back upstairs to the saloon where the Nephew was sitting chewing his nails. As the storm didn't seem to be getting any worse for the moment, it was decided that they should have a meeting. Jessica, the Poet and Stinkhorn were roused from their bunks and they all crowded round the map while Miss Quill patiently went over the calculations and explained what was going to happen. The Poet turned even paler than normal, Jessica began whimpering, and Stinkhorn kept shaking his head and saying that he might not be very clever or well educated but it didn't make any kind of sense to him.

A little while later they heard whistling in the passageway and Ahab, obviously refreshed by his sleep, came in carrying the Sloth as Songspinner had done earlier in the day. They looked up at him but said nothing.

"You're all looking rather gloomy," he said. "What's the matter, did somebody die?"

"Not yet, but it looks as though most of us are about to," said the Poet morosely. This started Jessica wailing again.

Ahab thought for a moment, then he sat the Sloth down on a chair next to one of the tables and fetched a banana from the galley.

"Okay, who wants to have a race with the Sloth?"

"What would be the point of that?" said Stinkhorn. "We'd all win."

"Are you sure?" said the Captain.

"Of course we would," said Miss Quill. "A Sloth's reflexes are among the slowest in the animal kingdom."

"All right, so who will challenge it to a quick-draw competition?"

"I'm too depressed," said the Poet. "Here I find myself, confronted by my own mortality and even if I did write the finest poem in the world, no one would ever publish it."

"I'll do it," said Alma, thinking that they needed something to take their minds off their fate.

"Okay," said Ahab, "this is how it works: I will place this banana on the table and then it will be a straight race between you and the Sloth to see who gets to it first. The

Sloth will begin to reach for it as soon as she sees it, because sloths like bananas and this one hasn't eaten for a couple of hours. For the Sloth it is merely a question of reflexes – slow reflexes perhaps, but uncomplicated ones. You on the other hand will have a number of decisions to make: first you will have to decide that you want the banana, then you will have to send messages from your brain to your muscles. Now just think how many muscles are involved in a simple action like picking up a banana. So, Alma, when I put the banana down make sure that you are ready to perform all the necessary actions. Remember: first decide that you want the banana, then send the message from your brain to the muscles in your shoulder, pass the signals along from there to your upper arm, then bend your elbow and at the same time turn your hand to be ready to pick up the banana. Spread your fingers out and get ready to contract them at just the right moment, co-ordinate all the muscles in your upper body so that you lean forward at just the right angle so that your hand comes down over the banana. When your hand is in exactly the right place contract the muscles in your fingers and hand, grip the banana with just the right amount of pressure – not too little or you'll drop it, not too much or you'll damage it."

Alma could feel her mind beginning to fog and the muscles in her right arm beginning to tense.

"And don't forget, you can pick it up with either your right arm or your left arm. Ready?"

She wanted to say, "No wait", but somehow she couldn't summon the will to even speak the words.

"Okay, here comes the banana." He slapped it down on the table.

As soon as the Sloth saw it she began to reach out her clawed hand, but Alma felt completely paralysed. It was just like the time her mother had told her to *just be herself*, and the very thought of it had caused her to completely forget *how* to be herself. Somehow there seemed to be no connection between her brain and her arms. She stared at the yellow shape on the table and couldn't even be sure that she knew what it was for. The Sloth was stretching across the table. Alma felt her left foot twitch but all communication between brain and body seemed to have broken down. The Sloth picked up the banana and was peeling it before Alma had lifted her hand from the table.

The others were cheering and applauding the Sloth.

"You didn't even try," said Jessica.

"I did," said Alma, who now found she could move quite easily. "It's really difficult. You have a go."

They each took it in turns to try. The Captain would explain the process very carefully and then put down another banana, but even though the Sloth was getting progressively less hungry it still won every time. Even Stinkhorn, who was absolutely convinced that he could win easily, found that he could only move his right arm by picking it up with his left, and even then he could do no more than push it down on top of the banana. The Sloth nipped in before he could get a grip and hooked it away with a claw.

"Why couldn't we do it?" asked Alma when she saw that Ahab was smiling.

"It was not a fair contest," he said. "In a way I hypnotised each one of you. I got you so involved in breaking up your single action into many tiny actions, that you could hardly even begin the first one, let alone complete them all in the right order. The Sloth saw the whole thing as one – she took the banana. You saw the one as many fractured pieces, and were unable to make a start. In the same way, I see this journey we are on as one thing, whereas you have got into a panic and are seeing it as many little steps – you think of distance and speed and size and curses and storms and you have decided that we will never arrive at our destination. But the journey is one. The setting out and the travelling and the arriving, it is all part of the same action. We will arrive at our destination eventually, though where that destination is we cannot say. It may be that our destination is the bottom of the sea, but if that is so it will be a very good destination and we will find something wonderful there."

They were all looking at him, trying to get their heads around what he was saying.

"Consider the case of the Bee and the Scientist," he went on. "The Scientist decreed that the Bee was unable to fly. Now the fact was that according to the science of aerodynamics neither of them could fly, but the Bee wanted nectar and the Scientist wanted to be right. In order to get the nectar the Bee had to fly, but the Scientist only had to do some calculations on a piece of paper in order to convince himself that he was right."

He paused.

"What is the point of that story?" said the Poet.

"I'm not absolutely sure," said Ahab.

"Perhaps that they both lived happily ever after?" suggested Stinkhorn.

"I would rather be a scientist I think," said Jessica

thoughtfully. "Being a bee sounds exhausting."

"But the point is," said the Secretary, impatiently, "are we, or are we not shrinking?"

"Perhaps it works like this," said Ahab slowly, "the more we worry, the smaller our minds become. That is the effect of a curse. If you fear it, then it may find a landing place; if you do not fear it, then it will simply return to the person who sent it."

The ship suddenly pitched forward and they all had to cling on to the table as the rest of the furniture went sliding across the floor of the saloon. At the same time the light faded dramatically, and within less than a minute they could barely see each other at all.

"The storm has been kind to us," said Ahab's voice in Alma's ear.

"Aren't we sinking?" she said.

"No, we are arriving."

"Arriving where?"

"In Aeonia, and much sooner than I expected."

CHAPTER EIGHTEEN

A Fountain in Aeonia

At Ahab's suggestion the members of the team staggered down the pitching passageway and groped their way into their cabins. Some emergency lighting had come on to compensate for the darkness outside. The ship was now making a sort of slalom movement, which reminded Alma of going down a water slide. From her bunk she stared at the porthole but she could see no sign of stars or moon. It seemed incredible to think that it could so suddenly have become night-time. She wondered if they might have entered some sort of canal tunnel, but she could not work out why their speed should be increasing so rapidly. She wedged herself in the bunk, stretching out her arms and legs to stop herself from rolling out onto the floor. She closed her eyes and found that it wasn't such an unpleasant feeling if you didn't try to resist it. It was like a state she sometimes got into just before going to sleep, when she imagined that she was on a swing, going backwards and forwards in dreamy slow motion. Now she imagined herself to be on a fairground ride in a capsule hurtling down a cylindrical slide towards a swimming pool full of semolina. Then the motion began to change again. The speed was increasing and they were going into a left hand bend. The centrifugal force was pushing her against the wall of the cabin. She moved her pillow across to stop her head from bumping against the wooden panel. "At least it looks as though we will arrive somewhere eventually," she thought. "Unless of course we have shrunk so much that we are already only the size of an atom, or perhaps we are like an electron spinning around the centre of an atom..." She tried to remember what the centre of an atom was called. A nucleus? That sounded about right. She closed her eyes again and wondered if this was the end of the journey, if they were now trapped inside an atom and destined to spin and spin forever.

*

In a silent courtyard, a boy sat on the edge of a fountain and watched as a stream of water poured into a pool. In the centre of the fountain was a statue of a woman with braided hair, kneeling and pouring water from a bronze urn into the pool. The boy sat so still that one might have supposed that he too was a statue. His attention was fixed on the mouth of the urn, and nothing distracted him. A breeze ruffled the sleeve of his shirt, and the trees in the courtyard swayed like dancers. At the same time the sound of music came floating into the courtyard, and with each wave of music the trees bowed their branches, as if they had been conducting the music themselves, or somehow sweeping it around the courtyard. The boy may or may not have heard the music. His brown eyes never blinked, and though he had been sitting in the same position for a long time he did not seem to grow stiff or uncomfortable. He did not scratch his nose or cross and uncross his legs. He did not sigh or pout or show signs of boredom. His concentration was similar to that of an animal watching its prey, but without the shifting of muscles, the gathering for the spring. He was utterly at peace and utterly at rest.

And then his eyes grew wider and he let out a laugh of such beauty that had anyone been listening they could not have helped laughing as well. He clapped his hands together, stood to his feet, turned away from the fountain and walked out of the courtyard through a vine-covered portico. As he went he moved in time to the music, and his walk, though it was nothing more than motion from one place to another, had the quality of a dance. It was obvious that even in this simple action he took the profoundest pleasure.

He turned back before he left the courtyard and looked at the object that had caused him to laugh when it had suddenly emerged from the mouth of the urn. There, floating serenely on the surface of the pool was a toy ship, about a foot long, made of dark wood, its tin funnel emitting a plume of smoke.

*

When the ship had stopped spinning Alma thought about getting off her bunk and going over to the porthole. Their momentum had slowed and she felt relatively safe at last. But with a great creaking of timbers the prow of the ship began to tip downwards. She braced herself once again as her head came up and her feet went down and things started sliding across the cabin. The cupboard doors opened and she was just in time to catch the water bottle which she had wedged upright in one of the drawers next to the bed. The ship was plunging straight downwards. From the cabin next-door Alma heard someone scream and across the corridor she could hear Sanderby Coriander crying out for mercy.

Then there was a crash and water hit the porthole with great force. Their downward motion was checked and had she not been bracing herself she would have been thrown out of her bunk against the far wall. A blue light was streaming in through the porthole and she realised that they were actually under water. With a groaning and creaking the ship slowed in its dive, came to a halt and then began to be forced back towards the surface. Alma braced her arms to prevent her head from banging against the panel behind her as the ship surged back towards the surface like a cork.

As they came up into the daylight the ship seemed to give a sigh of relief, and she heard the sound of water pouring off the decks. It pitched from side to side for a few seconds then began to settle, and soon they were floating on a calm sea and all was silent again. Alma listened to the moaning of her friends and wondered if any of them had been seriously injured. After a couple of minutes she heard Ahab coming down the passageway and checking each cabin. Shaky voices answered his enquiries. When she stood up her legs were trembling. The door of her cabin opened and Ahab looked in.

"Still alive in there?"

Sitting back on the edge of her bunk Alma nodded.

"Sorry about the rough landing, I didn't know we'd be coming in this way."

"So are we here?"

"In Aeonia? Yes we are, just pulling up to the jetty. Our size hasn't adjusted yet. I'd better be on my way before it does or I'll be stuck here. You okay to go on deck? Take anything with you that you want."

She took her water bottle and put on her own jeans again with the bits of paper in the pockets, but when she looked out of the window the sky looked so clear and sunny that she decided she wouldn't probably need any extra sweaters. Apart from the sky she could see nothing except a wall of sandstone that towered above the ship, which she took to be the harbour wall. When she went out into the passageway, the first person she met was Stinkhorn, yawning and stretching. When she asked him how he was he said "fine" in such a matter of fact way that she realised he had slept through the whole thing.

"Weren't you thrown out of bed?" she asked.

"Certainly not!" he said. "When the funny stuff started happening I made sure I was really well tucked in and then got right down to the bottom of the bed."

The Secretary came out of her cabin looking very pale. Jessica had to be supported down the gangplank. The Poet had been hurled out of his bunk when they began the vertical plunge. He was rubbing his arm and had a lump on his forehead. The Nephew was clutching his suitcase and looking bewildered. "Someone should have stayed with him," thought Alma. "We really need to look after one another a bit better."

Ahab came down the passageway carrying the Sloth. "She's good in a storm," he said. "She grabs hold of the side of the bunk and digs her claws right into the wood. We could turn turtle and she wouldn't budge."

"She doesn't look as though she wants to come with us," said the Secretary.

"Nobody has to," said Alma, suddenly feeling a great concern for all these people who seemed to have been drawn into this strange voyage without having much say in the matter.

"What about you Miss Quill? Don't you want to go back? You only wanted a holiday by the seaside."

"Oh, a cruise is even better," she said, "and a foreign holiday is best of all. I've never been abroad before."

The Poet was breathing in the air.

"Ah yes," he said, "there is something here that excites me. I feel that this is a place where at last my talents will be appreciated and where I shall be inspired to begin my magnum opus: an epic poem of three hundred and sixty stanzas, all in flawless iambic pentameter."

They went on deck. Ahab went first, jumping from the ship onto the quayside with one of the cables. The Nephew flung across another cable and Ahab pulled the ship right up to the quay. The gangplank was pushed across and they stepped ashore. In front of them rose the mighty harbour wall. They turned and looked out to sea, and found that they were in an enclosed harbour, and opposite them, towering into the sky was an enormous statue as tall as a mountain. They all stood gazing upwards, trying to take in the scale of the place, trying to work out what it all meant.

Ahab was now releasing the cables. "So, how many are staying and how many are coming back with me?" he said.

They looked at him in some confusion and watched,

speechless, as he went back up the gangplank. There was something strange about the way he looked at them, for he looked up at them when by rights he should have been looking down, as the gangplank had been sloping up to the door in the side of the ship from the quayside.

"You're all staying then," he said. "Perhaps we will meet again, perhaps not. I hope you find what you're looking for." He hauled in the gangplank and at once the ship began to move away.

Alma stared after the little vessel which had brought them safely through such a dangerous journey. Ahab was waving and the Sloth, sitting contentedly on the rail waved as well. They must have moved away very rapidly because in no time at all the two figures had all but disappeared from view and the ship looked like a model bobbing on a boating lake. Alma realised she was standing far too close to the edge of the dock, and had to step backwards. She looked up at the mountainous statue again but now everything had changed. They were no longer in a harbour but in a courtyard looking at a pool, in the centre of which was a statue of a woman with an urn. Alma turned in surprise and nearly fell over a low wall which hadn't been there a moment ago.

"Well blow me down," said Stinkhorn, "we've grown!"

"Look!" shouted Jessica pointing across the pool to where the little brown ship was climbing steadily up the stream of water that came pouring out of the urn, like a salmon swimming up a waterfall. It hovered for a moment in the mouth of the urn and then it was gone.

CHAPTER NINETEEN

The Shuttered Houses

They swung their legs over the wall of the fountain and looked around at the courtyard. The ground was covered in smooth, sand-coloured flagstones. Beyond a ring of silver-green willow trees were the walls of houses with red tiled roofs and balconies with wrought iron railings. Vines heavy with fruit climbed wooden trellises and here and there bougainvillea blossomed crimson and pink.

"I feel like I've been heretofore," whispered the Nephew.

"I know what you mean," said Miss Quill.

"Nah," said Stinkhorn, "the likes of us have never been in a place like this. This is a classy joint."

"And at last the sun has come up," said Jessica. They looked around then to see where the sun was, but though they looked in every direction they couldn't see it.

"It must be low in the sky," said Miss Quill.

"Yes but where?" said the Poet. "It's so bright you'd expect the sun to be right overhead. And look – our shadows are barely visible."

"Let's get out in the open," said Alma, "then we'll get the lie of the land."

They headed through an open portico into a tree-lined

street with low houses on either side. The houses were all different colours and had carved wooden front doors.

"Oh I could live here," said Alma.

"The climate!" said the Poet. "It's almost perfect."

Just then a breeze moved through the trees.

"Now it is perfect," he said.

"Listen!" said Stinkhorn. "Did you hear that?"

They had all heard it, and it made them stop in their tracks and strain their ears in the hope of hearing a bit more.

"That was the most beautiful thing..." said Alma.

It had just been the briefest snatch of a song brought from far away on the wind, and yet it made every song that she had ever heard seem hollow by comparison. The breeze dropped and with it the music faded. They walked on, stepping as quietly as they could, partly because the place was so peaceful and partly so as not to miss any of the music should it come again.

"Who do you think lives here?" said Jessica.

"Angels!" said the Poet. "I'm sure this is where the Angels live."

There was a sign on a wall just ahead of them. It had a picture of a fish and some wavy lines, and it was pointing down a street that branched off at right angles to the one they were on.

"That must be the way to the harbour," said Miss Quill.

"But I thought we'd just come from the harbour," said Alma.

"No, we came into a fountain of some sort. It seemed like a harbour to us because we were so small. But there must be another harbour, a real one, down this street."

They set off in the direction indicated by the sign. The street was a lot narrower than the one they had left; it had no trees and the houses didn't look quite as nice, in fact the further they went the dingier they became. They came to another sign and turned to the right. And here the windows of the houses were all shuttered and the paint was peeling off their walls and doors.

"This is the poor part of town," said Jessica.

"But it wasn't always poor," said the Secretary. "These were once grand houses too, it's just that they haven't been looked after as well as the ones on the main street."

"Do you think it's siesta time?" said the Poet. "There doesn't seem to be anyone about."

"Perhaps it's still early in the morning and no one's up yet," suggested Jessica.

"I wonder if angels sleep..." mused the Poet.

"I think angels would keep their houses in a better sate of repair," said Miss Quill.

"Well here comes someone," said Stinkhorn. "We can ask them."

A dark figure had appeared at the far end of the street; it was shuffling along, keeping close to the wall. When it saw them it stopped for a moment and seemed to be thinking about turning back, but finally it came on, its head turned to the wall. As it came closer they could see that it was a woman with an old-fashioned shopping basket on wheels. While she was still twenty yards away they could hear a terrible wheezing, snuffling sound.

Alma called out, "Hello! Excuse me, I wonder if you can help us?"

The woman kept her face to the wall.

"Do you speak any English?" said the Secretary.

The woman muttered something, but as she had a scarf over her mouth and her head turned away from them, she had to repeat herself several times before they could understand what she was saying.

"I've just been out for a book. Always go out for a book about this time."

"A book? Is there a bookshop?" asked the Poet with great interest.

"Or a library?" suggested Jessica.

"Both," said the lady, "but I don't go to the library, I go to the bookshop, only he won't let you take them away."

All the time she was speaking the dreadful wheezing was still going on and Alma realised that it wasn't the woman who was making the sound, it was coming from the shopping basket. Under a lot of old newspapers something was moving.

"What have you got in there?" Alma asked, and for the first time since they had arrived in this place she felt afraid: afraid of what might be in the shopping basket, that it might be something that shouldn't be in a shopping basket, something that might be leaving a trail of blood all the way down the street. She remembered what Ahab had said about Aeonia being better and worse than the other places they had been. She looked back down the way that the old woman had come. There was a line of something nasty and sticky on the ground.

"What is that?" said Alma in a horrified whisper.

The woman spun round and saw what Alma was pointing at.

"What?" she snapped. "What are you looking at? Things that don't concern you?"

As the woman turned Alma caught a glimpse of an incredibly lined face; a face of unimaginable age, yet caked with crude pink makeup, rouged cheeks and false eyelashes.

"My molasses!" shrieked the lady. "Sookie, you bad dog!" She began ripping out the newspaper from the shopping basket, tossing it into the street. As she did so the wheezing and snuffling got louder, until finally she pulled out a black pug dog with bulging, blood-shot eyes. It was snuffling and growling, licking its chops and sticking its tongue into its nose.

"Sookie, have you been at my molasses?" She reached into the bottom of the basket and pulled out a jam jar half full of a dark and treacly substance.

"You're a bad, bad, greedy dog!" she scolded, giving him little pats on the nose. He snapped at her but there were no teeth in his pink gums. There was something reassuringly familiar about the way she scolded the dog.

"Excuse me," said Alma, "we were just wondering if you could tell us where we are?"

The woman went on addressing the dog.

"Oh yes and all these people coming asking questions, Sookie! They'll be wanting to know where they are I shouldn't wonder. Well we all asked that at first, didn't we? They tried to make us do things we didn't want to do and see things we didn't want to see, but they can't get at us if we don't want them to, can they poppet? And we won't let them get at us, will we?"

"Who are you talking about?" asked Miss Quill gently.

"There are the lurkers, aren't there my lovely? The waiters

and the watchers with their long faces, the knockers on the door trying to get their size nines into the house, trying to peer through the shutters, but we have good shutters don't we, and we have our little trips to the corner store for the sweet things and the bookshop for entertainment."

"Excuse me," said Miss Quill again, and she reached out and touched the woman on the arm. Without any warning she spun round and spat into the Secretary's face.

"NO!" she shrieked. "You can't pin that on me! It's that Harold's fault! It's all his fault. He's the one you want and I don't know where he is, see? He hasn't been here and I haven't seen him so you can all naff off and stop harassing me! I know my rights!"

The Secretary had staggered back in surprise and was wiping the spittle from her cheek.

"But we weren't accusing you of anything," said Alma. She saw the wild look in the woman's eyes and realised she wasn't actually listening to anything they were saying to her.

"Disguises won't work!" she said. "You can't make me do anything I don't want to do and I don't want to talk to *you*."

She hurried off down the street, keeping close to the wall, looking back over her shoulder every few yards. The pug put its paws over the edge of the shopping basket and let out a few feeble yips. Then the woman reached a black door and fumbled for a key that she had on a piece of elastic round her neck. She put it into the lock and let herself into the house. The last thing they saw was the dog in its basket being pulled bumpily up the steps and disappearing into the house. As soon as it was inside the door slammed, chains were fastened and they were alone in the silent street.

"What a horrid woman," said Alma.

"Who do you think Harold was?" asked Jessica.

"Probably her son," said Alma authoritatively. "Women like that always have ne'er-do-well sons."

"I thought I liked this place, but now I'm not so sure," said the Poet.

"I don't know," said Stinkhorn, "I thought she had a point. She doesn't have to talk to us if she doesn't want to."

They were all standing close to the wall, looking up and down the street, feeling suddenly exposed.

"There's someone watching us from the house opposite," whispered the Poet. They all looked and saw a face behind a broken shutter. Slowly it withdrew. They moved off again in the direction of the harbour. Now that the idea was in their minds they couldn't shake the conviction that behind each shutter someone or something malevolent was watching them.

"It'll be better once we're at the harbour," said Alma.

"Don't know what they're watching us for," said Jessica. "If they're anything like that old woman, we're the ones who should be staring at them."

They followed the signs through several more streets. All of the houses were shuttered and menacing. But then finally the streets became broader and were once more tree-lined, the houses again friendly and inviting. They looked in through some of the ground floor windows and saw rooms that were beautifully furnished. In this part of town everything was clean outside as well as in. There was no litter, no weeds growing between the paving stones, no fallen leaves. There was earth in the flower beds, but none on the street – there wasn't even any dust.

"They must hose down these streets every day," said the Secretary.

They came into a large square with a magnificent fountain, the centrepiece of which was a huge piece of rock as smooth as ice and full of holes and indentations. Jets of water shot out intermittently and seemed to be playing, trying to catch each other unawares. They stood and watched the patterns the water made. Sometimes there would seem to be a symmetry to the ballet, at other times they would wait in vain for a pattern to repeat itself as the water shot out from at least twenty different carefully concealed pipes.

"It's like a lot of children having a fight with water pistols," said Jessica.

They soon found themselves laughing at the bizarre aquatic warfare. Some of the jets were obviously jokers – one pipe would keep pretending to fire a jet but it would just bubble a little bit of water out and as soon as it did ten of the other pipes would all fire at it. Then it would try again and the ten would once again smother it. Then it produced a stream that went straight up into the air and split into two jets of exactly the same strength which poured down on either side; then it began to rotate and the jets formed spirals spinning faster and faster until it was just one sheet of water in the shape of an hourglass.

They decided that there were actually different teams involved: at one point it would be all against one, then five against fifteen, then ten against ten; alliances were made and then broken by sudden betrayals. But through everything there ran the idea that a magnificent game was being played. It was like watching a family of young animals. The variety was endless. It was like a play and a ballet and a war and a brilliant game of football.

"It just doesn't get boring, does it," said Alma.

"I don't know why," said Jessica. "There's nothing much going on, it's just water falling into a pool and being sucked up and squirted out again; nothing is being added or subtracted, it will just go on and on."

"We can always come back," said the Secretary.

"Oh, I don't want to miss anything," said the Poet.

"I feel like I could stand here and watch for ever," said Jessica. "Come to think of it, how long have we been standing here?"

"Oh my goodness!" said Alma with a sudden rush of horror, and looked at her watch. With relief she saw that it was still only 4.29.

"We should get on though," she said, "we don't know how long we've got."

"It's that way," said Stinkhorn, pointing to another sign on the far side of the square.

The Nephew had become so engrossed in watching the fountain that they actually had to drag him away.

"It's weird," said Alma, "but though we were standing quite still for what seemed like a really long time I don't feel tired or stiff or anything."

"It must be the air in this place," said Stinkhorn. "My leg feels better than it has for years and years. In fact I don't have any aches and pains at all. And for once I don't feel hungry."

"Nor thirsty," said Jessica.

"And Stinkhorn doesn't smell so bad," said the Poet.

"Oi! Watch it!" said Stinkhorn.

Of course once it had been mentioned they all had to gather round him and sniff, much to his embarrassment.

"It's true," said Jessica. "He doesn't smell at all."

"Well I never did much," he protested.

"Or rather he does, but he smells quite nice," corrected the Secretary.

"It's because he's stopped smoking that horrid tobacco," said Jessica.

"That's weird too," said Stinkhorn. "I had completely forgotten about smoking." He waited for a few seconds.

"It's gone," he said. "I have absolutely no desire to smoke."

"The Harbour!" shouted Jessica. And everything else was suddenly forgotten as they came round a corner and were confronted by a scene of such size and beauty that for several minutes they just stood there with their mouths open.

They looked out over a dark blue ocean, on the far side of which they could just make out a hazy shoreline. Following this line round to left or right they saw that it swung far out into the distance and then began to curve in towards them.

"It's like a huge round pond," gasped Alma.

"But how can anything be that big?" said Jessica. "How can we see something so far away?"

"There's no curvature," said the Secretary, "so there is no horizon. This sea is completely flat."

There was no beach to speak of, and ships of all shapes and sizes were moored at intervals along the coast, some tied up at the quay, some resting at anchor a little way off from the shore. The harbour could have been any distance across, even hundreds of miles, it was impossible to say, and beyond it on every side spread an immense city, and beyond the city, though this was hazy and difficult to see in the far distance, there were green, forest-covered hills, and running along the ridge of hills a fine golden strip that formed the dividing line between the green and the immense canopy of perfectly blue sky. Not only were there no clouds in the sky, there was neither sun nor moon. Once again they turned round and round trying to work out where the light was coming from, but it didn't seem to be coming from anywhere, it just was. There were soft diffused shadows as if the light were coming from all around.

Alma felt her legs beginning to go a bit wobbly and she sat down on the quayside.

"Are you all right Alma?" asked Jessica.

"I feel a bit faint again."

"Perhaps you should have a bit of air," said Miss Quill, coming over to her. "How's your head?"

The Nephew helped her to get the bottle from her belt.

"I just don't know how much there is left," she said.

"Just try a little bit," said Miss Quill.

Alma twisted off the cork and put the neck of the bottle in her mouth, then tipped it back and half breathed, half drank some of the contents. Instantly her mind began to clear. She carefully replaced the stopper.

"I'm okay now."

They all turned again and gazed at the enormous panorama.

"Where are the people?" said Stinkhorn.

This was the missing element. There all these ships, the huge harbour, which should have been a bustle of activity and yet there was no bustle.

"There's a ship coming in!" called the Poet. "Look at it!"

A three-masted schooner, in full sail, was racing towards them, and there were the passengers on the deck, waving. And then Alma thought she could see a lot of people on the quayside who had come out to meet the ship. There were dockworkers getting ready to catch the cables, and the others were the friends and relatives of the passengers who were returning from a long journey. And she knew, without quite knowing how, that some of them had been away for a very long time, and that they were greatly looking forward to returning. That was why the ship was travelling so fast, they just couldn't wait to get back to the ones they had left behind. It was like emigration in reverse, as if these people had all decided to go abroad when they were very young, and had spent their entire lives in a distant continent and now they were coming home with wonderful stories to tell. They had a cargo of treasures for those waiting on the quay, gifts perfectly suited to each person.

Alma turned to look at the others to make sure that it wasn't just her imagination running away with her.

"Can you see it?" she said.

They all turned to her and nodded. But when she looked back to the ship she found that just in those few seconds things had moved on rapidly. The ship had now drawn alongside the harbour, tied up, let down its gangplanks and the company were streaming onto the dockside. There were reunions and tears and shouts of joy and laughter. And then they caught snatches of singing that was just like the music they had heard in the courtyard when they first landed.

But already the people were heading away from the harbour towards the various streets that opened onto it, with their arms around each other and smiles on their faces. Alma wasn't quite sure how she knew this because something seemed to have happened to her vision. The people were slightly out of focus and she sensed rather than saw what they were feeling. They all seemed to be quite young, but she couldn't make out their features; whenever she tried to focus on a face it would turn away or become smudged and indistinct. The harbour and the sky and the scenery were all quite easy to get into focus; the boats were more tricky, but the people were hardest of all, and in a few moments they had all melted away. Several of them, she was sure, had come up the street where they were standing and must have passed quite close to them, but somehow she hadn't seen them except from a distance.

"Did we all see that?" said Alma, turning to Jessica.

"I saw something," she said. "There were shadows, but it could have just been the light reflecting off the water."

"A ghost ship," said the Poet, "a magnificent ghost ship with no crew and no passengers, running before the wind."

"But didn't you see the people?" asked Alma.

"I thought I saw something," said the Secretary, "but now I'm not sure. Wasn't that ship already tied up at the quayside?"

"Did you see them Stinkhorn?" asked Alma, who was beginning to feel the whole thing slipping away, like a dream upon waking.

Stinkhorn didn't answer. She looked around and caught the worried expression on his face.

"Where's the Nephew?" he said.

Everyone started looking around and calling, "Nephew! Nephew!" Their voices sounded strange echoing down the silent street. They waited and waited but there was no answer. Then up at the far end of the street they heard footsteps approaching and a figure came into view.

"Nephew!" shouted Alma, much relieved.

But as the figure came closer they could see that it was not the Nephew.

CHAPTER TWENTY

Mr Tarantullus

"My friends, what are you doing out here?"

Coming towards them down the street was a short man in a brown corduroy suit. His face was so grey and leathery that he looked more than anything like a lizard.

"Have you just arrived?" he asked.

"Well, we've been here for an hour or two, but..."

"You didn't come off the ship then?" he said, looking at them rather uncertainly.

"Well, not that one, but we've..."

"Did you slip ashore in a long boat? Or did you come from one of the islands?"

"I think we came through a fountain," said Alma.

His eyes opened very wide.

"But we've lost someone," she continued.

"I see," he said, and there was a note of interest in his voice. "You have lost someone, and you came through one of the fountains..."

"Can you help us?" said Alma. "He was with us a few moments ago, but now he's disappeared."

This latest piece of information seemed to confuse him. "He was with you a few moments ago? Do you mean he came here with you?"

"Yes, he came here with us and he was with us until just a few moments ago. He's in his late teens and dressed in a black suit with long tails."

"And he almost never speaks," said the Secretary.

"But when he does he nearly always says just the right thing," said Jessica.

"Except when he's talking complete rubbish," added Stinkhorn.

"I see, I see..." said the man. "Well this is most serious." He looked around. "You haven't... seen anyone since you arrived here have you?"

"We saw an old woman," said Miss Quill.

"And some of us thought we saw a lot of people here in the harbour," said Alma.

"This old woman," he said, "did she have a shopping basket?"

"Yes, and a weird little dog," said Alma.

"Mrs Trimble," said the man, nodding. "I think I know where your friend will be."

"But he won't be with her," said Stinkhorn. "We saw her go into her house."

"And lock the door," Alma agreed. "We would have seen if he'd gone in there with her."

"But did you see him come down the street with you?"

"He was walking behind," said the Secretary. "I remember because ever since we were at the fountain he'd been hanging back."

"Wait – perhaps he's gone back to the fountain!" said Alma.

They hurried back down the street to the square where the fountain was still playing its mesmerising game, but the

Nephew was nowhere to be seen. Next they found their way back to the courtyard where they had landed in Ahab's ship, but it was as still and deserted as ever. In fact it was so peaceful they were tempted just to sit on the wall and watch the water pouring lazily from the amphora and listen to the soothing sound it made, hoping for another snatch of the beautiful music. Alma had to shake herself to remember that the Nephew needed to be found.

"I suppose he might have got lost trying to find his way back to us," she said.

"But he only needed to follow the signs," said Stinkhorn. "Even he could have managed that."

"I suppose it is possible he might have gone to the old lady's house, if he was lost," said the Secretary.

"Let us try," said the stranger. "But before we go there I must introduce myself to you. I am Tarantullus, I run the local bookshop."

"The bookshop!" said the Poet with interest. "I wonder if you may have heard of me..."

"I doubt it," said Tarantullus, "but I think we really should be looking for your friend, he may be in some danger."

They followed Tarantullus back down the street to the house with its faded black door and creepy shutters. He rapped briskly and waited.

"Mrs Trimble!" he cooed. "Mrs Trimble, it's Mr Tarantullus here, why don't you open the door? I would very much like a word, Mrs Trimble."

They listened for a moment, and from within they heard the wheezing snuffling noise of the pug.

"I know you can hear me Mrs Trimble..."

"What do you want?" came the old woman's voice.

"I would just like you to open the door for two minutes Mrs Trimble, just so's I can have a word with you."

"Well you can naff off," said Mrs Trimble. "I know you've got a great crowd of them there with you."

"I don't have a great crowd with me Mrs Trimble, it is quite safe."

There was a shuffling noise and one of the shutters of the downstairs room twitched.

"I can see them!" she shouted. "I wasn't born yesterday. You can all just go away, 'cos I'm not opening my door to no one."

"But these people are not who you think Mrs Trimble, you met them earlier on and they are now looking for their friend."

"Well he isn't here! Nobody's here 'cept me and Sookie. There's no one else. And Harold isn't here either."

"Very well Mrs Trimble, not to worry. I'll see you very soon at the shop."

There was no reply from inside the house. They heard her shuffle away from the door, though the pug remained, wheezing and growling. Mr Tarantullus stood with his hands on his hips, breathing heavily.

"Are you all right?" asked Alma.

"Asthma," he said. "Sorry, it's these stressful situations, they take their toll. I am not in the best of health to be quite honest."

"Do you think he's in there," asked Miss Quill.

"I can't be completely sure," he said. "It is possible your friend could have been taken into any of these houses."

"Are they all occupied?" asked Alma.

"I believe so. I know some of the residents, quite a few come to my shop, but there are many more who never leave their houses at all."

"They never leave?" said Jessica. "But they must get out sometimes."

"Some make it as far as the corner store, but there are plenty who simply never go out. Anyway my friends, why don't you come to my bookshop? People are more relaxed when they come in there, and we are more likely to get news of your friend. I'm afraid these doorstep tactics have very little chance of success. It's not far, just round the corner."

They followed him into an alleyway between two houses. This opened out into a shady square on the far side of which was the bookshop. There was no sign, but there were displays of books in the windows. He went down two steps and unlocked the door. A bell tinged as he pushed it open.

"Come in and don't bother to wipe your feet. Nobody here just at the moment. It's a quiet time of day."

They stepped through the low doorway into a dingy shop. There were shelves of leather bound volumes along every wall from floor to ceiling. In the centre of the shop were more bookcases, and there were piles of dusty books scattered everywhere. In the windows the displays of books were covered with cobwebs.

"Have a seat anywhere," he said.

They looked around for somewhere to sit but the only chair was wedged behind a desk.

"Just pull up some books," he said. Taking a cloth from a drawer he began to flick the dust off some of the piles of books.

"Don't you ever clean this place?" said Jessica coughing as she was enveloped in a cloud of dust.

Mr Tarantullus looked at her strangely. "Clean? No my dear, on the contrary, I spend half my time making the place look dirty. Of course, I was forgetting how recently you have arrived here. You see, in this country things don't get dirty – there is no naturally occurring accumulation of dust. I have to make all this myself by specially drying out and grinding to powder earth from the flowerbeds. The cobwebs are actually made of very fine cotton – I have stitched them all myself. There are no spiders you see. But to my way of thinking a bookshop needs dust and cobwebs or it isn't a real bookshop, and of course my customers love it."

"And where are we exactly?" said Alma, relieved to have at last found someone who might be able to answer some of her questions.

"You are in the country known by some as Aeonia."

Alma could feel the drumming in her temples again, and the tramping footsteps, which had been lurking for some time in the back of her head, marched from the back to the front. The room had suddenly got very cold. Then she saw that instead of sitting down on the pile of books as she had intended she had managed to miss them and was sitting on the floor. The smell of old books was replaced by the smell of rotten vegetables and a yellow light was shining into her eyes. She heard her own voice saying, "I can't go back yet; I have to stay here, I haven't found out anything." She braced her feet against the side of the kitchen cabinet and pushed as hard as she could, at the same time closing her eyes and trying to concentrate, but she could feel her grip on the other world slipping away. With an enormous effort she tried to move her hand to her belt where the bottle was hanging, but she knew even as she did so that it would not be there. She opened her eyelids a crack and saw the yellow street lamp, the dark outline of the bin, the familiar dark shapes of the kitchen.

"Don't struggle," said a voice in her ear, but fearing that this was the voice of her spirit admitting defeat she struggled even harder.

"Put your head back."

She felt the hard neck of the bottle between her teeth, felt it being lifted and felt herself draining the last breath of air. She sucked it in and felt its warmth spread through her body. The yellow light began to mellow into the dusty shadows of the bookshop.

"We almost lost you," said Miss Quill.

"But that's the end of the air," said Stinkhorn shaking the bottle. "What will happen next time?"

"How long do you think we have?" said Jessica gloomily.

"I may be able to help in some small way," said Mr Tarantullus.

He went to a cupboard behind his desk and unlocked it. Inside were shelves full of boxes, half a dozen stone jugs and some green bottles. Each of these had a hand-written label. He selected one and brought it to Alma.

"I believe this one still has some air from your world left in it. It will keep you going just a little longer, unfortunately it is the last I have."

She thanked him and they all helped her up off the floor and sat her once again on the pile of books.

"Mr Tarantullus," she said earnestly, "we have come a very long way and we really, really don't want to have to leave here without finding out..." she struggled for the words. "I'm not even quite sure what it is that I want to know, but there was something missing from my life and I feel as though that is why I have come here. But I only have a very short time left in which to find it, and when I've gone I don't know what will happen to my friends here, because they are not from my world, they're from somewhere called the Wastelands and from what we have been told it seems that they may become stranded. Can you tell us what we should do? Should we try to go back across the sea now before it's too late?"

"You would never make it," he said. "But don't worry too much about your friends. What is the worst that can happen to them? If you go back, or should I say when you go back, they will remain here, and there are many worse places in which to be stranded. Who would not rather be here than in the Wastelands? You have been drawn here for a reason. Let me explain some things to you, for I have seen groups like you enter Aeonia before. Not, I must say, through that particular fountain, but it has been known for anomalies to occur."

"What do you mean, anomanies?" said Stinkhorn, sensing an insult.

"I simply mean that it is unusual for souls to enter this place mid-term."

"What do you mean by mid-term?" said Alma.

Mr Tarantullus considered for a moment.

"I am sorry," he said, "once again I have been making certain assumptions. You really have no idea where you are, do you?"

"We only know what the Customs man told us, and a

little that Ahab said, but everyone seems so vague about everything," she said.

"In which case allow me to speak plainly. To use the language of your Age, you are in *The Next World*".

He waited for a while and watched Alma. She was blinking, trying to take this in. After a few moments she looked up at him.

"Yes," she said, "I think I sort of half knew that. But does that mean we've died?"

"No my dear, that is why I have called you an anomaly. Unlike myself, you have not died, nor, in my opinion, are you about to die – hence the strong link back to the earth. But for some reason you have been drawn here at an unusual time. Exceptions of this kind are not unknown, but they are usually associated with some form of bereavement. I have met wives who have recently lost their husbands, fathers who have lost their children, but from what you told me earlier this is not the case with you."

"No," she said, "both my grandfathers died before I was born, and my great aunt died a couple of years ago..."

"No, that is not it. Not it at all," said Tarantullus.

"I know why she's here," said Stinkhorn.

They all turned to look at him.

"She's here because she felt like she was a mistake. That's why we're all here. That's how we all felt in the Wastelands. We all felt like failures, misprints, people who shouldn't have ever been born, who wouldn't have been born but for some clerical error. Or perhaps when we were born we didn't meet the required standards and we should have been scratched, you know, put out of our misery, but somehow that didn't happen either and we ended up in the Wastelands. And Alma here, well she was sort of the same, and she felt like she'd been thrown in the bin, that her parents hadn't really wanted her and nobody particularly liked her and everyone seemed to want her to be a bit different from what she was. And I saw her through the wall when she was sitting behind the rubbish bin, and I thought she was like me in a way, and I'd heard rumours of people finding things out across the sea, over the Wall..."

He was sitting slumped on his pile of books. They were all a bit slumped now, feeling their lostness and disappointment with life in general. Jessica was crying.

"My parents don't even know where I am," she sobbed, "and if they did know they wouldn't be particularly bothered."

"I have been fooling myself," said the Poet, joining in with the gloomy mood. "No one is interested in my verses. Why should they be? Most people have better things to do with their lives than read my ramblings."

"And what about you Madam?" said Mr Tarantullus, addressing Miss Quill.

"In a word... redundant." she said. "All I have ever done is pointless jobs for pointless people."

"You see it is very simple," said Mr Tarantullus, after he had waited a few moments in case anyone else wanted to speak. "You have all lost someone! You all feel, to a greater or lesser extent, that you have lost yourselves. You may perhaps have been fearful of disappearing altogether. May I venture to suggest that you have come here in search of a meaning and a purpose?"

There was silence in the Bookshop. Then they heard

footsteps scraping down the alley outside. The Bookdealer looked out of the window and then spoke quickly and quietly. "My friends, I wonder if I could ask you to step behind that curtain. It might be best if my customers were not aware of your presence just for the moment. It may help me to discover the whereabouts of your friend if these people who are approaching do not know they are overheard."

He pulled aside a curtain and the five of them all hurried behind it. Just as he drew it back again they heard the bell tinkle as the door opened. They heard the voices of a man and a woman, apparently in the middle of a heated argument.

"That is typical!" said the woman. "You can't see anyone else's point of view, can you? You are completely locked into your own pathetic cycle of wants and needs. It never even occurs to you that I might be suffering."

"Well, excuse me for breathing!" said the man. "If you hadn't suddenly decided to take matters into your own hands, without consulting me I should point out..." he paused and addressed Mr Tarantullus.

"We'll take that one again."

"Yes Sir, of course. If you wouldn't mind just stepping through into the back of the shop. Thank you Madam."

They heard a door open and close. The conversation was now barely audible. After a few minutes the door opened again and then the Bookdealer was once more opening the curtain.

"There we are," he said. "They'll be gone for a few hours."

"Where did they go?" asked Alma.

Mr Tarantullus looked embarrassed. "They have... erm... taken a book. Don't concern yourself my dear, they are regular customers."

"But did you ask them about the Nephew?" asked the Secretary.

"I did, of course I did. Unfortunately they were unable to give any clue as to his whereabouts. But look, I tell you what, why don't you all come upstairs to my apartment, that way if anyone else calls I won't have to hide you behind the curtain like so many spies."

They followed him up a staircase to a glass door, from the other side of which came the sound of a tinny radio. He took out a key, unlocked the door and ushered them in. It was a rather scruffy flat, and once again the walls were all lined with books. The furniture looked tatty, the carpets threadbare. He went over to the radio, which was on a gate-legged table by the window. There were heavy shutters on the inside of the windows, most of them partially closed. Alma expected him to turn off the radio but instead he turned the volume up, in spite of the fact that the reception was so bad they could only hear the crackle of interference and the occasional word as the program came and went. At one point a woman's voice said, "I may be many things Roger, but I am certainly not a quitter!"

"*The Archers*," said Mr Tarantullus. "Yes, we can just barely pick up Radio 4 here."

There were several sofas and armchairs and they all found somewhere comfortable to sit.

"So are you really dead then?" said Jessica, causing the others to wince.

"Well, I don't actually think of myself as being dead," said Mr Tarantullus with a little laugh. "I have passed through the experience which you would refer to as death, but as you can see my life continues, it has just taken another form."

"So are all the people here... dead, in our sense of the word, as well? Mrs Trimble and the people in the houses?" said Alma, feeling that she would soon be able to get things straight in her mind.

"Most certainly! Although," he added in a confidential whisper, "I can't say you've landed in one of the best parts of town."

"What do you mean?"

He looked at Alma, as if wondering how much he ought to say.

"It is difficult to explain," he said at last. "Let us just say that some people cope with death and its immediate aftermath better than others."

"Oh please tell us more," she said. "This is just the sort of thing I've always wanted to know about. Are you talking about Heaven and Hell, and if so which are we in?" As soon as she had spoken she felt quite foolish. She was sure of one thing: if her mother's religious beliefs were anything to go by they certainly weren't in Hell.

The radio reception cleared for a couple of seconds – just long enough for them to hear some reference to *Eddie* being *no earthly good*. Then Mr Tarantullus spoke again.

"Aeonia is not a final destination," he said. "It is, if you like, a staging post. This is the place from which you set out on a life and the place you return to when that life is over. It is also the place where a part of you stays while the life is in progress."

"I'm sorry, I don't quite understand," said Alma. "How can you set out on a life and yet also partly stay here?"

"These are all matters which you have forgotten about my dear. When you return here across the sea at the end of your life it will all come back to you."

"But I have come across the sea."

"Indeed you have, but you came in a very special vessel; one which was able to avoid the usual processes. Had you really been through a death you would have come on quite a different ship."

"Like the one we thought we saw earlier on?"

"Yes, it might not have been a sailing ship like that one, it might have been a steam ship or a submarine or a huge cruise liner, but you would have come across the sea and gradually you would have remembered things."

"So as soon as you die you wake up on a ship?"

"Not straight away. There is usually a journey of some sort to be made first. It may be a long journey or a short one, but most people have some terrain to cross before they reach the sea. The experiences are quite dreamlike at this stage; they may be pleasant or unpleasant, but eventually you reach the sea. There you are met and taken on board a vessel and guided through your voyage. Very gently you are helped to review your life, to go over it and understand all the things that have happened. This can be a painful process at times, particularly when you have to face up to all the missed opportunities. Some find that part quite unendurable. Sometimes they throw themselves into the sea, or else hide in the bowels of the ship and sneak ashore once the ship docks."

"What happens to them then?"

"Generally they come and live in a part of the city like this, in one of the shuttered houses."

"And what happens to the ones who throw themselves into the sea? Do they drown?"

"No, they do not drown, though many of them wish they could. But it is not so easy to die once you are dead. Some are eventually washed up in the city; others swim to one of the islands and live there. Some construct their own little kingdoms; some even get the idea that they are gods, and persuade others to come and worship them."

"I think we may have met one of those," said Stinkhorn.

"But what happens to the ones who don't jump ship?" continued Alma, feeling that at last she was getting somewhere.

"Well, as the voyage progresses gradually they remember the things they knew before their life on earth began." Mr Tarantullus paused. They were all staring at him intently.

"I'm not sure that I will be helping you by telling you all this," he said. "Besides I would not be speaking from direct experience."

"What do you mean?" said Alma slowly.

"I simply mean that I jumped ship myself."

This latest piece of information was greeted by a stunned silence.

"There now," said Mr Tarantullus. "That is perhaps not what you hoped to hear. Suffice it to say that if I were not in my current state, I would not have been able to hold this conversation with you. Those of you who thought you saw people on the quayside will have noticed something strange about them, am I right?"

"Yes, they kept drifting in and out of focus," said Alma.

"Yes, that is how it seems. It is because they operate in a very different time frame to you. It may help you to imagine that for them time moves much more rapidly, though in fact the relationship is more complex than that. Time for those of us who live in these streets drags abominably, but for them it flies. It is as difficult for them to focus on you as it is for you to focus on them."

"They seemed so happy," said Alma, in a distant sort of voice. She wasn't quite sure how she knew this, but it was the thing she remembered more strongly than what she had actually seen.

"Well, certainly they are happy," he said. "They have been reunited with their loved ones. Not just the people they knew in their most recent lives, but friends from other incarnations as well, and friends that they have made while they have been here. But most of all..." He checked himself. "I wasn't going to tell you any of this," he said. Then he sighed, "Ah well, perhaps this is why you came. They are not just happy because they have met their companions, they are happy because they are once again *whole*."

"You mean they are well, like they have been healed of whatever killed them in the first place?" said Alma.

"That is not what I mean at all. In most cases the illnesses and causes of death are done with as soon as death is accomplished. No, they are whole in the sense that they are once again united with their Watchers."

"What is a Watcher?" said three or four of them at the same time.

"The Watcher is that part of the Self, the greater part I might add, which remains here in Aeonia and watches over the life that the earthly soul is leading. When that life is over the Watcher comes to meet its soul and, all things being equal, is reunited with it. As I have indicated this is not always an easy process."

Alma was wondering about Mr Tarantullus. "And your Watcher...?" she began hesitantly.

He shot her a glance that was not quite of annoyance – perhaps of pain, she thought.

"There are sins..." He broke off. "There are things which people do while they are on earth; certain things which they later have cause to regret, sometimes for a very long time. But I have said enough, indeed I fear I have said far too much, and your friend – we are still no nearer to finding him."

Voices could once more be heard downstairs though no bell had sounded.

"Ah, that will be Mr and Mrs Lewis back from their little trip," he said. He hurried downstairs and left the five remaining members of the team in the flat.

"Do you think we can trust him?" asked Stinkhorn.

The consensus seemed to be that they thought they could trust him, and that he had been telling them the truth about himself and about Aeonia, though obviously there was a lot he was withholding.

"Could someone turn down that radio a bit," said the Poet. "The standard of the script writing is starting to get on my nerves."

Jessica was nearest to the radio and had to try several knobs before she found the volume control. When she had turned it down they heard a few notes of a song coming from somewhere nearby.

"Oh, the music again!" said Alma. "Do you think he'd mind if we opened the window?"

The Poet went to the window and managed to pull back the shutter, but getting the window open was a more difficult prospect, as the sash seemed to have been nailed down.

Suddenly Mr Tarantullus was once more striding into the room.

"My favourite programme!" he said, in a tone of slight annoyance. He went straight to the radio and turned up the volume again.

"There that's better. I know it's silly but you would be surprised how much of a comfort it can be. Life can be very lonely."

"Can I ask you something else?" said Alma.

"Of course, I am at your disposal. You can ask, but I can't promise to be able to answer."

"I don't understand that about the Watchers," said Alma. "If it is the case that part of us stays behind when we go down to earth then that must mean we all have Watchers somewhere up here right now. I wonder if it's possible to meet them?"

"It is possible, but not advisable. If you came face to face with your Watcher you would blank out, and no matter how much air you breathed you would be right back in your own world. That is why it is best if you don't go out too much. You have been brought here by a different sort of attraction, but now that you are here, there will be a strong pull between you and your Watcher, for the two are always longing to be made one again."

He paused and paced up and down the room for a moment. When he spoke again there was sadness in his voice. "It is a very hard thing to embark on a life. It is an enormous challenge that we take on when we choose to be born. To be separated from your greater Self is not an easy thing to bear, for the bonds are very strong. Indeed the attractions you feel to other people, the loves in your life, are but shadows and reflections of the love you feel towards your Watcher."

"Do you think perhaps the Nephew has met with his Watcher?" said Miss Quill.

"I should think it most unlikely," said Mr Tarantullus quickly. "No I believe your friend has been taken into one of the houses."

Downstairs the bell sounded again and Mr Tarantullus went down to attend to another customer. A few moments later he came back upstairs.

"There is some news," he said. "One of my customers tells me she saw a young man talking to a Watcher by the fountain."

CHAPTER TWENTY-ONE

The Backpack

On the advice of Mr Tarantullus, they split up into search parties. Alma privately thought the Nephew's meeting with a Watcher would probably have catapulted him back to the Wastelands. She imagined him returning to his Uncles' office and being greeted by the dog Tennyson. Of all the group she thought he would probably be the least disappointed to be returning home; and yet in another way she felt sad at the thought of it, as though she had lost a part of herself. Whatever the case it was clear that they had to do whatever they could and not just give up on him. It could be that he was being held in one of the shuttered houses, and presumably there were ship-jumpers even stranger than Mrs Trimble; desperate people who had done terrible things in their lives.

So they went out in three teams: Stinkhorn went with Alma, the Poet with Miss Quill, and Mr Tarantullus offered to accompany Jessica. It was agreed that they would meet back at the shop, though no one could quite work out when they were to meet, what with time being such an uncertain commodity in Aeonia. They decided that they would search for approximately an hour. This turned out to be almost impossible to judge, partly because of the fact that none of them seemed to be growing tired any more, and partly because there were so many interesting things to look at that you could find yourself becoming completely engrossed in a statue, or the façade of one of the big houses, or a flowering tree and just not be aware of the passing of time. Stinkhorn and Alma went down to the docks again and caught glimpses of several more vessels: a Chinese Junk, a gaudy paddle steamer and a silver submarine. Once again Alma was aware of the crowds of people waiting on the quayside, while Stinkhorn claimed he had seen nothing except for some white birds flying high up in the air. There was no sign, however, of the Nephew.

"I don't see how he can have been talking to a Watcher anyway," said Stinkhorn. "I thought we weren't supposed to be able to talk to Watchers."

"Mr Tarantullus did say that the Watchers can slow themselves down to our speed for short periods of time."

"I'm not sure about that bloke. There's something not quite right there. What do those people want who come to his shop?"

"Books!" said Alma innocently.

"If they come for books why don't they leave with books? That Mrs Trimble said he didn't let anyone take books out. Why did those people go through into the back of the shop and then come out later on? And why does he always have the radio playing?"

"Well, like he said, he gets lonely." Alma wasn't quite sure why she was defending the Bookdealer.

"And," said Stinkhorn ominously, "why was he so keen to go with Jessica?"

"He wasn't keen to go with Jessica," said Alma, "he offered. The rest of us had all paired off if you remember."

"Well I can't help wondering how many of us will turn up back at the shop."

"Stinkhorn, you are so mistrustful."

They had sat down on a bollard by the quayside. There were no ships coming or going as far as they could tell. The sea was a deep, dark blue and the mighty city was shimmering in the distance. It was another strange aspect of life in Aeonia that unlike in her own world where Alma would find herself worrying for hours about tiny things, in this place she found that she tended to forget things that should have caused her concern. This made it a pleasant but dangerous place to be.

"Look, there's one of those binocular things over there," said Alma.

They wandered over to it. It looked like the sort of contraption they have at the seaside which people put twenty pence in for half a minute's worth of staring at an out-of-focus sand bank and a few sea birds, only this one was free of charge and worked amazingly well. Alma looked through first; almost immediately she stood up and checked that she was pointing it in the right direction. She felt as though she was looking at the quayside just a few yards away, but the binoculars were pointed directly out to sea. Somehow, she could make out the far side of the bay with remarkable clarity. It was very similar to this side in that there was a quay with bollards and ships bobbing in the water. She pointed the scope a little higher and saw the roofs spreading back further and further from the shore, then beyond the houses there were the green hills and the pine forests; then the trees thinned out and running along the top of a ridge was a wall of golden sandstone.

"It is *The Wall*..." she thought.

"Here let's have a go," said Stinkhorn. "You've been on it for ages."

He shoved her aside and got up onto the little pedestal.

The first thing he wanted to see was the water. He pointed the telescope as far down as it would go and kept saying "Wow!" Then, as Alma had done, he would raise his head to check where it was pointing.

"That is unbelievable..." he said. "That is just the most incredible..."

"What Stinkhorn? What are you looking at? Can you see fish, or the monsters?"

"Fish and monsters? There wouldn't be many fish or monsters in that sea. Have a look."

He stepped down and Alma took his place. The binoculars seemed to focus themselves automatically on whatever you pointed them at. Now that she was pointing them downwards she understood what Stinkhorn had found so amazing. At first she thought she was not seeing the sea but the sky reflected in it. The strange thing about this was that she was not looking at the blue, cloudless expanse above them, but at a night sky.

"How can it do that?" said Alma

"Do what?"

"How can it be reflecting a night sky when it isn't night-time?"

"I don't think it is reflecting," said Stinkhorn, "I think it isn't really a sea at all. The surface looks like water I'll admit, but that's just a thin layer, and beneath that – is Space."

"Space? What do you mean?"

"Space! Stars and the like; the sky the way it looks from your world."

"Of course!" said Alma. "That's what I couldn't understand – where the ships were coming from. Because obviously when the ships come in they're not coming from across the bay. Somehow they must be coming up from beneath the surface."

Alma got down from the binoculars and went right up to the edge of the quay. She lay on her belly and leant her head out over the water. There was a slight reflection of the sky from the top of the water, but when you tried to focus your eyes at a deeper level you could see it quite clearly: the stars, the swirling galaxies, the clouds of what might have been multi-coloured gases. And here and there in between she could see objects flitting back and forth very quickly. These she suspected were the ships she couldn't quite see properly, coming and going.

"Here let me show you," said a deep voice behind her.

Thinking it was Stinkhorn trying to make his voice sound impressive she said,

"Leave it out Stinkhorn."

"Erm... Alma..." said Stinkhorn. She turned and saw the little black figure standing looking up at a much bigger person. For a moment she wasn't quite sure if it was a man or a woman; if it was a man he was very beautiful and if it was a woman she was very muscular.

"Look again," said the stranger.

("No, definitely a man," thought Alma.)

"Only this time don't use your eyes alone. Imagine..." He knelt down by her side and touched her forehead very gently. "Imagine that you have another eye right in the middle of your forehead, one that you don't have to focus, one that has no eyelids, that you don't have to blink. Now look again."

She looked into the water and tried to imagine this eye in the middle of her forehead, and suddenly found she could see the flitting things quite well. There were silver mini-submarines, and canoes with one or two people in them that were moving at a remarkable speed. There were bigger ships coming and going all the time, landing at different parts of the great port, and there were crowds of people and passengers, and this overwhelming sense of happiness, but there were still traces of darkness and sadness and confusion, and every so often she was aware of shadows breaking away from the incoming ships.

"Those must be the souls jumping ship," she thought, "the ones who can't bear it." And then she saw the islands, and people swimming ashore, and there was this one little place that looked just like a desert island and a wild man with a beard was shaking his fist at people who were trying to swim ashore and he was beating them off with a branch. They turned and swam away and she could see him talking to himself. And then there was a canoe with two people in it, which rowed right up to the shore and followed him as he walked along the beach. She could tell that they were trying to reason with him, and he was getting angry and cursing and swearing but the two beings in the canoe remained very calm and then they didn't speak at all but waited, paddling gently, and the man sat down and looked weary. After a while the canoe paddled away, and the man gazed after them.

Suddenly remembering where she was, Alma fully opened her eyes and looked around. There was the stranger with Stinkhorn standing just behind him looking over his shoulder.

"You all right Alma?" said Stinkhorn.

"I'm okay," she said, "but... how did I see all that?"

"Think how much you can see if you actually go in," said the man. "It is possible to know many things, for this is the Sea of Knowing."

"But I thought people forgot when they went through it."

"Going out you forget, coming back you remember, and afterwards you can go wherever you want, and find out about anything in the Universe."

Alma sat up and looked into the man's eyes.

"I have been watching you," he said.

"Are you... my Watcher?"

"No, I am not. If I was you would not quite be able to bear it. But I know your Watcher."

"How come we can see you so well?" said Stinkhorn.

"I have slowed myself in order to talk to you."

He reached out and touched Alma's forehead. She could feel the blood beginning to pump.

"You don't have long," he said. "Do you have more air?"

"Yes," said Alma, "I have a bottle that Mr Tarantullus gave me." She searched in her pocket and found the bottle. The man was looking rather doubtful. "Try," he said.

She took out the cork and put the bottle to her lips, but when she poured she couldn't seem to get anything out of it. She looked at the neck to see if she'd really got the whole cork out.

The man took it from her and studied it. "This bottle is empty," he said.

"But Mr Tarantullus said it had air from my world in it."

The man said, "Where are your friends?"

"We split up to look for the Nephew," she said. "We were going to meet back at the Bookshop. In fact we should probably be back there already."

"I think you should go," said the man and he helped Alma to her feet, "and you had best hurry."

"Are you coming with us?" she said, but the man only smiled at her, a little sadly, and slowly faded from view.

There was something different about the Bookshop when they got there. The windows looked even dustier and more cobwebby than usual. They tried the door but it was locked.

Alma pressed her face against the glass but the place was dark and seemed to be quite abandoned.

"Where could they be?" said Alma in an anguished voice. She felt dizzy and her head was aching; she feared the tramping footsteps would reach the top of the stairs at any minute.

"What should we do?" she said, turning to Stinkhorn.

"Alma!" said a weary voice. They both turned and saw Jessica on her hands and knees crawling into the courtyard. Alma and Stinkhorn ran to her. She was terribly pale and weak. They took an arm each and tried to lift her, but she seemed too exhausted to stand.

"It's this blasted backpack," she said. "I think if you could just take it off I might be able to get up."

They got the straps undone, and Alma began to lift the

little grey bag away from Jessica's back, but it seemed to be stuck; she pulled and pulled but couldn't get it free.

"Have we undone all the straps?" she said.

"It's loose," said Stinkhorn, "it just seems to be really heavy."

He put both arms round Jessica's waist and twisted her free, while Alma took the weight of the backpack. And what a weight! It fell to the floor and Alma tried to let go of it, but her hands would not release. The weight of the backpack made a dent in the pavement and then the paving stones began to crack. Stinkhorn let go of Jessica and leapt forward to help Alma, but now the ground was giving way all around her like thawing ice, and Alma could feel herself beginning to sink.

"I've got you Alma!" said Stinkhorn. "I won't let you go." But even as he spoke she felt his grip slipping away. The weight was dragging her down and down and yet she found she couldn't let go of it. It seemed to have become a part of her. And then she felt someone grab her by the collar and at last she was being pulled up again. As she came out she bashed her head on a ledge of some sort. She cried out in pain but whoever it was just kept pulling and she kept coming up and out into bright fluorescent light.

"What do you think you are doing down here!" shouted a familiar voice.

She opened her eyes and stared into her mother's furious face.

"I... I don't know..."

"Look at the state of you! I've told you not to go there, haven't I? I cannot imagine why any normal person would want to sit behind a filthy rubbish bin. And why do you have your clothes on?"

"What's happening?" Her father appeared in the doorway. He came in wrapping his dressing gown around him, yawning and rearranging his hair.

"Has she been sleepwalking again?"

Her mother shot her another look. "Well?" she said.

"I think I may have been sleepwalking," stammered Alma in a tiny voice. She felt confused and utterly drained of energy. Her mother's expression softened and she put a hand on her forehead.

"You're burning up," said her mother. "Right – into your pyjamas and back to bed my girl. We'll see how you are in the morning." Alma felt her mother's arm around her shoulder steering her out of the kitchen and up the stairs.

"What time is it?" she said.

"It's half past four," said her father looking at the clock.

When she had put her back into bed and covered her up, her mother spoke to her more kindly.

"Did you have a bad dream?" she asked.

"I... can't really remember," said Alma. "I think I did have a dream but I can't remember what it was."

"A bad dream?" queried her mother. Alma could sense her looking for something to worry about.

"I can't really remember it."

Well let me pray for you anyway.

She saw her mother's tightly closed eyes and heard her begin to mutter under her breath, "O Sanderby, Sanderby Coriander..." And for a moment Alma felt that there was something she should remember, something that was just out of reach and a little behind her. With her eyes closed she tried to turn around inside her head to catch a corner of that thing which had slipped out of her grasp. She had an image of crumbling paving stones and the sea opening, but then it all drained away like water spilled on hot sand. The shape of it was all there for a second and she felt if she could just have drawn it she would have been able to remember what it was. But even as she watched, it disappeared.

CHAPTER TWENTY-TWO

Home

Alma felt very strange when she woke up.

"How do you feel this morning dear?" said her mother, putting a thermometer into her mouth.

"Small... and empty," said Alma out of the corner of her mouth.

Her mother took the thermometer out and looked at it.

"Right, well, no school for you today." She shook the thermometer, making an efficient snapping sound with her wrist.

"Your father was not best pleased, I can tell you. It took him hours to get back to sleep last night."

"I'm sorry," said Alma.

Her mother said, "Are you hungry?"

"Not very."

"I'll bring you some hot Bovril."

"Can I just sleep a bit more?"

"You can sleep if you want to, but let's get you well. You don't want to miss any more school."

She slept most of the morning, waking up only long enough to drink Bovril and stagger to the loo. When she woke up at around two o'clock it was from a dream in which she was trying to open a safe on a frozen lake. She kept trying to type in the combination on a telephone keypad, but every time she tried she pressed the wrong buttons and had to start all over again. When she finally got through, a voice said, "I'm sorry, that number does not exist. Please consult your directory and try again."

Her mother checked her temperature again and told her she must stay in bed, but that she might read a book if she wished. She read a chapter of something dull called *The Afternoon Adventure*. Then laying her head on the pillow she stared out of the window at the sky. Outside she could hear the marching feet of the children heading towards the science block. There were shrill calls and laughter, some of it happy, some of it cruel. Someone was being chased and she heard the scatter of a bag being emptied, the books hitting the road, a ring-binder exploding, a pencil case opening and losing its contents. A teacher intervened and voices protested innocence, someone was invited to give names and declined. Then the tramp, tramp, tramp of the feet going past...

Alma sat up in bed with a start. She had just remembered the hole in the kitchen wall. She could not imagine how it could have been out of her mind for the whole day. Hadn't she planned to get through it only last night? She had been going to get up and go through the ritual. In fact she thought she could remember getting up and going downstairs and... And what had happened? She must have fallen asleep under the worktop. She grabbed for her jeans and found the notes in the pocket. She spread them out on the bedside table and looked at them again. The strange black handwriting with its air of mystery seemed so infinitely enticing. But she knew she would never get past her mother while she was ill.

"I must get better," she said to herself, "I will feel better. I will bring down my temperature by sheer concentration."

For the next hour she lay in bed trying to will her temperature to fall. In the late afternoon it was down a couple of degrees and she was allowed downstairs to watch *Eastenders*. Her mother didn't approve of soap operas as a general rule but *Eastenders* was her only concession and she would half-watch it herself, setting up the ironing board in front of the TV and pretending that she wasn't really interested.

Her father came home at six o'clock. Alma had her supper upstairs in her room. She could hear her parents' voices downstairs droning on and on over their meal. They rarely had full-scale arguments; it was more like a war of attrition. She heard her mother's relentless whine and her father's occasional defensive grunt. She was on at him to do something. He would have to do it. Later she heard the thud of furniture being moved around.

Around nine o'clock her mother came up and made Alma wash and change into clean pyjamas, then she drew the curtains and put out the light.

"You get a good night's sleep and hopefully you'll be all right in the morning, but if you even have a tiny bit of a temperature I'm not going to risk sending you back."

The alarm woke her at 5.30 am. She had the clock under the bedclothes again. And she knew that her temperature was back to normal. She put on her clothes and tiptoed down to the kitchen. She eased open the door and made her way reverently towards the first square, but something was wrong. The floor was covered with a sheet of polythene.

The kitchen was empty; the furniture had been moved into the living room. In the corner she could see the green carpet tiles sticking out of the top of some black plastic bags. She went across the crinkly polythene and quietly pulled out the bin. She tapped on the hardboard and knew instantly that the wall was solid behind it. Inside herself she felt something crumble.

"I have been feverish," she said reluctantly, "and I have had some very strange dreams."

She went back to bed.

That weekend her father completed the renovation of the kitchen floor. When he had finished laying the laminate he was so proud of himself and the kitchen looked so good that he took Alma's mother to Comet and they bought a dishwasher. He had plumbed it in before *Songs of Praise,* and that evening, for the first time since they moved to the house, her mother didn't do the washing up.

THE BOOK OF SLIGHTS

I was put on a different table for lunch today, with the year below. I didn't know most of them, and they didn't know me, and Mr Smith was in charge of the table, and it was a kind of déjà vu because this little kid told a joke and as soon as he started I knew it wasn't going to work, and I knew what kind of a kid he was, and the reason I knew was because he was just like me. His name is Roland Perkins and he is small for his age. So when the joke was over, I think maybe people like trying to tell jokes to Mr Smith, I could feel the words in my head even before he'd finished, and there was the gap, the pause while people tried to work out in their minds why anyone would want to tell such a pathetic joke, and before I could stop the words they slipped out and I said, "It speaks!" And everyone burst out laughing, because I timed it just right, and I said it in just the same way that Paula said it to me. I say everyone burst out laughing, but Mr Smith didn't, he just gave me a strange look, though no one else noticed.

I don't know why I did that. You would think that having been through it myself I would not want to put someone else through it. Roland tried to laugh as well, but I bet it hurt him.

I feel like I am a bad person.

This really happened, and I feel so empty inside, like there is just something rotten like an old rotten apple rolling around inside an empty barrel and I am the empty barrel. Up until now I think I had in the back of my mind, well maybe if people don't like me it's because there's something wrong with them rather than something wrong with me, but now I feel like there is nothing right with me. And the only thing I had left, the thing in the kitchen, that has all gone now, and it was just stupid anyway, and I know that I scribbled that thing in black crayon myself. So what is there? There's just nothing at all, it is all as black as anything. That is what is on the other side of The Wall - a place that is entirely black and in it I am paralysed and I can't move or anything, and I can't cry out and if I do cry out it won't make any difference because no one will come.

CHAPTER TWENTY-THREE

Rag and Bone

FIVE YEARS LATER

Grass stalks tickled her neck as Alma lay on her back and watched the banks of cloud drift through the square she had made with her fingers.

"Nicki, would you please come and finish packing your room," called her mother from the kitchen.

She rolled over, stretched her arms out as far as they would go and murmured into the grass, "All right, old woman, keep your hair on."

She dragged her long body to its knees, then rocked back and stood up. Her father came out of the garage carrying a large cardboard box.

"Door!" he shouted. She pushed open the back door for him and he eased his way into the kitchen.

"There's a pile of stuff for Oxfam and there's a pile of stuff for the tip," said her mother, "and for God's sake don't mix up the two."

"Mother!" scolded Alma. "Thou shalt not take the name of the Lord Thy God in vain!" Her mother grunted. Alma went up to her room, sat on the edge of the bed and looked out of the window.

"Just when I'm getting to like this place..." she said.

"Nicki!" Someone was calling from the front garden. She looked out and saw Robert swinging on the front gate.

"Nicki!" His hair was hanging down over his left eye. She ran down the stairs then casually wandered out through the open front door and leant against the fence.

"What?"

"Address," he said, "phone number, the lot. Come on girl, were you going to sneak off and leave me to hire a private detective?"

"I was going to call round before we left," she said. "The van hasn't even arrived yet. It'll be the evening before we go. And it's not like we're going that far. It's a bus ride for goodness sake."

"I'll be down to see you," he said.

Impulsively she leant over the fence, grabbed him by the collar, pulled him close and kissed him.

"You better bloody well had."

"Nicki!" called her mother.

"I'll call round before we go," she said and ran back into the house.

It was nearly three o'clock and her mother had been shouting ultimatums and threats at her to bring down the stuff for Oxfam. Then Alma heard the sound of horses' hooves. She went to the window and saw a horse-drawn cart come creeping up the road.

"What about the Rag and Bone Man?" she called down.

"What?"

"Why don't we ask the Rag and Bone Man to come in? He might pay us something, instead of giving all the stuff away."

"What are you talking about?" shouted her mother.

"I am TALKING about the RAG AND BONE MAN!" shouted Alma.

"They don't have Rag and Bone Men any more."

"They damn well do – there's one in the street!"

She waited for a reply but her mother had evidently given up the struggle; she could hear her boxing crockery in the kitchen.

"Well I'm going to give him some of my stuff!" she yelled, and grabbing a bin bag she went out of the front door just as the horse and cart were passing the gate.

"Hey, we might have something for you!"

The man didn't hear her and kept going.

"Hey wait!" She ran along the pavement, "Wait! Hey, don't you want to have a look at what I've got at least?" She was shouting at the top of her voice but he still didn't seem to hear. In the back of the cart were some old carpets, a distressed wicker chair, a coal scuttle with its bottom knocked out and a pile of old clothes, under which something was moving. When the dog poked its face out Alma had the strongest sensation of déjà vu. She was looking at the brown and white muzzle of a Jack Russell cross, and instantly a line of poetry came into her mind: "*Half a league, half a league half a league onward...*"

Alma became aware of a number of loud noises – a bang followed by a screeching sound. She turned and saw a red Post Office van coming towards her at a strange angle, limping on a flat front tyre and jumping as it mounted the pavement. She could see the frightened, pleading eyes of the driver. In slow motion the bonnet came up close and nuzzled her like a friendly horse looking for sugar lumps. It seemed quite normal that this should propel her effortlessly into the cart to land on the split plastic seat right next to the Rag and Bone Man.

"Ahab!" she said looking at the dark face of the driver. "Fancy seeing you again after all this time!"

"The pleasure is all mine," he said with the briefest sideways glance.

"Where are we going?" she asked after they had rumbled on in silence for a few minutes.

"I couldn't say precisely," he said. "Unfinished business of some sort."

The dog came, pushing his way between them.

"Hello Tennyson," she said.

"How are you doing?" said the dog, and offered a paw, which she shook affectionately.

"I remember some people," said Alma absently. "There were four or five of them."

"Five," said Ahab.

"I don't really remember that much... It seems like a long time ago."

"They used to call you Alma," he said.

"I know, but now everyone calls me Nicki. I was really screwed up, but I feel a bit better now."

"Unfinished business." he repeated.

"So you keep saying, but where and what?"

"It will come back to you as we go," he said.

After a while she said, "That was a bit of a close squeak with the post office van. I'm surprised it didn't scare your horse. Where's your ship?"

"Oh, you remember that do you?"

She was quiet again for a moment. "Ahab," she said at last, letting her hands fall palms upward on the seat, "how could I have forgotten all this?"

"That is how it goes," he said slowly. "The same thing happens to me. Coming out you forget things that you would think it impossible to forget."

She was silent for a while. They were passing through a pine forest that seemed very familiar.

"I have been here before," she said. "It was a much longer journey last time."

"Everything is different now," said Ahab.

They came to a striped pole barring the way; a barbed-wire fence stretched away in both directions. Ahab got down from the cart and raised the barrier. Alma braced herself for something, she wasn't quite sure what, but nothing happened. He got back into the cart and the horse plodded forward, then he got out again and closed the barrier.

"I'm sure something happened the last time I went through there. Something to do with raspberries."

Ahab said nothing. Tennyson was peering into her face.

"So you didn't stay with the Lawyers?" she asked.

"I stayed for a while," he said. "They were nice to me, and they never twigged that I could talk, but they were involved in some dodgy dealings. I didn't like some of their clients at all – creepy people, always asking questions. So one day while I was out for my walk I bumped into the Captain here and we sort of threw in our lot together."

There were sea birds calling now, and she could hear the sound of the surf breaking on the shore and smell the sea air. They came over the brow of the hill and there was the bay with the little ship tied up to the jetty.

"Now this I do remember..." said Alma. "And Stinkhorn!" She found her eyes were filling with tears. Everything was coming back in a rush, memories tumbling over themselves like a litter of puppies.

"The Nephew! The poor Nephew, whatever happened to him? And Miss Quill, and that conceited Poet person... and... and..."

"Jessica," said Ahab.

"Yes, Jessica. She gave me something to carry for her, only it was too heavy. I couldn't bear it." The memory was unclear but she could feel the weight of it, the strange metallic feeling of plunging through ice and being torn apart. And then she thought she could hear the tramping of many feet in the forest. She thought that at any moment she would see the sharp points of pikestaffs come poking through the trees. But the tramping was only that of the horse's hooves on the needle-covered path. She allowed herself to relax again. They came down to the beach. Alma looked out at the sea stretching to the horizon.

"I seem to remember that they were kind to me," she said. "I think they all really cared about me."

"They did."

"Even Stinkhorn. We had a bit of a tiff at the start, and I told him off a couple of times, but he would have done anything for me."

"Of course."

"They were like a family, though I didn't know them for very long."

The cart had stopped close to the driftwood hut and Ahab went inside.

"I've just remembered something," she said. "They must all still be there, in Aeonia I mean. Have they been there all this time?"

"They are still there," said Ahab coming out of the hut dressed in his old clothes.

"So they never came back to the Wastelands?"

"No. Perhaps they hoped you would come back for them."

"But how could I? I mean I couldn't remember anything." She thought for a moment. "No that isn't quite true, I would have got back in, even though I didn't remember being there, except that the floor was redone, and then the hole in the wall was blocked up. But I have had dreams... I thought they were just a recurring dream, and so much nicer than the recurring dreams I used to have before. Not dreams about darkness, but about a beautiful fountain and a sea full of stars."

"The tide is turning," said Ahab looking at the ship. He helped Alma down from the cart. Tennyson jumped down and ran up the gangplank. As Alma went aboard she sniffed the tar smell of the timber. "Can I have my old cabin?" she said.

"It has been waiting for you," he said. "I'll set the horse free and then cast off. You go and have a lie down if you want to."

She was feeling pleasantly sleepy in spite of the strangeness of the day and the uncertainty of what they were to face at the end of the voyage. She felt that there was nothing much to be done until they got there, and that she might need all her strength when they did. Also she felt safe in this little ship with Ahab and Tennyson. They seemed to emanate calmness and rest. She felt something hard tickle the back of her hand and looking down she burst out laughing as she saw the Sloth reaching out its arms to be picked up.

"The Sloth!" she cried, scooping it up. She hugged it and in the tenderest way it reached up and stroked her hair. She couldn't resist kissing it on each eye patch. Its fur was coarse and clean and smelled of tar and the sea and bananas. When she put it down again it went off down the passageway in the direction of the galley. She remembered the way to her cabin as clearly as if she had been there the week before. In the cabin everything was just the same. She went and sniffed the sheets and felt their starchiness. She looked in the drawers and there were the spare clothes, and to her surprise the blue and yellow bottle was in there too. She tipped it from side to side hoping to find that it had somehow been refilled, but it was empty. She thought she would probably have enough air to last for a few days, seeing as this time they had found a faster path through the Wastelands.

She pulled on some soft pyjamas. She even found the ones she had used on the last trip; they seemed so tiny now.

"You can sleep as long as you like," called Ahab through the door. "We'll eat something when you wake up."

"Thank you!" she called sleepily, stifling a yawn. Then she drew the curtain across the porthole, crept into the bunk and was asleep almost before she had pulled up the blankets.

CHAPTER TWENTY-FOUR

The Cavern

When he had let go of Alma's hand and seen the flagstones once again become solid, Stinkhorn had directed his anger at Jessica.

"What did you do that for?" he yelled.

"What did I do what for?" said Jessica, rubbing her shoulder.

"Why did you make her take the backpack? It's blown her fuse."

"Well I didn't know that's what would happen did I?"

"And how come it suddenly got so heavy?"

"It was Mr Tarantullus," she said. "He did something to it when I wasn't looking and then he helped me put it on again and suddenly it was really heavy, worse than the one at Sunny Towers. I thought it was going to finish me off. I still don't feel so good."

"Where is he?" growled Stinkhorn. "Just wait till I get my hands on him!" Just then a wave of weakness swept over him. He leant against the wall and waited for it to pass.

"Ah there you are!" said a voice from the top of the alleyway. "I've been looking for you everywhere!" Stinkhorn turned and saw Mr Tarantullus striding towards them.

"So how are the remains of my little anomaly?" he said.

"Your companions are inside." He unlocked the door. "Perhaps you would like to come in and join them." Bending down he pulled Jessica to her feet and pushed her through the door, then he turned to Stinkhorn.

"And now you, you unpleasant little thing..." he reached out a scrawny hand.

With his last remaining strength Stinkhorn grabbed the hand, pulled it into his mouth and bit down hard. He heard the man scream, then he felt the full force of his other hand as it came round and smacked him on the side of the head. He felt himself being dragged into the darkness of the shop, then there was the swish of a curtain and just before he lost consciousness, the sensation of fine cords tightening about him.

*

"I have been longing to taste this again you know," said Alma, pulling a bowl of Ahab's Sea Chowder towards her, "and this bread." She dunked it in the creamy soup then slurped off the soggy end. She stared out of the window at the great calmness of the sea.

"No curses and no storms this time," said Ahab. "We'll be coming in somewhere different."

"Do you know where?"

"No two journeys are the same," he said.

Later they went out onto the deck. There was a small island on the port bow. A gaggle of wild looking people came down to the shore to watch them go past. They were comical in a way, and yet at the same time so hopelessly forlorn that Alma didn't know whether to laugh or cry. Then one of them ran into the surf and hurled a makeshift spear at the ship. It flew all of ten yards and splashed harmlessly into the water. The man stood and stared at them. Some of the little crowd were women and all of them had matted hair and were dressed in rags.

"Will they be there forever?" Alma asked, remembering what she had heard about people jumping ship and swimming to the islands.

"Nothing is forever," he said. "Everyone will be rescued in the end, but you can't rush people. Some hold out longer than others."

"But what will happen to them? Will they suddenly decide they've had enough and try to swim to the harbour?"

"Oh, they get loads of visits," said Ahab.

"Who visits them, the Watchers?

"Their own Watchers have to be careful, because they are very vulnerable to capture. It's usually people who have known them in other lives. They visit them and try to talk to them. Eventually they wear them down, but it can take a long time."

They were silent for a while and Alma stared at the sea, and tried half closing her eyes; she realised that she could see the stars and galaxies beneath the surface out here in the open sea, just as she had seen them in the harbour all those years before.

"Could you just explain about this sea? Is this the water I saw in the harbour in Aeonia?"

"All the seas are linked together, but this one is in a slightly different dimension. The transition is not always easy to make, as you may remember from our last voyage."

"Ahab," she said, uncertainly, giving voice to a creeping apprehension. "How long is this trip going to last?"

He didn't answer her.

"Ahab, have I died?"

He didn't answer.

*

THE BOOK OF SLIGHTS

There is this dream, not as bad as my recurring nightmare, but quite frightening. In it I have to climb around the outside of a house, using ledges and drainpipes, and it is all quite familiar. I have been in this situation before, but I also know that there is one bit that is really difficult, if not impossible, because there is just too far to reach and no handhold. And I don't know how I get out of this situation. In the dream I always come to this point and can get no further. The dream goes on to other things, but I never really get the hang of the difficult corner, and I know that I will come up against it again.

Alma went back inside and lay down on a sofa. "If I am dead," she thought, "what do I really regret about dying so young?"

She had been feeling much closer to her parents recently, and of course Robert had been a very good thing, and her friends at school, the small circle that had gradually grown over the four or five years since she had stopped worrying so much about life – in fact which had begun to grow shortly after her hitherto forgotten visit to Aeonia. But she knew that during that time she had done some terrible things: she had twisted herself into strange shapes to fit in with the world in which she found herself. She had made some unhealthy alliances; she had betrayed people...

Ahab came and stood in the doorway.

"Is this my final voyage then?" said Alma quietly.

"I'm not sure," said Ahab, "but I think if you were actually dead you wouldn't be travelling with me again, you would be on one of the regular sailings."

"So why am I coming here again?"

"Like I said, unfinished business."

"What happened to everyone when I went?" she asked.

"That I can't tell you. I haven't been to that part of Aeonia since I left you there the last time. But we'll be there soon enough," he said, looking up at the white birds that had started to fly alongside the ship.

"Ahab, I've just thought of something: if time passes so slowly here, and I've been away for years, then how long will they have been in Aeonia without me? It must be thousands of years!"

"In Aeonia, time obeys its own rules," he said, "and they are surprisingly flexible. Time there flows like water – it goes to the places where it is needed most and drains from the places where it is not needed at all. To some, a day will seem like a hundred years, to others a hundred years is gone in a day."

Alma thought she could almost understand this.

"And how will we get in, if not through that fountain?"

"I'm not sure, but we seem to be approaching one of the caverns. It might be best if we took to our bunks."

Alma went to her cabin and before she got into her bunk she pressed her face against the thick glass of the porthole. Outside the sky was beginning to darken and they were sailing into a fog; she could see it settling on the surface of the water. She lay down and braced herself for another helter-skelter ride, but it did not come. They sailed on and on and the ship barely even rocked from side to side. They sailed on so smoothly that she imagined the ship had sprout-ed trolley wheels and was gliding across an enormous lake whose frozen surface had been polished so that it mirrored the sky. The air in the cabin had become cold; Alma could see her breath condensing and pulled the blankets up around her neck. They were accelerating and she could hear the wind whistling past, but still their progress was remarkably smooth.

Shivering, she got off the bunk, wrapped one of the blankets around her shoulders and went to look out of the porthole again. The light outside was dim but she could see a frosty shoreline a few hundred yards away. The surface of the water was now white and she realised that they were indeed skating or sliding across a frozen sea. Above her the sky was black and there seemed to be some luminous prop-erty within the sea, for all the light was coming from below. Then the ship changed direction and they began to turn in towards the shore. At the same time their speed checked, and a vibration made itself felt through the timbers of the ship. They were now heading straight for the rocky shoreline. Then once again the ship turned, but their motion continued in the same direction, and slowed yet more as they came gliding sideways into a little inlet. She saw a line of flat rocks like a quay and a huge metal ring in one of the rocks. There were smaller rings too, and tied to them with ropes were several canoes. They were creeping towards the quayside now, and the grinding vibration was more pronounced. Then the ship settled and they came to a halt.

"All right Alma?" she heard Ahab's voice outside.

"I'm all right," she said, "but it's really cold."

"Put some more clothes on, there's plenty of stuff in the drawers."

She took out a woollen sweater and pulled it over her head, also she put on some thick socks and a pair of gloves. When she came on deck Ahab was already on the rocks tying the ship to the big ring.

"Just in case we get a sudden thaw," he said.

Alma went down the gangplank. The light from the phosphorescent sea gave an eerie tinge to everything. She looked up and saw, far above, a cavernous roof just barely illuminated. Looking back the way they had come she saw the tracks, like tramlines, that the ship had made coming across the frozen sea. Now that she looked at the bottom of the ship she saw that there were two steel blades which ran the whole length of the hull, either side of the keel.

"We skated in!" she said.

"Indeed we did!" said Ahab. "A bit smoother than last time if I remember."

"Yes, but I preferred the fountain. This is a horrible place. Are we really in Aeonia?"

"We are beneath Aeonia," he said. "I think our route lies

up that way." He pointed to some stone steps carved in the rock which spiralled upwards from the underground shore.

"Have we shrunk again?" she asked.

"We have," he said, "but we won't adjust for a while, not until we get closer to the surface."

Tennyson and the Sloth were left on board. Tennyson came to say goodbye and promised he would keep watch. There was no sign of the Sloth; Ahab said she was curled up in a pile blankets trying to hibernate.

Alma and Ahab began the trek up the cold stone steps. They had to walk carefully because the whole place was very icy. After they had been climbing for a few minutes they came to the top of the stairs and saw that the path led along a narrow ledge. Alma looked down and noticed for the first time that there were lots of dark holes in the rocks, potholes about three feet in diameter. They continued along the path with Ahab leading the way. They were moving away from the frozen sea now, and as they looked back they could see the ship, a dark silhouette on the glowing ice and next to it the smaller shapes of the canoes. Alma stopped suddenly – she had seen a shape scuttling across the rocks twenty yards below them.

"Ahab," she hissed. He stopped and turned.

"They won't harm us," he said. As they watched, the figure disappeared into one of the holes and Alma shuddered, remembering an earwig she had once found in a seedpod in the garden of their old house. Two figures appeared on the path further up, coming towards them. They were dressed in black cloaks with hoods. The leader had a large book clasped to his chest. Ahab kept walking and Alma hurried to get up close behind him. The figures kept coming and they passed without acknowledgement. She saw their faces only dimly, and what she saw did not encourage her to look more closely or to wish that the light were stronger.

The air was beginning to get warmer, but the light was fading as they got further away from the sea. They didn't pass anyone else on the path, but they did see some black, chimney-like openings in the rock face, about the same size as the ones they had seen by the shore. Alma imagined something more horrible with each one they passed: long giant centipedes with hundreds of waving legs, fat pulsating grubs, giant ants, cockroaches. Then she noticed that Ahab had taken a piece of paper out of his pocket and was holding it to catch the weak light from the sea behind them. She looked over his shoulder and saw that it was a crude map.

"A little further I think," he said, folding the paper and slipping it back into his jacket.

They came to a fork in the path and Ahab veered off to the right. After about ten yards the path ended and they were faced with a wall of rock, into which had been carved three steps. Above these was another black hole, just big enough for them to crawl into.

"This is the way in," said Ahab.

"Do you think it's safe?" she said. And then with a little shock, "What if we start to get bigger once we've got in there?"

"Well, we can always crawl back; we'd get smaller again if we did that..."

This made her feel a little better, but then he added, "I think..." which made her feel worse again.

"Well," he said with a shrug, "it's all part of the journey."

"Who were those people?" whispered Alma, "and what if we meet some more coming down?"

"We'll have to back up or they'll have to back up, one or the other. We'll get there eventually."

"Can't we go back now?" said Alma.

Ahab turned and looked at her in surprise. "Is that really what you want?" he said.

She thought about this for a moment. Then shook her head.

"This is going back, isn't it," she said. "This is what we have to do just now."

Ahab nodded.

"Nothing can harm us," he said.

"Let's give it a try," she said.

Ahab climbed up the three steps and pulled himself into the mouth of the tunnel, then turned and reached down a hand and pulled Alma in after him.

Then the long crawl began.

CHAPTER TWENTY-FIVE

The Bookshop Again

When Stinkhorn came round everything was completely dark. It was so dark that it made no difference whether his eyes were open or shut. In fact he couldn't even be sure he had opened his eyes, because he couldn't feel his eyelids move. There were no sensations of any sort. He didn't feel hungry or thirsty, or cold, or warm. He felt no pain or physical discomfort. Even the ache from his leg wasn't there. He tried to move his legs and then his head but nothing happened. He tried to struggle but soon realised that he wasn't even able to strain against anything. It wasn't just that he couldn't move, he couldn't even try to move; he was paralysed from head to toe. The next thing to do was obviously to cry out, but he found he was also unable to make any sound. Nor could he swallow, and then he wondered if he was actually breathing, and realised that he probably wasn't.

"Well that's it then," he thought. "I must be dead. This isn't much fun. Still, could be worse; I could be in agony, or I could have an itch – that would be hell." He decided he'd better stop thinking about having an itch in case just thinking about it might bring one on. It would only need to be a very mild itch, he thought, to drive you completely mad.

He thought about going mad for a moment and then decided to stop thinking about going mad because that would be the very thing to start him screaming. "Only I wouldn't be able to scream," he thought, but this didn't encourage him very much either. He began to wonder how long he might have been in this state and in this dark place. The really worrying thing was that he might be nowhere at all and that he might have been there forever. He tried consulting his memory, but drew a blank. He tried for his own name, but nothing came to him. He had once had a name – not a very nice name, but it had been his. There had been a little girl... He tried to hold onto a picture of her, but he knew he was only stalling, that pacing around the little campfire of comforting thoughts were... What were those animals called? Creatures with teeth and claws. This was the madness that was coming to tear him to shreds. In the meantime he thought he might as well go to sleep.

But then he realised that he didn't feel in the least bit sleepy. On the contrary he felt wide-awake. And a further worry was that in this state of paralysis he was unlikely to tire himself out. He tried to think of some jokes, some funny stories, but all that seemed to have been wiped from his memory too.

"So that means I've just got... I've just got..."

But now even that had gone, he could no longer remember what it was that had given him that little spark of hope.

"And now I shall go mad and I shall scream here in my mind without the relief that a real scream gives."

But then, just before he began his silent scream, he heard a noise in the darkness: a cool clear sound, followed by another, similar yet distinct from the first, and then a whole succession of sounds. They reminded him of something, and they lifted his spirit. They were... What was that word? It hovered just out of reach. He felt as if he were hacking through brambles to reach some interesting mushroom... Wait, he had hold of it now, it was *music*.

The notes grew and multiplied and they made him think of shapes and colours and he imagined these shapes and colours dancing around him and he found that he could almost see them in his mind's eye.

And still the music grew and changed and swirled and he thought, "As long as this continues I shall be all right. I could listen to this forever."

And so poor, abandoned Stinkhorn, floating in his dark place, relaxed into the music.

*

The tunnel was definitely growing narrower. So far they hadn't met anyone coming down, but Alma thought it was only a matter of time before they would meet someone or, worse still, somet*hing*, and she was glad not to have to be making this journey alone. She was also beginning to wish that she hadn't put on so many clothes as the air in the tunnel had grown warmer as they climbed. It was growing steeper as well, but fortunately its surface was ribbed, providing just enough in the way of handholds. It looked as though many people had used these tunnels in the past, though she couldn't imagine why they would want to go down into such an inhospitable cavern.

They had been climbing through darkness for ten minutes or so, but now she became aware of daylight up ahead and she could see Ahab's outline again. The tunnel had been sloping at a gentle gradient but now they could see that a few yards further on it came to an end and a ladder led up towards the light. The tunnel had widened now and they found they could stand upright.

"Do you know where this comes out?" whispered Alma.

"I have only been following the vaguest of instructions," said Ahab. "In fact," he came closer to her and lowered his voice. "In fact I cannot even be sure that they were instructions. It was a message in a bottle, you see, that piece of paper; it arrived in a bottle, sealed up, and I thought it might mean something so I kept it, and then I felt like going for a ride in the cart with the pony and somehow we met you. That is how my life works. And when we came to this place I remembered the map and it seemed that we were to take that fork in the path and at the end of the path was this tunnel and we appear to be close to the end of the tunnel now, but what we will meet there I do not know. But we will be somewhere in Aeonia."

Just then they heard voices. Instinctively they flattened themselves against the wall. A man and a woman were arguing, and the voices were familiar. The woman was saying, "That is typical! You just can't see anyone else's point of view can you? You are completely locked into your own pathetic cycle of wants and needs. It never even occurs to you that I might be suffering."

"They're coming down," whispered Alma, huddling behind Ahab and shutting her eyes.

She heard the voices get louder.

"Right, well, this time we'll sort it out once and for all."

"That's what you said last time..."

So engrossed were they in their argument that the couple passed Alma and Ahab without seeing them.

"Did you see that?" said Alma. "They were wearing cloaks like the other ones. Where are all these people going?"

Ahab didn't answer. After they had listened for a while he said, "I think I should go up first." He climbed cautiously up the steps and Alma, waiting in the wide part of the tunnel, watched his feet disappear. He was gone for a minute or two, then she heard him call.

"Alma. It's okay, but come up quietly."

She followed him up the steps and soon they were standing in a small room lined on three sides with shelves full of leather bound books. The fourth wall was a wood and glass partition.

"We're in the Bookshop!" said Alma.

"You know where we are?" whispered Ahab.

"Yes, this is the last place I saw the others. Well, it was outside in the courtyard actually. The Bookdealer went off with Jessica to look for the Nephew, but I never saw him again, just Jessica. And her backpack was so heavy, when I tried to lift it I literally sank into the ground." She looked around. "But we never came in here last time. This is where the customers came. And I think I've seen those people before too."

"Haunters," muttered Ahab, but when she asked him what he meant he just said he would explain it later.

"Do you think the Bookdealer may know what happened

to the others?" she asked.

"Oh, I think he'll know exactly what happened to them," said Ahab.

They crept to the door and listened. All seemed quiet, so Ahab turned the doorknob as gently as he could and pushed the door open. The main part of the shop appeared to be empty. There was the desk with the chair still wedged behind it, just as it had been on Alma's last visit. The piles of books were still scattered all around the shop with their thin layer of dust, and the carefully embroidered cobwebs were still in the window. The sign in the door said OPEN, which must mean that the shop was closed. And now they could hear a faint noise coming from upstairs.

"The radio," she said. "He always tries to tune in to Radio Four."

Ahab paused and considered for a moment, then he went to the foot of the stairs and looked up at the door to the flat.

"It was locked last time," Alma said. "He had a key."

"Have a look in the desk," said Ahab.

Alma went and opened the drawers. In the top left hand one there was a bunch of keys. She brought them to Ahab and together they went up the stairs. The door was locked so he tried the keys in turn. At the fifth attempt there was a click and the door swung open.

The sound of the crackling radio was louder as they stepped into the hallway. They went along the corridor and looked into the living room. The flat appeared to be empty.

"He must have gone out and shut up the shop," said Alma.

Ahab was standing in front of the radio and listening.

"Do you hear that?" he said.

"I can hear interference but not much else," she said.

"No, there's another sound."

Alma listened very hard.

"It's music, but it's not coming from the radio…" Ahab looked around the room.

"Perhaps from outside?" Alma said. "We heard music the last time we were here."

He went to the window and listened, then came back to the radio and switched it off. The silence was shocking. They stood and listened, and sure enough there was another sound.

"It's someone singing," said Alma, "but where's it coming from?"

Ahab went over to the wall and put his ear to a gap between two bookshelves. Then he looked back to Alma and beckoned her over. The sound was quite distinct now. Ahab tried tapping on the wall. Immediately the music stopped. He tapped again. No response.

"It must be the neighbours," said Alma.

"It can't be the neighbours," he said. "This is an interior wall, so it must be someone in the next room."

They went out into the hall again and down the corridor. The door to the next room was ajar. They listened for a moment but there was no sound. Ahab went in and Alma followed him. The room was quite bare, apart from some rolls of paper and a bucket full of tools and brushes in the corner. The shutters were open but there were steel bars across the window. Ahab ran his hand over the wall.

"This room has just been decorated," he said.

Suddenly, Alma went to the wall and called, "Hello! Hello,

is there someone in there?"

They heard a movement somewhere in the flat. Footsteps striding down the corridor, they looked around for somewhere to hide, but before they could move the door burst open and Mr Tarantullus was looking at them, his reptilian face cold with suppressed fury. He took out another bunch of keys and swiftly locked the door.

"My dear," he said, "you have found your way back to us after all this time. And I see you have brought an old friend with you."

He turned to Ahab.

"Ahab, what a surprise. I was forgetting that I am not the only one with a roving commission in the Wastelands."

Ahab staggered back towards the window as if he had been struck in the stomach.

"Tarantullus..." he breathed, "what have you done?"

"I should have thought you of all people would know better than to poke your nose into my affairs," said the Bookdealer.

He turned to Alma. "Now my dear, how can I help you?"

"Where are my friends?" said Alma, feeling the rage building up inside her.

"Probably wandering aimlessly in the Wastelands where they belong. And how are you feeling? A little light headed again? Here, let me see if I can find another of those bottles for you."

Alma looked at Ahab, but he was leaning against the wall and the strength had gone out of him.

"What is it?" she wailed. "What is he doing to us?"

"We have come into his house uninvited. He is free to do

as he wishes."

"No!" screamed Alma.

Suddenly there was a shout from outside the door.

"Hey! Tarantullus, are you in there?" It was the man they had heard earlier in the tunnel.

"What's the meaning of this?" said the man. "The shop door is locked. Are you trying to keep us here against our will?"

"I shall be with you directly," called Tarantullus. He stared at Alma for a moment, then he pulled the keys out of his pocket and unlocked the door. He slipped out and locked the door behind him, leaving Alma and Ahab alone in the room.

"What does it all mean?" she pleaded.

"Listen Alma, if he comes back there is nothing I can do to stop him."

"But who is he?"

"Someone who greatly prefers darkness to light."

He took from his pocket the bunch of keys Alma had found in the drawer.

"We can escape!" she said.

"No, he'll catch us in the shop. Here, wedge the key in the lock on this side and if he tries to poke it through then hold it there so he can't."

"What are you going to do?"

Ahab was rooting through the bucket of tools. He pulled out a chisel and a mallet and began chipping away at the plaster. Alma held her key in the lock. She could hear footsteps coming up the stairs two at a time, pounding and pounding up the stairs. For a moment she thought it was the onset of another fainting spell, but this time the footsteps were real, and in a second she felt the key scratching around the lock, then pushing against the key she was holding. She twisted it to one side, wedging it so that no matter how hard Tarantullus pushed he wouldn't be able to dislodge it. He was hammering on the door and she could hear him making desperate whimpering noises.

"Don't do that!" he was saying. "Come on Ahab old chap, you know you can't do that sort of thing. Alma my dear, I have another bottle for you."

Inside the room Ahab was hacking at the wall as fast as he could.

"AHAB!" screamed the Bookdealer through the door. "AHAB, I FORBID YOU TO TOUCH THAT WALL!"

Ahab called back, "I'm sorry Tarantullus, but you have something in here that doesn't belong to you."

"Oh come on Ahab, they're just a few fragments, she didn't even want them. She threw them out! And she brought them to me. She wanted me to get rid of them for her. But if you want them you can have them, it's not a problem. I'll get them for you. I tell you what, I'll get them for you and then she can take them with her and go back and we'll forget all about it. But I beg of you Ahab don't knock down that wall, let me do it for you."

Ahab, who had now regained some of his strength, took up the mallet again and continued to hammer away at the wall. Several bricks had already shattered and there was a hole about a foot square.

"My dear," said Mr Tarantullus in a soft voice. "Alma my dear, I can set your friends free if you'll let me in. I'll help him; if he does it himself he may hurt them. Just let me in, there's a good girl. I mean you no harm."

The bricks were coming away easily now. Ahab put down the chisel and mallet and began to pull them away in the shape of a door. Outside Alma heard the sound of the Bookdealer sliding down to the floor. Ahab had gone into the cavity behind the wall now, and checking that the key was still wedged, Alma went in after him.

Hanging in the centre of the room, swinging gently from side to side, suspended from hooks in the ceiling, were five sacks. Ahab took the weight of the first one and lifted it up and off the hook and staggered with it out into the room. Alma helped him to lay it down gently on the floor. She found a knife in the bucket and carefully cut away the strange fabric. It burst open and the limp body of the Nephew wallowed out onto the floor like a newborn calf. At first she thought he must be dead, but he was warm and seemed to be in a deep sleep.

Meanwhile Ahab was bringing out the others. Alma released the Secretary, the Poet, Jessica and last of all the black furry body of Stinkhorn. She held his little unconscious form in her arms and hugged him.

"Why don't they wake up?" she said.

"He's sedated them," said Ahab. "He has some very clever tricks." He felt the fabric with his fingers. "This stuff suspends all physical animation but leaves the mind perfectly conscious. They should come round now that we've set them free."

"Are you satisfied now," came a cold voice from the door. "If you've quite finished would you please leave my house!"

"What are we going to do?" said Alma. "If we let him in what's to stop him capturing all of us?"

"He wouldn't try to take us all on at once," said Ahab, "but there's something not right here." The same thing had occurred to Alma. They still hadn't found the source of the singing. Ahab went back through the wall and Alma heard him chiselling again.

"NOOOO!" screamed the voice from the door. Tarantullus began pounding on the door again, then she heard him run off and come back dragging some heavy object, and in seconds the wood was splintering beneath his frantic blows.

"You fools!" he fumed. "Why did you have to come back?! Why couldn't you just leave things as they were? Why go poking about in things that don't concern you? Why can't people just stay in their own worlds?"

Most of the door had been smashed now and he was stepping through it. But even as he came into the room, Ahab came out through the hole in the wall, leading by the hand a frail little woman, whose long silver hair fell down over her shoulders to her waist. Her face, though lined with age, was so beautiful that it made Alma gasp. When the Bookdealer saw her, he crumpled to the floor.

"Don't look at me like that!" he said. "You don't have to accuse me. I know what you think of me. I know what I am."

He had his face on the floor now, his tears mingling with dust. The woman went to him, knelt down and put her slender hand on his head.

"Come on Jerry," she said gently.

"Don't touch me!" he said, jerking back into a sitting position and pulling his head away so that she couldn't look into his eyes.

"I know what you think of me."

"Jerry..." she said.

"Don't call me that! I know what I am. Don't pretend with me."

"I am not pretending," she said, with infinite gentleness.

"You are a *liar!*" he said. "You want to mock me with your phoney sympathy. You pretend to want to make me *better!*" He spat the word out. "You want to pour the acid of your purity all over me."

"Jerry," said the old lady very quietly, "look at me."

"I cannot bear to see it in your eyes. I acknowledge it all, but don't make me see it in your eyes. From now on I will live quietly. I will shut the shop. I will let her go – I have let her go already. I will not do this sort of thing any more."

"Look in my eyes," she said.

"I tell you what," he said, "I will start to do some good things instead! I will help people, like Ahab here. I can be of some use. I... I could understand what people have been through."

"Jerry, you know you can do all of these things but only after you have looked into my eyes."

"I will look, but after a little while. I will reform myself just a little, then I will be able to look, but I really can't do it just now. You go with these people now, and I will come and find you... I'll come and find you in a little while and we can have a good old chat."

He was still turned away with his head pressed into his shoulder and his hands covering his eyes. The woman was stroking his hair and leaning very close to him. Voices floated up from outside in the courtyard, and then Alma heard the music, the same extraordinary music they had heard on their first visit.

"Who is that outside?" whimpered Tarantullus, now trembling with fear.

"They are all there," said Ahab who was looking out of the window.

"ALL OF THEM?" screamed the miserable creature. "No, no, no…" He was blubbering like a child. "No, no, no… Please don't make me do this."

"We are not making you," said the woman, still in a voice filled with kindness.

"You ARE! You are FORCING ME! You are NOT ALLOWED TO FORCE ME!"

"No one can force you," said the woman in such a gentle voice that Alma could not believe anyone could resist its power. A wonderful scent was now filling the room. Mr Tarantullus was twisting his hands and trying to scratch himself, scratching at his face, trying to scratch out his own eyes, but his fingers seemed to have grown weak and soft.

"Can't you see what you are doing to me!" he screamed. "How can you make me suffer like this if you say you lo… If you lo… If you care so much for me then why are you doing this?"

"You can say it Jerry."

"No! You don't! You cannot! No one can. I hate myself! I would tear myself in tiny pieces if I could, and grind every piece to powder. I would burn myself again and again, I would inflict such unimaginable pain on myself."

"But that is what you have been doing."

"And I do not intend to stop!"

"Look at me darling." She was still stroking his hair, and now she ran her fingers over his wrinkled skin.

"That would be much worse than all the rest!" he screamed.

"Then do it! If you think you deserve so much punishment, look into my eyes and see it there, see the hatred, see how *much* I hate you."

This seemed to wrong-foot the miserable man. For a moment he stopped trembling and shaking. The tears stopped as well. He sniffed, but he still had his head turned away and his hand over his eyes. Outside, the music had ceased and the crowd were silent. The silence trembled with anticipation, and the room seemed to be full of people. Alma saw that while her attention had been fixed on the man, the five limp bodies had opened their eyes and were raising themselves and staring at Mr Tarantullus and the old woman.

"Look at me Jerry."

He took his right hand away from his eyes and wiped his nose but his head was still turned away from the woman. And then he made a little movement towards her. It was such a tiny movement that Alma was not quite sure she had seen anything, but the whole room caught its breath in amazement, for something had rippled across him, some nascent transformation. He had glimpsed the woman's face from the very corner of his eye and then immediately turned away again. From outside there came just a few notes of music, bass notes, like the introduction to a symphony.

He was covering his eyes again, but weakening. He darted her a glance, and the woman remained as still and calm as ever, her hand still stoking his hair. Then he looked at her again, only the movement was more deliberate this time. He looked for perhaps a second, then turned away, then it seemed he couldn't help but look again, and she held his

331

gaze and nodded her head.

Suddenly, he spluttered and the tears leapt from his eyes, his mouth twisted and he let out a terrible cry, a cry of the deepest misery and regret. It was the scream of a guilty soul seeing the full depth of its own wrongdoing; it was a cry of doom as from one who stands on the brink of the abyss and leaps expecting eternal agony... And at that moment the woman clasped him in her arms and held him. For a second he was like her newborn baby screaming its birth cry, and she held him and covered his leathery face with her kisses. Alma could hardly see for the tears that were filling her own eyes. She kept wiping them away, and then a fountain erupted inside her and she just let them flow and didn't bother about seeing anything, for the music was soaring and the window seemed to have imploded and the sweet air and the music and the most amazing singing she had ever heard filled the room, swirling them around.

The singing was of unbelievable richness, with harmony building on harmony. She had heard four-part harmony in her own world and thought it beautiful, but this was a harmony of fifty parts and in a host of different languages, and yet all blending perfectly, the tongues of men and women and angels. Someone had taken her by the hand and her feet were dancing around the room and she saw that Stinkhorn was holding her on one side and the Nephew on the other and their faces were beaming, and they were all dancing round and round.

Alma had no idea what her feet were doing but when she looked down she saw that they seemed to know the steps, so she didn't worry about them. In the centre of the room

Mr Tarantullus was now standing with his arms wrapped around the beautiful old lady and he was crying and laughing for joy and she was kissing him and stroking him and as Alma watched they seemed to undergo some sort of transfiguration. They were growing younger and a change was coming over their bodies and their clothes. They pulled apart and turned to look at Alma, then they looked around the room at Ahab and the others, and the ring of dancers moved towards them. Alma understood that the two in the centre were asking for forgiveness and that all the others were only too happy to grant it. They were all leaning together and it felt so good and peaceful and complete that they could have stayed like that forever, but the door opened and other hands were grasping them and the music swelled once again as the dance swirled them out of the room and down the stairs and out into the courtyard which was filled with the singers and dancers who were now standing all around, singing and clapping to a rhythm which was at once simple and complicated and which stirred your blood to a fever of excitement. Alma and her friends and Ahab were now with the crowd outside, but Mr Tarantullus and the old woman were still inside the house.

The rhythm of the music slowed and the singing grew softer. People gradually stopped moving and all attention was fixed on the door of the bookshop. Everyone was clapping now, a simple, gentle beat that grew louder and more insistent as they waited for the couple to appear. When at last Alma felt she couldn't stand the suspense a second longer, a single figure stepped through the door. A gorgeous lithe young... Alma stared in disbelief: this was neither man nor woman; it was neither Mr Tarantullus nor the beautiful lady, but a younger and in every way more wonderful version of them both!

And what a reception greeted them! Alma realised that she was able to see all the people in the courtyard quite clearly. She looked around at them and saw that many were similar to this new creature that had been restored to them. And they were taking it in turns to greet him – or her. There was much hugging and laughter and tears and then more singing. And then the being that had once been Tarantullus came up to Alma and lifted her off her feet and hugged her. He put her down again and then other people were coming to him (or her) to hug and be hugged.

The music and the dancing crowd were heading off down the alleyway and joining with other groups that had appeared now in the street.

"Come on!" said Ahab.

"What's happening?" asked Alma.

"The Chaos Waltz!" he called. "In the Great Hall."

CHAPTER TWENTY-SIX

The Chaos Waltz

Alma could feel the dancing reaching her feet again and as before she seemed to know just what the steps were; something was completely bypassing her brain and going straight into her body. Her hands were grasped and grasping and she was part of the crowd that was flying down street after street. Soon they had left the shuttered houses far behind and were gliding down avenues with rows of palm trees and houses set back from the road with lush lawns and beds full of the most amazing flowers. The whole thing was like a wild living flower show that has got just slightly out of control.

Suddenly they were joined by a pack of animals: cats and dogs and ferrets and stoats and rabbits and guinea pigs. The animals were both wild and tame at the same time, and quite calm in company of these magnificent and loving humans. And then in the midst of the crowd of animals Alma saw two that stood out. They were larger than the others and one of them was moving very slowly.

"Tennyson!" she cried.

The dog came up to her, wagging his tail.

"Hello Alma" he said.

"However did you get here?" asked Alma.

Ahab joined them, the Sloth now clinging round his neck.

"She woke up after you'd left and just set off like she knew where she was going," Tennyson explained. "I tried to stop her, but Sloths are stubborn animals. I suppose she didn't want to miss all of this. So I gave her a piggy back most of the way here. I'm sorry about deserting my post Captain."

"Don't worry," said Ahab, patting Tennyson's head. "The ship will be fine. I'm glad you are both here. We are about to see something amazing. Come on."

All this time the music and the rhythm had been building. Alma was alternately laughing and weeping with the thrill of it. "I hope I'm not going to black out and miss any of this," she thought. But she didn't feel faint at all, she felt utterly enlivened.

Now they were crossing a huge square and people were pouring out of the houses and joining the throng. It was a little difficult to get used to these tall, androgynous beings at first. There was something overpowering about them, they exuded life at such a rate that Alma didn't know quite how much she would be able to take. But this seemed to be an extreme event even for them; some great conclusion had been reached.

They streamed up the steps of a magnificent building between fluted pillars and through doors twenty feet high and ten feet wide. These opened onto a hall whose ceiling was an animated fresco of a colourful dancing procession; it was so rich and vivid that Alma could hardly take her eyes off it. It was like a huge living mural – a painting that moved with the music and the dancers. The floor of the hall was made of deeply polished wood. She looked for the joints to see where one plank ended and the next began, but it was perfect and seamless.

By now upwards of a thousand people had gathered in the hall. Alma still had hold of Stinkhorn's little rough paw. They smiled at each other and she felt that she knew what he had been through, what they had all been through, since they last met. Though there might have been a lot for them to say, somehow this was not a time for talking.

The music had dwindled slightly, though the bass rhythm continued. The dancers seemed to be taking up preordained positions, and Alma had to admit to herself that she was about to be out of her depth. Then Ahab was standing behind her with his hand on her shoulder.

"I think we'll see things best from up there," he said, pointing to a gallery that ran all the way round the hall.

The team ran up a flight of stairs and leant against the balcony rail, Ahab still carrying the Sloth and Tennyson running behind. They greeted one another properly now. There were few words, but hugs and smiles and long stares and much nodding. Tennyson went round to each of the team in turn and introduced himself to the Poet and Miss Quill and Jessica. The music was building again in volume and complexity and they looked down with a sense that something was about to begin, though they didn't know what.

"What is it?" shouted Alma into Ahab's ear.

"I told you! It's the Chaos Waltz!" Ahab shouted back.

Alma looked around for the orchestra but could see no musical instruments anywhere. There were people standing in rows all round the outside of the hall and these were now the singers, who formed three or four rings around some five hundred people who were standing in the centre of the hall rocking gently from side to side. As she watched, their timing seemed to interlock and they began to move as one. She had never seen people moving so perfectly in time. The only thing that came near it was a flock of starlings she had once watched as they turned and wheeled back and forth, up and down, all seeming to know exactly when and in which direction to turn without having any visible leader.

The dancers continued to sway in time, each exactly the right distance from those around them, and then they began to spin on the spot. As the music changed they broke out of their individual cycles and joined hands with their partners, turning round and round in pairs, perfectly spaced, all turning together. The music changed again and the spinning pairs began to split off and join hands with members of other pairs. The whole room was now peeling off and lines appeared, flowing this way and that as they weaved in and out; beautiful harmonic patterns were created by the music and echoed in the dancing. She looked up and saw the painting on the ceiling producing a wonderful counterpoint, its rhythm just slightly syncopated with that on the dance floor.

Now the patterns became more complicated and unusual; there were concentric circles, then spirals as dancers ceased their lateral movements and again began to turn round and round. Up until now everything had been symmetrical, but the movements were becoming increasingly difficult to follow. Alma tried to recognise a pattern, but if there was one it was too complex to understand; it just looked like a random mass of bodies, each moving independently. It was chaotic, but there was a different sort of beauty involved in the shapes and movements of the dancers now; there was only variety, original and inspiring; everyone seemed to be expressing their own individual nature, interpreting the dance from their own perspective. The same thing was happening with the music, as each singer improvised a song of their own, and while every song was different, yet they were not discordant. Everything remained in tune and harmony, but it was no longer of fifty parts but five hundred parts, and the invisible orchestra was doing the same thing, each instrument playing its own series of apparently random notes.

Alma found that her mouth was hanging open; she felt that everything in her had opened as wide as it would go. She realised that she wasn't blinking any more, and she didn't think she was breathing either. Her ears seemed to have opened to all sound and her eyes to all vision, so now she could hear all the individual voices and instruments and see each individual dancer and be aware of all their movements. At the same time she could see the dancers in the ceiling who were doing their own thing as well, and she was aware of her friends with her on the balcony. She was gone into the music and movement and she could barely distinguish herself from the sound or the movement or even the building, for they were all moving as one in this fantastic random chaotic stream of sound and motion and emotion.

"And I am crying because it is all Love," she thought, "that is all it is!" She wanted her parents to be there, and Robert, and Roland and the children from the school, even Julia and Mrs Benson and her grandmother.

The dance floor was now a seething mass, all semblance of order had gone. Gaps had appeared here and there, and in other places people seemed to have become entangled. The music was now discordant, though strangely this was not ugly, rather it was exciting and interesting. The dancers seemed to be completely off their heads. Some had stopped moving altogether, others had gone berserk, some were in writhing groups, others limping around on their own, some staggering drunkenly and bumping into people, some tripping over. Alma was beginning to feel a little worried in case they hurt themselves.

"This is *Utter Chaos*!" she thought.

The music was growing louder and more and more strident. She could feel that things were building to some sort of climax and she felt sure that at any minute they would either start fighting or there would be a huge explosion and they would all fall flat on the floor. But neither of these things happened; what did happen surpassed everything she had witnessed so far. Just when it seemed that the music and movement could not become any more confused, a single piercing note made itself heard in the far corner of the room. It was a note of absolute purity. Whether it was being played or sung Alma could not say, but the note came up through the cacophony and at that moment a pattern appeared in the same corner of the room among the staggering dancers, and this spread in a fraction of a second across the whole hall. They got a very good view of it from where they were on the balcony. What had happened was that every single dancer had somehow got themselves to exactly the right place to pick up the dance again, for each one was back with their original partner, and when, as one, they moved off, not a dancer missed a beat. The singers too were instantly in unison, yet the transition had been as seamless as the great wooden dance floor.

The music grew softer; the movements of the dancers more and more gentle. Now they were all rocking again from side to side; the instruments faded and the voices dropped to a hum; then there were just the bass notes, and then there was silence and stillness. The painting on the ceiling had also ceased moving and the hall was perfectly still.

Full of life and completely still.

Alma wondered if she should clap.

"Oh my goodness," she thought, "what if I start clapping and everyone glares at me? Oh, but it was so beautiful..." She began to clap, and everyone turned to look at her, and next to her Stinkhorn also began to clap and so did the Nephew and the Secretary and the Poet and Jessica, and then Ahab and down in the hall someone also began to clap, and then the whole hall were clapping and then cheering and shouting and whooping for joy and embracing and hugging one another. And on the balcony there was more back slapping and hugging too. Tennyson was barking and spinning round in circles, chasing his tail, and the Sloth was standing on the handrail with her mouth wide open and her arms in the air.

When they looked down again the Singers and Dancers were all leaving the hall.

"I think we should follow them," said Ahab.

By the time they had come down the steps the hall was almost empty. One of the last to leave was the being that had been Mr Tarantullus. He stood in the doorway and waited for them with his arms outstretched. They went and stood around him and he (or she) managed to embrace them all.

"What do we call you?" asked Alma a little shyly.

"Not Tarantullus," he said. "Names are a bit redundant now."

"But who was the beautiful lady?" asked Alma.

He looked at her with a thoughtful smile and she understood, understood perfectly without him having to say anything because she saw that she was looking into the eyes of the woman and of Mr Tarantullus at one and the same time.

"Thank you coming here and for asking your questions," he said. "It was my misguided goal to guard all the trapdoors in the Wastelands. I tried to keep out the seekers and questioners because they reminded me of what I had done, and what I should have done with my own life. When you came through the door you brought light with you, and I was only comfortable with darkness. I saw you at the Lawyers' house and feared that sooner or later you would find me. When you did, I was determined to send you back. But you didn't give up – nor did you, Ahab. You have our everlasting gratitude."

"You're fading," said Alma.

"Our companions are calling us. We must go over the Wall."

"Over the Wall?"

"We are all going home now, this age has finished for us."

"Will you ever come here again?"

"If we choose to, some of us may, we don't really know. There are things we cannot remember between Aeonia and our home over the Wall, just as there are things we forget when we leave here to go to earth."

"It was a wonderful dance," said Alma, "the most

wonderful thing I have ever seen."

"Thank you, Alma. Farewell!"

They were coming and going, like a poor television signal. They would freeze for a moment, then she would catch sight of them again and find that they had moved. Alma looked at Stinkhorn and realised that he was doing the same thing.

"Stinkhorn what's happening to you?"

"I don't know Alma, I think we're going too..."

"But you can't go!"

The others were looking confused. She felt the Nephew touch her arm and saw the look of dismay on his face. Jessica said, "We're so tired Alma."

"Ahab?" she looked at him for support.

The Sloth was climbing down Ahab's body and joining the others. Tennyson was with them too.

"They will be safe," said Ahab.

"But I can't just let them go again..."

"It is only for a little while."

CHAPTER TWENTY-SEVEN

Through The Wall

They were alone once more, sitting on the wall by the fountain. She stood up and looked all around, calling their names, but the place was deserted but for herself and Ahab.

"Where have they gone?" asked Alma.

"Don't worry – you will join them soon."

"It was like a dream," she said.

Ahab nodded.

"And who were all those other people? Were they Mr Tarantullus's friends?"

"He was the last of a group that came here together. They had all completed many lives and were beginning to long for their home again. As soon as he was reconciled they knew that it was time for them to be going back over the Wall."

"But how long had they been waiting for him?"

"It was exactly the right length of time," said Ahab. "He had spent many ages trying to relive moments in his last life. That became his obsession and he had taken to helping others go through the same hopeless routine. While he was experiencing all that it seemed to Tarantullus that he was in the shuttered houses for millennia, but to his friends it was just a few days.

"Over the Wall, life-stories are told. Those who go back there carry their stories with them and tell them in great detail and with great skill. Each life teaches something, and each incident in each life teaches something, so that nothing is wasted. There is no anger or retribution, because in that place not only the actions are seen, but the causes of every action. And the stories are told so beautifully, that when you have listened to a life you are not sure whether or not you have lived it yourself. And so people who have lived great lives are not proud, and likewise people who have lived very sad lives are not ashamed. You will have heard the saying, 'He that is forgiven much, loves much.' In this way those who have lived very bad lives become very loving people."

"Jesus said something like that," said Alma; then she said, "Hey! What about Jesus?"

"No one knows which of us played the part of Jesus," said Ahab. "It could have been you, it could have been me; it could have been almost anyone."

"And who is God? Or where is he?" she said.

"My sense is that God will be all of us, when we are back together. Until then God cannot truly be said to exist."

"So the atheists were right then?"

"Right... and wrong."

Alma had to think about this for a while. She wondered if she would remember enough of what she had seen and heard to be able to tell some of it to her mother.

"And what about you Ahab? What are you?"

"For now I am a wanderer and a helper. And I'm afraid I must be setting off again."

"I am not to come with you then?"

He shook his head.

"Am I to meet with my Watcher?" she asked. "And if I am, does that mean that I have died?"

"That is what I cannot work out," said Ahab. "If that were the case then your Watcher would have been here to meet you, but he is not."

"And Stinkhorn and the others? You said I would follow them."

"And so you shall."

"Where have they gone?"

"Come, I will show you."

He walked with her through the city. As they got further away from the harbour the houses grew more and more beautiful. Some of the gardens were like jungles and she caught glimpses of brightly coloured birds in the trees. After a while they came out into open countryside and the land began to climb towards the foothills. It didn't seem that they had been walking for very long, but when Alma looked back they had left the city far behind; it stretched out in both directions along the bay and disappeared into the distance. When they reached the top of the ridge they saw that the ground fell away before them, before climbing once more up to the Wall.

"And here I must leave you," said Ahab.

Alma went up to him and he held her in his arms for a long time.

"You have many more questions, but I am not the one who can give you the answers. Follow this path now. Things will become clearer."

"Will we meet again, you and I?" she asked, but she already knew the answer: that it would not be soon, but that she would recognise him instantly.

"Goodbye," she said, "and thank you for everything. Thank you for coming to get me, for reminding me."

He smiled down at her, and as she watched his feet lifted off the floor and he rose gently into the air. In a few moments he was a tiny dot in the sky above Aeonia; then she saw him begin to descend, heading back towards the abandoned Bookshop and his ship in the underground cavern.

Alma turned and walked down the slope, then up again towards the Wall. As she got closer she noticed that there was a little door at the base of the Wall, with a sandy path leading up to it. The last few yards of the path were paved with square paving stones. Some of them had symbols and letters carved on them. The first one she came to had an elaborate letter E over a pattern of circles and cylinders. She had to study it for some time before she realised what it was.

"It's a train!" she said, and then she almost shouted, "Euselessness!"

Without thinking, she began jumping from stone to stone: "Fenchurch, St Pancras, Marylebone to the right, then Charing Cross, then Kings Cross straight ahead and finally..." But the last stone, which should have been Mortlake, wasn't there. Instead she was standing right in front of the door. She looked up for a moment at the great Wall that towered above her, then down at the little door. It was about three feet tall and two feet wide, made of fine dark wood like the floor of the great hall. The doorknob was of brightly polished copper. The lintel was just like the one she had passed through from her secret place behind the bin in the kitchen.

"Is this the way home?" she thought, and waited to see

how that made her feel. Her first emotion was disappointment; if this was the way back into her old life, it meant she was going to leave without answers to her questions, and without seeing her friends again. But Ahab had said she was going to see them again.

"Perhaps it means that I'm still alive. Or that I have to choose between life and answers. Oh, I don't know what to do..."

She felt a tickling sensation around her ankles. She looked down and saw that sand from the path was beginning to swirl towards the door. Although there was no breeze blowing, somehow the air was being drawn under the door.

"Something's calling me," she thought, and gripping the handle, she opened the door and crawled through the Wall.

Alma was on her hands and knees looking into a walled garden. Through the trees and bushes she could see the far side of it. There was another wall, not as high as the great Wall, but made of the same golden sandstone, only about fifty yards away. Stopping half way through the door, she looked to her right, then to her left. She crawled out again, back into Aeonia, and looked along the length of the Wall, then crawled back into the garden.

"This is crazy," she thought, "it bends both ways at the same time! On one side the Wall encloses the whole of Aeonia, the city and the sea and everything, and on this side, the same wall contains this tiny garden."

She spent some time crawling back and forth through the doorway. It was like flicking a switch in her mind. At first it made her feel giddy, but when she got used to it, it seemed to make perfect sense. She closed the door to Aeonia behind her and set off to explore the garden.

She walked among rose bushes and flowerbeds; there were laburnum trees with heavy bunches of yellow flowers which gave off a lazy and intoxicating smell; fat, furry bees were burrowing into petals everywhere, covering themselves in dusty pollen. Alma became engrossed in watching the activity in and around a rose bush that arched over the path; the bees were making such ecstatic noises that she couldn't tear herself away. Somewhere she could hear the sound of running water and she followed the path through the garden to a flight of steps. There was running water in the banisters, and she walked down trailing her fingers in its coolness.

The garden opened out into an orchard of crab apple trees that were both in blossom and weighed down with red and yellow fruit. And then there was the music again, only this time it was, if possible, even more beautiful than it had been at the Chaos Waltz. The music seemed to be coming from somewhere below her.

Now the path followed a stream which descended in a series of miniature waterfalls, and at the heart of the garden she caught sight of the bright green leaf-umbrella of a strange tree. The tree looked incredibly ancient, and though it was not very tall, its trunk was massive. Beyond the tree, the stream ran over a rockery into a pond.

Alma came to a turn in the path and froze. On the other side of the pond there was a lawn, and in the middle of the lawn a boy about her own age was throwing a blue and golden ball up into the air and catching it. He had his back to her and seemed to be unaware of her presence. Almost at the same instant Alma spotted the bent form of Jessica, crouching behind the ancient tree, watching the boy. In front of Jessica, also with his back to her, was Stinkhorn, and in front of him Alma could just see the back of Miss Quill. Presumably the Poet, the Nephew, Tennyson and the Sloth were out of sight on the other side of the tree.

Keeping close to the ground, Alma crept up to Jessica and knelt down behind her. The garden was so still and peaceful that it would have seemed wrong to speak, so she reached out her hand to touch her friend on the shoulder. But just as she did, she saw Jessica reach out with her hand to touch Stinkhorn, and something made Alma draw back. As she withdrew her hand Jessica also withdrew her hand. Alma reached out her hand again, and Jessica mirrored her movement exactly. Just as her hand reached Jessica's shoulder, Alma felt a hand touch her own shoulder. She turned round slowly and was aware as she did so that Jessica was doing exactly the same thing. She sensed, though she did not see, that all around the tree each member of the team was looking over their shoulder. She fully expected to look into the face of the Poet or the Nephew.

But as she turned she found she was looking at a girl with ginger hair. She couldn't see her face properly because she was turning away. Alma looked back to Jessica, and as she did she saw that it was not Jessica at all. With a shock she realised that she was looking at the back of her own head! The girl in front of her was herself and so was the girl behind, and it seemed logical to suppose that each figure around the tree was also a version of herself.

"Hello," said a voice behind her.

She turned and found herself looking into the shining eyes of the boy with the ball.

"Oh it's you!" she said, suddenly filled with inexplicable happiness.

"Yes it's me."

Alma stood up, and now there were just the two of them in the garden.

"Oh what a relief!" she said. "It's so good to see you again." She went to embrace him, but he took a pace back, and she understood that this was necessary for now.

"Where have the others gone?" she asked.

"They are still here," said the Boy, "but you're all back together now."

"What do you mean?"

He did not answer, but looked into her eyes.

Alma returned his gaze and they were silent for a long time, but without any sense of awkwardness. She felt she could have stood there and looked into his eyes forever. Eventually she said, "They were bits of me, weren't they."

He nodded slowly.

"My mother would have hated Stinkhorn," she said, "he was everything she could not abide. And then there was the Poet, the one who was hurt and tried to hide away."

She tried to place Miss Quill.

"The efficient, outspoken one," said the Boy, "the one who was taken for granted?"

Alma nodded. "And I could be pretty vengeful, in my mind at least," she said. "And The Nephew – that was me whenever I was floating in the corner of the room... Tennyson?"

"The reluctant performer – forced to do things in public

against her will," said the Boy.

"And the Sloth? Was I really slothful?" asked Alma.

"No," he said, "you just wanted to take things slowly."

"I suppose. And Jessica?"

"You didn't really know, but your parents partly blamed you for their unhappiness."

"I was partly to blame though," she said.

"You had a lot to cope with," he said.

"I walled them up, didn't I, all those feelings. No wonder I felt so lost."

"But you came back for them."

Alma looked at the Boy. She felt so comfortable and at home with him, but this did not surprise her. How else would she feel about... She searched in her mind for his name. "Oh this is ridiculous," she thought. "It's completely gone. Why it's... But I know him so well, he's like my brother – closer than a brother..."

"Alma!" he said.

"Yes dear?" she said.

"Alma, do you think you want to stay with me?"

"Of course," she said. "Now that we're together again what else would we do?"

He kept looking into her eyes.

"There is a problem," he said.

"A problem?"

"Yes," he said. "You have not fully remembered yet, you see. And if you stayed with me now you would begin to remember, and you would be very disappointed."

"How do you mean?"

"Well, the life you have been living, the life as Nicki, is not done with yet."

"But I'm her."

"Yes, but do you know why you are here?"

"Because I was hit by a post office van and I died."

"No, you were hit by a post office van and you are in the hospital. Your parents are sitting at your bedside. Your mother is holding your hand and weeping. The reason you came here the first time, and the reason you came back, is because you..." The Boy paused and looked down for a moment. "Do you remember what it was your Granny said when you were listening in the kitchen that time?"

Alma stood very still and looked into his eyes again. Then she felt something moving in her mind. It wasn't so much a thought as a picture, or a vision. There was a creature that had been lying for many years in the mud at the bottom of a pond, but was now waking up and deciding it wanted to swim to the surface. When it poked its ugly, toad-like head above the water, she saw that it bore a strange resemblance to her grandmother. The creature spoke. "It would have been better for all concerned if Veronica had never been born at all," it said.

Alma stood there gasping. The Boy's face was more serious now.

"Something got broken," he said. "The healing has been going on all this time, and it will continue now, if you go back."

"Go back? But I can't leave you again." She felt as if she had just been handed the best Christmas present she could imagine and then been told that she would have to wait a lifetime to open it.

He smiled again. "That is what we chose when we took

on this life; that is what we promised: *until death us do join*. We swore that we would see it through no matter how difficult it became. We said we would keep on until the end."

"It is all so hazy," she moaned, folding her arms and hugging herself.

"This was the challenge we chose. It was a difficult one, but we knew we could do it, that in the end we could forgive any amount of thoughtlessness, and repay it with love."

"But why does it have to be so hard?"

"Because perfection can only be reached through these many stages of imperfection. There are no shortcuts. You must go back to what is real for you now."

"I can't!" she wailed. "If I have to I'll... I'll..."

"If you did that," he said, very gently, "you would become lost, like Tarantullus, or the people in the shuttered houses. You would not be able to look me in the eye."

"Is that what he did?" she asked.

"We haven't heard his story yet," he said. "We are still in the middle of our story."

They stood for a while in silence, listening to the sound of the stream and breathing in the astonishing air of the garden.

"Will I remember any of this?" Alma asked at last.

The Boy did not answer, but tossed the ball he was holding up in the air and caught it again. Now that she saw it up close, she realised that it was not a ball after all, but some kind of fruit. The skin of it kept changing, swirling and glinting with a light that seemed to come from within it.

"Where did you get that?" she asked.

He pointed to the tree, and she saw that it was covered with these beautiful things, all swinging gently in the breeze.

They looked at each other again, and she knew that it was time for her to go.

"Will I recover?" she said with a sigh.

"I'm not sure, but I'll be with you, and we'll be together again a little later on."

"Can I hold you?"

"I don't think we'd ever prise ourselves apart if you did that," he said.

She felt cold inside now, and started to cry.

"Don't worry Alma," he said, "I will always be speaking to you; in your dreams, in books, in people; in things that seem significant or insignificant. I will be there in the people who love you and even in the people who seem not to."

"I can't bear it!" she said.

"I will show you something that may help, something you have always wanted to see."

He took her by the hand and led her to the pond. Alma could feel her temples beginning to throb.

"I think I'm going," she said.

"Just look in here," he said.

Still holding his hand she sat on the wall that encompassed the pond and looked into it. At first she could see nothing but the rippling reflection of herself and the Boy; then, with a whirring of small wings and a flash of blue and orange, a kingfisher dropped out of the air into the water, shattering the surface, and the whole picture opened up before her. She was following the bird into the depths and they were twisting and diving and dancing to the music as they made their way home. And around her were other dancers; she could see them to left and right, above and below, before and after; people from the future, people from the past, birds and animals, all twisting and turning, reaching upwards, like seeds struggling through hard ground towards the light.

"It's just like the Chaos Waltz," she thought. "And I am a part of it!"

She was ascending now, and above her the light was growing stronger, but the music was fading. She wanted to cling onto it, but more than that she wanted to keep dancing upwards towards the light. The other dancers seemed to be encouraging her to keep going, but they themselves were falling away, one by one. She turned to her right and there was the Boy, still holding her hand.

"Go on," he said, "you're almost home now."

Above her and to her left another voice spoke. "She's coming round," it said.

"Yes, I am!" she whispered. "I'm coming round and round."

The spinning sensation was slowing now; the music had faded to silence and though her eyes were closed she could tell that the light was now very bright. When she finally came to a halt, she found that he was still holding her hand.

"You came with me!" she said.

She opened her eyes and saw only a beige ceiling with a grey, kidney-shaped stain and peeling paint. There was a strange metallic smell and she was aware of a dull pain in her back. She turned her head to the left and saw her mother's tear-stained face and worried expression; her father was standing behind her mother with his hands on her shoulders. Alma turned to the right and there, on a chair next to the bed, was Robert. He squeezed her hand and smiled at her.

THE END

Acknowledgements

Thanks are due to these wonderful people:

Judith and Geoffrey Stephenson for encouraging me to open the box and making so many helpful suggestions; Duncan MacLaren for reading the story to his family over a period of several weeks, doing all the voices and sending me the recordings; Jane, Alexander, Lindsay, and Iona MacLaren for liking the story so much and taking the Sloth to their hearts and into their home; Freya Murray for reading it and even doing a book report at her school; Elspeth Murray (even though she hasn't read it yet I still love her); Nick Thorpe, Hannah Sheppard, David Heavenor, Richard Adams, Anke Green, Andonella Thomson, Liz Barr, Norma Austin Hart and Jo Cameron Duguid for wise advice; Sam and Joey Medrington for believing my stories when they were small; JRR Tolkien for inspiration; Wendy Ball for helping to bring it into the world and Paul Medrington, who had important things to do and went on ahead.